THE MAN IN THE RED COAT

The Fourth Gunfighter Gothic Novel

Written by Mark Bousquet

THEMARKBOUSQUET.COM

Space Buggy Press

THE MAN IN THE RED COAT is a holiday story featuring weird western characters in a non-weird western setting. Portions of this book have been previously published.

Originally published as BLACK CHRISTMAS. This volume has been edited for content.

ISBN: 9798669779047

A Space Buggy Press Publication

Cover by James, GoOnWrite.com

First Printing: November 2014
Second Printing: July 2019

The GUNFIGHTER GOTHIC Universe

The Train Where Jill Dies
Western Demons
Absinthe & Steam
The Man in the Red Coat
American Valkyrie
The Bandolier

Associated Novels
The Haunting of Kraken Moor

www.gunfightergothic.com

The Man in the Red Coat

Written by Mark Bousquet

THE MAN IN THE RED COAT

PROLOGUE
THE LAST CHRISTMAS IN
THE UNIVERSE

The End of Time
The Day the Man in the Red Coat Left Hell

The End of Time was a lonely place.

Billions upon billions of suns and stars had died and the empty, dead rocks that remained were eternally drifting away from the center of the Everything, solo travelers in the cold darkness. There were no civilizations left. There were few signs they had ever existed, the billions of years between their death and the end of the universe having ground buildings and ships and cities to dust.

The Metronome lived here.

There were several dozen of them, the last beings in existence, the witnesses who would watch the final victory of the Void.

The Metronome was the name of the collective and the name each of them called themselves, their original identities long lost to the march of time. They dressed in black latex, adorned with pulsating green symbols that looked like circuits, and generally amused themselves in the manner of the gods of old and interfered with the timeline.

They caused floods.

They started wars.

They built Universe Cutters.

Once upon a billion billion years ago, they had names and nationalities and personalities and mortgages and received free calendars from banks to mark the passage of time. They had once celebrated birthdays and holidays and had affairs on desks in small offices in meaningless towns. They killed for Gods and countries. They got runny noses and syphilis and breast cancer.

7

But that was then. Now they were all simply The Metronome in gestalt and the Metronome in detail.

What they didn't do was try to set themselves apart from one another.

Until now.

The Man in the Red Coat thought of himself as a traditionalist, and had once been a Christian before he realized the Egyptians had it right — it was not man who made God, but man who claimed Godhood for himself.

Several hours ago, he had left Hell, a debt paid to the demon Xogol, who had first trapped him in his domain and then begged for his help to teach another to use the gifts bestowed upon him by the Universe Cutter.

He'd agreed.

He'd done his service.

He'd left.

Physically, at least.

His mind was still in Hell, still caught up in the thoughts and images and visions of Jill Masters.

He stood on a dead planet of emerald rock that had once held life. A great and powerful empire had resided here, ruling its particular solar system with warmth and empathy and a fleet of destroyers powerful enough to eradicate a sun. He could visit them, if he liked, and he often did, stepping back through time as easily as King Ridge had once strolled across his ...

No, the Metronome frowned. Ridge was Aegean, not Ande'cardian. This was the world where Emperor Ande'meade had once ...

Or was it the home of ...

It didn't matter. Not anymore. Not until ...

Until what?

Until Jill Masters was back in his life.

What that meant, exactly, he did not know, but he knew he needed her, in some shape or form. And it had to be soon. Even for the most powerful beings in creation could not stop the final decay of the universe. The Metronome would fall, too.

It wouldn't be long now until it was all over.

Because he was in a foul mood and because he could do anything he wanted, the Man in the Red Coat decided that today would be a Thursday and it would be Christmas.

The last Christmas in the universe.

"Where am I?"

The Metronome spun in place, surprised to find a middle-aged woman in a bedraggled red coat, edged with white fur standing before him. She had a worn canvas sack at her side that she white-knuckled in her hand to keep it with her. The top of her face was covered by a cheap, plastic mask of a reindeer with a red nose.

"I fought through time to be here," she said weakly, running hands through tangled black and white hair as she fell to her knees. She kept the sack in her left hand as she did this, and the Metronome could hear the rattling of metal. Words spilled out of her in standalone, staccato sentences.

"I must undo the damage."

"I am looking for the man inside."

"I miss him."

"I am the Mistletoe Queen!"

"I have something for him!"

"I have the rings!"

There was some pity in the heart of the Man in the Red Coat, but not enough to help her. Perhaps if there had been more time left until the Everything collapsed ...

9

But there was not.

Without a word, the Metronome opened a hole in the fabric of space and time beneath the Mistletoe Queen, causing her to fall away from him.

"Now," he rubbed his chin, his mind turning back to the American woman that had captivated him, "what shall I do about Jill Masters?"

THE MAN IN THE RED COAT

ACT ONE
THE KRAMPUS SOCIETY

1866, December
The Day the Man in the Red Coat Left Hell

Roland Garteau pulled off his winter coat, and then removed his shirt to show his mother the bruises. "It's the Krampus, mama," he said, tears threatening to burst. "I know you don't believe me, but it's true! He came again last night!"

Sybil Garteau shook her head, and looked to Catholic Bishop Andre Salome. "Do you see what I have to put up with?" she asked, pointing to the child. "Would you tell him the Krampus is nothing but a myth spread to scare children?"

Bishop Salome was a middle-aged, roundish man with a bald head and a friendly demeanor that often hid the fervor of his passion for God. He smiled politely as Mrs. Garteau, the very young and very new wife of Leo Garteau, one of the richest businessmen in Le Mans, France. The family lived nearly 40 miles outside of the city, near Mayenne. Leo had left France eighteen months ago for a tour of the Americas with one wife, and returned with a different one.

Younger. Prettier. More likely to cause trouble.

"Our train was robbed in the American west," Leo had told the Bishop upon returning. "It is a savage place, full of naked men and women raising ignorant children outside the light of God. Sybil has been a great comfort to me in the time since Mrs. Garteau's passing. To Roland, as well," he would always add, as if remembering too late that he had a son who was effected by his decision.

Bishop Salome had wanted to say more than he did, but he kept his mouth shut. Le Mans Cathedral was a large and expensive building (especially now, in the winter, with Christmas only three weeks away) and Leo Garteau was among the building's largest contributors. Did it hurt the devoted Christian's soul to keep his mouth shut at the hard to believe story? It did, but Salome knew the Church often made uneasy alliances with those who provided money for the coffers. Better, he believed, to take the money and spread the Word of God than to accuse a man without knowing the full facts.

What he saw before him, however, demanded some kind of attention.

The Bishop dropped to one knee. The three of them were gathered in the southwestern corner of Cathédrale Saint-Julien du Mans, near a standing stone monument called a menhir, that had been with the church since 1778. He would not have chosen this location for a delicate conversation, but the new Mrs. Garteau did not have the old Mrs. Garteau's social graces. How could she? Bishop Solome guessed Sybil's age to be in the mid-20s, a full fifteen years younger than the woman she replaced in Leo's house. The Bishop missed the old Mrs. Garteau terribly, and was not satisfied with the story of her demise, but Leo's eyes had been forever more interested in business than his wife, and when Roland had confided in him that his mother has passed away whilst his father was out looking at farmland to purchase, that information felt as right as the Word of God.

"How are you, Roland?" Salome asked, looking at what appeared to be claw marks down the front of his chest.

"The Krampus wants to eat me!"

"Ridiculous!" Sybil scoffed. "Europe is a savage place," she insisted, but as the Catholic Bishop poked and prodded her clearly injured son, the native Pennsylvanian softened. "What is the Krampus, anyway?" she asked. "Roland says it's some kind of monster that wants to steal him away from us. That's poppycock, isn't it, Bishop?"

Salome ignored her questions concerning myths, focusing instead of the very real plight of the sandy-haired child before him. "Tell me about the Krampus, Roland," he said, peering closer at the scratches and finding flecks of what appeared to be small, metal flakes in the boy's wounds. "What's he like? When does he come?"

"Why are you humoring him?" Sybil demanded.

"Mrs. Garteau, please," the Bishop said forcefully, looking up at her. "You have come to me for help, so let me help. I am certain," he added quickly, to stop her from lodging a protest, "that is it not the Krampus who is after your son, but clearly, the boy has marks on his chest. I am sure you are not suggesting he has done this to himself."

Sybil was taken aback, and put up a weak defense. "He was playing in the hedges behind the estate and slipped in the snow. He's always playing in the hedges behind the estate, no matter how many times he is told not to go there. If we had better help ..."

Bishop Salome put up a hand to silence her, and turned back to Roland. It was curious to the old priest how the boy remained so still and calm, except when he had to talk. It was only then, when he gave a voice to his fears, that he showed emotion. After his outburst, he would stand still and placid again, as if he were an actor standing off-stage waiting for his cue to perform.

"Please, Roland, tell me how you acquired these scars."

Roland held up his hands as if they were claws and growled at the priest. "If you are a bad boy, I will steal you away from your parents on Krampus Day!" As soon as he finished, he returned to his docile state.

Bishop Salome nodded and told the boy to get dressed. Rising to his feet, he addressed Mrs. Garteau. "I do not think the Krampus is after your son."

Sybil rolled her eyes. "I could have told you that, Bishop. I left our home before the sunrise to travel by wretched carriage to speak to you, so do not tell me what I knew before I left Mayenne. Tell Roland."

Bishop Salome bit his tongue, hard, but knew there were pews that needed replacing after the holidays. Better the congregation pay for it than the Church. Giving the woman who was nearly half his age a small bow, the man of God turned down to Roland.

"My boy," he said, "whatever is causing those scars, it is not the Krampus. The legend of that particular demon is tied to the days when the wilderness controlled Europe, not civilized men and women and children of God. You are a child of God, aren't you, Roland?"

Roland clasped his hands together behind his back and his eyes suddenly found the floor to be a highly interesting place to look. "Yes," he said weakly. Behind his back, his stepmother saw that he had crossed his fingers, and reminded herself to still her tongue so as not to push the Bishop off-track. He was surely already making as big a show of all this as he could, in the hopes of getting even more money out of her husband.

Bishop Salome patted Roland on the head. "Someone is playing a very real and very mean-spirited trick on you, my son." He turned back to Mrs. Garteau. "He needs to be watched, day and night, by someone reliable. Those scars on his chest were not caused by any hedge, and I will not hear that lie spoken in this cathedral, again," he said in a firm, but controlled voice. "Do you have anyone that you can trust to watch him?"

Sybil stamped her foot and straightened her back. "I do not trust any of our servants. They dislike me because I'm an American."

"They dislike you because you are not the wife your husband left this country with," he said, sharply, instantly regretting it. "But no matter," he said, calming himself, "it is good they do not trust you because that will allow me to do you a favor. I know someone I can hire. Can you remain in town until nightfall?"

*

"What did you find?" Haneul Pak asked Jill Masters, her partner in Gunfighter Gothic, as she plopped down across from her at a small cafe in Le Mans, France. Their new career as investigators of the weird had them juggling multiple pursuits and they were tired from their recent efforts.

Both women wore variations of the same outfit: boots, jeans, blouse, cowboy hat. Hanna wore a black, leather vest above her green blouse, and Jill wore a maroon-colored bolero (or half-jacket, as Hanna liked to chide her) atop her white shirt. It was a chilly December morning, and Jill had picked a seat at a small, round table near the stove on the side wall.

"The coffee is delicious," Jill said, raising a small, white cup and taking a sip.

"Coffee is the drink of the devil," Hanna replied, sticking out her tongue and dropping her black hat into the seat beside her.

"That's why I had them bring you wine," Jill said, tapping the unopened bottle in the center of the table. A small plate of bread and cheese sat next to it, and Hanna helped herself to the food.

"It's a bit early for wine," Hanna said, despite reaching for the bottle.

"Except that you haven't been to sleep, yet, have you?" Jill asked. "Did you find anything in the library?"

"Nothing on the Mistletoe Queen," she sighed, popping the cork on the glass bottle. "Nothing in the legends, nothing in the papers. Look at my hands," she said, showing ink-stained fingers. "I feel all the wrong kinds of dirty. What did you find?"

"I found you a good bottle of Sauvignon Blanc," Jill said, making a point to let the words roll off her tongue in a thick, French accent as Hanna sniffed the now open bottle. Jill added, "Or, as you pronounce it, white."

"It's wet is all I care," Hanna replied, pouring the wine into a coffee cup. "Now, are you going to tell me if you found anything related to the Progenitors of Steam?"

A man's voice interrupted them. "What she found was me," Charles Francis Poseidon said, sitting down at the table with them. He was a demon hunter, aged nearly 80 years by the calendar, but with a body that cut that number in half, thanks to a steady treatment of African herbs. Of African parentage, he was raised in England and spoke in his adopted tongue.

Hanna sighed. "Are you still mad about us stealing your steam carriage?"

"Yes," Poseidon replied. He wore tan, khaki pants and an olive shirt, and both of them were freshly stained with blood and in need of repair. "I need your help."

"We don't come cheap," Jill smiled, popping a cube of Pont-l'Évêque cheese into her mouth.

"Neither did my carriage," Poseidon reminded her.

Jill chewed on the soft, creamy cheese and raised a finger into the air. "Point to the scary black man."

Hanna steered the conversation back to business. "We're on a case."

Poseidon waved his hand dismissively, and leaned back in his chair, folding his hands on his stomach. "Yes, the Mistletoe Queen and the Progenitors of Steam. Not to mention the ghostly orgies you see taking place in the old Roman baths," he said. "It's not really surprising you have yet to solve that case, is it?"

"You don't see that messed up stuff in America," Jill said, folding her arms across her chest. "Are you here to solve our case and take a cut of our pay?"

"I don't take renumeration for my services," Poseidon said, slowly shaking his head as he reached for a piece of still-warm bread, "but I can tell you that your friend, the Lady Carashire, has left Europe for Madagascar. The Anthon boy is with her, and she has taken a new lover."

"Shocking," Jill said.

"But that's a matter for another day," Poseidon continued. "For this day, simply put so we do not risk misunderstanding, I want you to leave the city."

Hanna and Jill both shot up in their seats. "Forget it," Hanna said.

"You're not stealing our case," Jill insisted, dropping a knife down into the demon hunter's bread and locking it to the table.

Poseidon looked at the white woman with a blank expression as he pulled the bread through the knife before plopping it into his mouth. "I hunt demons," he said, "and what's plaguing Le Mans is a demon. You, as your business card so eloquently says, 'shoot the weird in the face,' and you don't yet know how to shoot a ghost."

Jill scoffed. "Semantics."

"There's a whole lot of weird west of here that needs shooting and has large enough bodies that will make it terribly hard to miss."

"They're ghosts at the baths," Jill pointed out. "Not demons."

"They are demons," Poseidon corrected her, "in the visage of ghosts. Spirits of Christmases past, present, and future coming together."

Jill blinked. "Was that a sex pun from a dirty old man?"

Hanna interjected before Jill could derail the conversation any further. "What's happening out west?"

Poseidon sucked on his teeth to clean the bread from the crevices between them. "Children have gone missing," he said, accepting the bottle of wine from Hanna. "There is a rumor that it is related to the Krampus."

"If you're just gonna make up names," Jill pouted, "you can leave."

Hanna and Poseidon ignored her, and the Korean-American asked, "I thought the Krampus was a demon."

Poseidon shrugged. "It depends which legend you ascribe to," he said, "but as you know from our shared experience at Kraken Moor, most demons are tied to a specific location.

The Krampus myth is of Germanic origin, and it's only spread as far west as the Alsace region of France."

"Is that close?" Jill asked, eschewing her coffee for some of Hanna's wine.

"There is roughly 350 miles between us and Strasbourg," Poseidon said, "so no, not particularly close. That means," he added quickly, before Jill could ask another question, "that it's not likely a demonic attack, but a Krampus cult, or impersonator. I hear the verbiage 'Krampus Society' in the wind."

"Goddamn it," Jill scoffed. "When will I be cool enough to throw around phrases like that and sound awesome?"

"Never," Hanna chided with a smile as she chewed on a piece of cheese.

Poseidon ignored their chatter and sipped some of the Sauvignon Blanc. "I need you to check it out."

"Aw," Hanna smiled, leaning back in her chair and folding her arms across her green blouse, "you're so cute when you think you can give us orders."

Jill shook her head and crooked a thumb at the demon hunter. "I mean, I know he's hot and all, but I just can't forget he's like 172 years old."

"I'm eighty."

"Like there's a difference."

Poseidon dropped a bundle of French bank notes on the table. "I'll pay you to take over your case and pay you to solve this one. Included in this bundle is the upfront money Ignatius received."

"There he goes," Jill sighed, looking to Hanna, "making up names again. What kind of demon is Ignatius?"

Hanna shook her head. "No idea."

"Ignatius is not a demon," Poseidon said somberly, giving a slight bow of his head. "He is my son."

"You have a son?" Jill asked. "Is he, like, half-demon from some sexy devil woman who once stole your heart but you still sent back to Hell because of, like, ideals or something?"

Poseidon blinked at her. "If the world was powered by imagination and bluster, surely America would be the world's one true superpower," he said dryly. "Much like you, Ignatius likes to think he is highly skilled in this line of work. He took a job — also like you, he believes one should be paid for saving innocents from the denizens of Hell — to investigate a missing child in Flers, a town to the northwest of here. Three days ago, he informed his client he was going to follow a lead to Cherbourg." Poseidon made eye contact with both women, in turn. "Ignatius has not returned."

Hanna and Jill exchanged a glance, and it was Jill who spoke. "Shouldn't you go after your kid?"

"The matter of the Roman baths is more pressing."

Jill pointed a finger. "It's because it's an orgy, right?" She shook her head. "I hate how this continent makes me feel like a prude. Me!"

Poseidon leaned forward and could not keep a small smile from playing out across his lips. "One only sees what one wants to see at the baths," he said, "so if you are seeing an orgy, it is not Europe that is is obsessed with sex, but you."

Jill opened her mouth, and then shut it. She looked to Hanna for help, but her partner just shook her head. "Fine," Jill huffed. "We'll go save your kid."

"Find the missing children and uncover this Krampus plot," Poseidon said. "Save Ignatius only if it does not cost you an innocent life."

"How will we recognize him?" Jill asked as Poseidon rose to his feet.

"He hunts demons and he's black-skinned," Poseidon said, snatching the rest of their bread from off the table. "How many young men fitting that description do you think there are in France? Go to Cathédrale Saint-Julien du Mans and ask for Bishop Salome," Poseidon instructed. "He was Ignatius' client."

*

"We're babysitters?" Jill asked, staring at Roland Garteau's scratches. "Ugh. Pull your shirt down."

Bishop Salome looked apologetically at Sybil Garteau, and then at Hanna and Jill with an aghast expression on his face. "Where is Poseidon?" he asked nervously.

"At an orgy," Jill deadpanned.

Bishop Salome's face turned red.

"What's an orgy?" Roland asked, looking from Jill to his mother.

Sybil Garteau's face turned red.

The five people stood in an alley behind the hotel where Sybil and Roland had wasted away their day on socializing and ice cream, respectively. A steam-powered carriage waited for them, the driver a professionally courteous and handsome young man who stood off to the side, watching and listening.

Probably Colony, Hanna thought, but then had to admit that once you knew the Colony existed, you tended to see them everywhere.

"I am certain that if I could talk to Poseidon," Salome continued, "he would be swayed as to the importance of assisting Mrs. Garteau."

"Forget it, Bishop," Hanna said. "He's playing both sides against the middle. Believe me, if he had said we were going to babysit a kid, we'd have said no."

Sybil was instantly defensive. "You find my son beneath you?"

Jill nodded. "We find all kids beneath us."

"Stop it," Hanna grunted at Jill, putting an end to the argument. "We're going with you back to Mayenne, Mrs. Garteau. We'll find out who's after Roland. End of story." She opened the door to the carriage and ushered Roland inside. When the driver hesitated about stepping in to help, Hanna shot him a glare and pointed to the driver's seat. "Now, everybody get in the carriage and don't say anoth—"

"Mon Dieu!" a man yelled, bursting through the hotel's service door. It was Leo Garteau, nearing fifty and with a slight paunch, but clearly still a man who commanded most rooms he entered. "Sybil!" he yelled. "What have you done? Are you responsible for this?" he demanded, holding a handwritten note above his head.

Sybil was clearly taken aback, and her hand went to her face. "Leo! What are you talking about?"

"The kidnapping of our son!" he yelled. "A fine coincidence that you left to spend my money on the morning of ... of ... Roland?" he asked, seeing the boy's face in the carriage window. "But ... this note ... it says you were ... that ..."

All eyes turned to the little boy. "Oh, father," he said, smiling wickedly, "I'm going to eat your intestines after frying them in butter, white wine, coffee, and opium."

"What?" Leo asked. "Roland ... what are you talking about?"

Hanna and Jill moved to stand between father and son, their hands going to the pistols at their hips. They had taken some of the fancy guns that Lady Carashire's engineers had created, and so were rocking something beyond their normal Colts and Remingtons. Hanna suggested everyone move back.

No one did.

"What I'm talking about, dearest father," the boy sneered, "is that I replaced your Roland over a week ago while you slept, and you never noticed. Not once. Not you or this fool you married." The boy looked down to his stepmother. "You really should listen to the help. They knew." He smiled. "They know everything, Sybil. Everything."

The boy's stepmother blushed and the carriage driver again made like he wanted to step in, but forced himself to hold back.

"Roland!" Leo yelled. "You will stop this foolishness and get down immediately!"

"Roland is gone," the boy said, staring hate at the elder Garteau. "Food for the Krampus." He turned to Hanna and Jill and winked. "I'll eat the body of the others, but the things I will do to you two ..."

Hanna and Jill shot the boy in the face, the former with an electric shooter and the latter with a plasma blaster. The boy screamed, falling to the floor and out of sight as the combination of energy set the carriage aflame. The carriage driver jumped back down to the cobbled street, the image of the boy being shot spurring him to action. Before either he, the Garteaus, or the Bishop could say a word, Hanna drew on the carriage driver to halt his movement and Jill pulled the door open.

The fake Roland laughed, stuck his fingers through his eyeballs, and ripped off big slabs of flesh, revealing a swarming mass of bugs where his blood and bones should have been. The writhing bugs fell out of his body and onto the carriage floor, where they burned from the plasma fire as nothing more than confused slugs. In less than a minutes Roland's head had been completely removed and what was left of him simply stood there and burned.

Hanna turned to the stunned Garteaus, as the carriage driver looked for a place to put himself. "We're going to need to see Roland's bedroom. Now. Spring for a train."

Jill wrinkled her nose at Roland's skin and the bugs continued to burn.

"Don't be dramatic when we're in front of clients," Hanna said. "We've seen, and smelled, worse."

"It's not those things," she said, looking to Hanna. "I'm just confused."

"About where the slugs came from?"

"What? No, not that," Jill said, waving the thought aside.

"What, then?

"I can't figure out if this new twist is better or worse than babysitting? I mean, kids are horrendous, but this way, at least, we can shoot them."

Hanna rolled her eyes back to the Garteaus. "Tick tock, Leo. Time's wasting. We've been hired to help, so we're going to help. You will be okay with this."

"Of course, of course," a shaken Mr. Garteau said as he pulled his wife into his arms. It did not escape either Hanna or Jill's attention that while her arms went to her husband, her eyes went to the carriage driver.

*

An hour later, they were on the evening train out of Le Mans and headed to Mayenne. Christmas decorations were hung in the narrow aisles of the train, and the sounds of children singing "Stille Nacht" could occasionally be heard coming from one of the forward cars. Leo had bought them two private rooms, one for him, his wife, and Bishop Salome, and another in a separate car for the help: Hanna, Jill, and Anar, the carriage driver. The Americans sat on one bench and the driver sat opposite them. He was younger than them by at least a half-decade, making his age closer to twenty than thirty. He wore a fashionable black suit that made him, they reasoned, one of the finest dressed drivers in Europe. His face was angled with hard lines but covered with soft skin, and his shock of blonde hair seemed to refuse proper styling, sticking slightly up instead of being slicked back.

"You're from Finland, right?" Jill asked.

"Iceland," he said with a smile that he knew from experience opened more than doors.

"Take off your shirt," Jill ordered.

"Excuse me?" he asked, glancing to the door.

"Stop," Jill said. "You're hot. Like ridiculously hot. Hot people are never modest, so take off your shirt or I'm going to reach for my fire pistol and burn your jacket off you."

Anar's eyes went wide. "Is this necessary?" he asked, sending Hanna one of his charming smiles.

"Hey, Mr. Devilishly Handsome," Jill said, snapping her fingers to bring his eyes back to her, "you can smile at her all day, that's one lock you ain't gonna open."

"I don't know what you're talking about," he said with a smile. Always a smile.

"Do you have a sister?" Hanna asked.

Anar was puzzled for a moment and then he realized what Jill was saying. "I do, actually," he said to Hanna. "She is—"

"Shirt," Jill said, pulling her fire pistol off her hip. "Off."

Raising his hands in surrender, Anar slowly and uncomfortably removed his jacket, then his waistcoat, and finally his shirt.

Hanna frowned. "No scars."

"Scars?"

"The Garteau boy — or whatever it was that was pretending to be him — had scars. Jill wanted to see if you hand them, too."

"No, I didn't."

"Stop."

"I'll stop, but that doesn't mean you're right."

Anar kept smiling. "I do not know English well enough to understand half of what you said."

Jill sheathed her pistol and leaned back against the bench. "God. Hot and stupid," she sighed. "Where have you been all my life?"

"Iceland."

Hanna snorted. "Funny, too."

Jill waved a hand in her partner's direction. "Forget that," she said. "How long have you been sleeping with the boss' wife?"

Anar's smile vanished, and he shook his head. "Never," he insisted.

"Oh, please," Jill said, leaning forward to poke him in his chiseled chest. "Why else would she have you around?"

Anar looked wounded. "I'm an excellent driver."

Crossing her arms and leaning back in her seat, she turned to Hanna with a dead serious look on her face. "Colony, then."

Hanna nodded, but this did nothing save confuse Anar even more. "Colony?" he asked. "No, I am the driver."

Before either American could accuse him of lying, a scream cut through the early evening and the train's brakes were deployed, sending Hanna and Jill crashing into the handsome Icelander.

The door to their cabin opened, and a disapproving Bishop Salome looked in on the scene of the two American women draped over the body of the shirtless carriage driver. "Really," he scowled, "if you two are quite finished, there is a sight you must see. You are, after all, what passes for experts aboard this train."

*

Passengers were spilling out of their cabins and seats to see why they had stopped, clogging the aisle in the process, so Hanna and Jill improvised. The merchant's daughter knelt in the aisle so her ex-servant could climb onto her shoulders, then rose up so Hanna could open the roof's escape hatche. The Korean-American pulled herself up, then reached down to pull Jill through the opening.

"You buying Anar's act?" Hanna asked.

"Yes," Jill nodded. "He is definitely hot."

"About not sleeping with Sybil Garteau."

"He might be stupid, but she's not."

It was a cold evening, their breaths evident against the darkening sky. The fields around them were covered with a thick snow that the train's passengers were having difficulty moving through. Hanna and Jill gave them only the slightest glance before heading forward, running across the top of the steam train's cars. The large stack at the engine obscured their vision of what lay ahead of them due to its size and lingering expulsions of steam, but by looking to either side of the tracks, they could see that a large contingent of the train's employees were busy pointing at something up ahead and talking in panicked tones.

When they reached the engine car, Hanna jumped onto the small roof of the driver's cab as Jill scurried down to the snow. With the steam still climbing above the stack, Hanna still could not see anything, so she looked down to Jill.

Her friend was vomiting in the snow.

Hanna could feel the heat coming from the stack, and decided it was time to jump down. Once landing the snow (and surprising several passengers nearby), she looked forward.

"My god," she whispered.

"God has nothing to do with this," Leo Garteau said, coming up beside her, his face as ashen white as the snow.

Ahead of them, lining both sides of the tracks, were the bodies of at least twenty children nailed to "X"-shaped crucifixes, their bodies spread wide and their faces frozen forever in a look of absolute terror and pain.

"Come on," Jill said as she walked right past Hanna, "someone's got to check."

Hanna blinked at Jill's backside, slightly surprised at her partner's willingness to move forward, but understanding that this needed to be done, no matter how grim. Hanna jumped onto the tracks, where the snow had been beaten down and pushed aside by an earlier train, and moved forward after Jill.

Someone yelled for them to stop, and Leo Garteau told them to shut their mouth.

They reached the first child, a small girl of no more than four or five years old. She wore black, leather shoes, white stockings, and a crimson velvet dress. Her brown hair was curled, and her face looked up into the heavens.

"One last prayer for a disinterested God," Jill mumbled, pulling a hunter's knife off her thigh holster with a slightly shaking hand. "Times like this," she said, looking to Hanna with dead eyes, "I can see why you don't believe in anyone living upstairs."

Hanna said nothing; this was not the time for clever retorts and smart replies. Instead, she reached a hand out to steady Jill's, and together they plunged the knife into the girl's right leg. The knife sliced easily into the girl, offering little more than cold pudding. They pushed the knife through until the tip hit the wood of the "X," and then pulled it out.

The knife was coated with a brownish, whitish puss. More of the substance followed the knife out, dripping the thick, milky liquid into the snow. Small bugs began to force themselves out of the body, dropping to the earth.

The dead little girl began to laugh.

"The Krampus," she whispered, "is coming for your children. The Krampus," she yelled to the gathered passengers, "is coming for all your naughty children, just as it came for me!"

Jill's face went hard and cold. "I'm going to burn them all," she grunted, sheathing the knife and pulling out her fire shooter.

"Líta!" Anar yelled from back at the train. "Í skóginum! The woods!"

Turning to look past Jill, Hanna caught sight of something large in the forest off to their right. "Hey, stop!" she yelled, and the tall creature turned and ran from them. "Come on," she said to Jill, taking off after whatever it was that she had seen. It looked like a man draped in heavy furs, but he was abnormally tall.

A trick of the light? Hanna wondered.

Or the Krampus?

She pushed the latter thought out of her mind; Gunfighter Gothic had dealt with numerous demons and they all had one thing in common - they ran to you, not away from you.

The snow drifts were thick as they approached the woods (she could hear Jill huffing a few feet behind her), but once they reached the tree line, the ground swooped up and the snow thinned out. Darkness was beginning to be a problem, but she could see the large tracks in the snow and took off after whatever had made them.

Because while she wasn't ready to say she was chasing a European myth that stole children, the footprints she followed were too large to be that of a man.

The trees were densely packed, and Hanna had to spend more time than she wanted looking down to follow the footsteps, realizing that if the creature she was following could squeeze through, she could, too.

"There!" Jill yelled. "To your left!"

Hanna followed Jill's instructions and saw that the creature (big, covered in gray fur, large horns) had made a sharp turn ahead of them and if they risked going that way, they could cut him off. "Follow the tracks!" she ordered Jill. "I'll try to head him off!"

Jill didn't think it was a good idea, but she did what she was told, and kept following the tracks that curved off to the right as Hanna took off to the left to find her own way. The trees became increasingly thick as the snow became increasingly thin, and Jill noted the presence of tufts of fur clinging to some of the trees that the creature had to push his large body through. Whatever it was they were chasing, Jill was getting her mind to the point to do it real harm.

With nearly every step forward, her mind forced the image of a young boy named Timmy into her mind. Though they did not like to talk about it, Hanna and Jill used to take a friend on their adventures.

Used to.

Until he couldn't.

She grit her teeth, physically forcing Timmy's image from her mind, and saw the reason the creature had turned left - the ground sloped sharply up to a ridge, absent of trees. Breathing hard, Jill tore ahead on the nearly snowless ridge. Her eyes danced to the left, checking for any sign of Hanna, and she would appear and disappear through the trees as her own pursuit continued.

Ahead of her partner, she reached a clearing, and saw the large, furry beast bounding towards a small pond.

"Move!" she yelled back to Hanna, and then tore off after the creature.

Hanna swore as she had to keep stopping and figuring out the best way forward. The forest was simply too thick for her to plunge ahead blindly. She reached the edge of the clearing only to find a series of hedges in her way. Peering through the leafless branches, she could see Jill closing in on the creature, who was closing in on a pond.

Knowing it was going to leave scars, Hanna pushed through the branches, her mind flashing back to the scratches that had befallen the pretend Roland Garteau. What the hell was going in with this case? Pushing her way free, Hanna slipped and landed with a thud in the snow. Looking up from her prone position, she saw Jill squeeze off two blasts from her fire shooter. The first slid past the creature's head and Hanna could clearly see his horns. The second hit the creature square in the back, sending a fireball into the sky.

The creature roared and jumped into the pond before quickly sinking beneath the surface.

Jill moved into the pond, sloshing in down to her knees. "Come back!" she yelled, sending a long burst of flame over the water's surface.

By the time Hanna had scrambled to the pond's edge, Jill's fire shooter was empty and her friend was screeching wildly, her hand slapping the water. "Get back here, you bastard!"

"Jill!" Hanna called. While she was only a few feet behind her, Jill keep wailing and wading deeper. "Jill!" the Korean-American shouted again. Jill's only response was to toss her fire shooter towards the center of the pond. "Well, that's just stupid," Hanna said.

Jill spun hard on her friend. "Don't you tell me—!" Her eyes went wide. "Not good," she said at something behind the Korean-American.

Hanna turned in the snow, and saw three more of the creatures standing at the edge of the forest. Setting her jaw, her hand reached for her electric blaster. "Let's try not to burn the forest down," she said as Jill slushed out of the water.

"No promises," her partner replied.

The three, horned and hairy creatures slipped back into the shadows.

As Hanna and Jill started to move after them, a bright light slammed onto them from above.

"Arrêtez!" a voice yelled.

The women looked up into the bright light to find a hot air balloon hovering above them. There were four men in the basket, one to hold the steam-powered lamp that lit Hanna and Jill up, and three more to point their rifles at them. They fired several bullets down into the snow near the women as warning shots.

"Arrêtez!" the man at the lamp repeated. "Vous êtes en état d'arrestation!"

*

"This is a first," Jill said as the hot air balloon rose into the sky. The gendarmerie, dressed in basic black coats and pants, had loaded them back into the balloon. They thought it odd there weapons were not taken, but they did not complain. Only one of the cops had entered the balloon with them, and they were now ascending over the tree line. Looking back towards the train, Hanna and Jill could see that the bodies of all the phony children had been set on fire.

"Is it your first time being arrested, ma chère femme?" the one remaining policeman asked. He was short and pear-shaped, but had a pleasant face.

"No," Jill said.

"Definitely not," Hanna added. "Why have we been arrested?"

"My name is Charles Oudry," he said, adding, "You are not being arrested."

"What's with the charade, then?" Jill asked.

Before Oudry could answer, Hanna added, "Where are you taking us?"

The gendarmerie smiled. "To Heaven," he said, sending more flames into the circular balloon above them, and causing the balloon to rise higher into the air. As Hanna and Jill exchanged a quick glance, Oudry placed his arm into the flame, causing his jacket to catch on fire.

"Balls," Jill grunted, reaching for the hunter's knife on her thigh and jamming it into the laughing face of the policeman. Pulling down, she cut a gash in his face and neck. Oudry continued to laugh as slugs and maggots fell out of his face and to the floor of the wooden basket.

"Jill," Hanna said urgently. "His arm."

"What?"

"Cut it off!"

Jill slashed down on his burning arm, but what was left of Oudry moved it in time and instead of cutting it off clean, it hung limply, cut in half. Bugs tumbled free, catching on fire as they fell to the basket floor.

"Great idea," Jill snapped.

"Nice execution," Hanna shot back.

Oudry took his burning, hanging arm and jammed it against the cut on his face, which erupted in flame. "If you do not return to Le Mans, the Krampus will come for you!"

"What do I cut off now?" Jill asked, as Hanna stepped into Oudry, grabbed his coat, and shoved him up and over the side of the burning basket.

Giving only a cursory glance over the edge to make sure Oudry had fallen away from the basket to land in the snowy clearing beneath them, the two women quickly assessed the situation. They were standing in a basket nearly five feet by five feet. It was on fire, as were the bugs that had fallen to the floor.

"We gotta get the fire out," Jill said, stomping on the bugs.

"I wish you wouldn't do that," Hanna said.

"Why?" Jill asked just before her boot cracked the basket's floor. "Oh, right."

"That's why I make the plans."

"Yeah, well, I'll just stand here and wait for your plan," Jill said, heading for the control mechanism.

"You don't know how to use that."

Jill paused, frowning. "I don't know how to use this."

Hanna stepped in and shut off the flame, then stood there.

"Well?" Jill asked as the flame began to lap their way up the wicker basket.

Hanna made a face. "I don't ... uh ... know how to use this, either. I think we just wait for the air to cool off and we'll gently float back to the ground."

Jill blinked, and looked around her. "Are we descending?"

"I don't think so."

"Cause we're still on fire, which has to make that, you know, tougher."

"Do you have any ideas?"

"Hanna Pak is asking me if I have any ideas?"

"I'll take that as a no."

Jill sighed and looked around at the flames. "I wish they were bigger."

"What? Why?"

Jill shook her head as the flames danced in the night around them. "This one's not fun," she said, her shoulders slumping. "Those are kids down there. I mean, I know, I know," she held up her hands, "I hate kids, but I don't want to see them dead or filled with bugs. We've had too many cases with kids." She hook her head, "I can't stop thinking about Timmy."

The name hit Hanna hard. "Yeah," she said.

"It's been almost twenty years," Jill said, as the flames danced higher. Her eyes began to water. "We never even talk about him. What's wrong with us?"

Hanna took a deep breath in and let it out slowly. Her eyes scanned the air around them, but there was nothing to see except the darkening sky. For the moment, the flames seemed unimportant. They were rising slowly, but Hanna didn't know what to do. The flames were too abundant to stamp out, but the air in the balloon above them wasn't going to normalize in time for the balloon to drift back to the ground. What kept her from doing something, anything, was that the balloon was drifting towards the nearby town, where there were roofs that perhaps they could reach if they jumped.

It was a situation where the best thing they could was wait.

"Jill," she said softly, "I ... back in Colorado. When you were fighting the kaiju in Colorado ... I saw him."

"What?" Jill asked, stepping forward, onto the crack in the floor without realizing it. "Why didn't you tell me?"

"Because it wasn't really him," Hanna insisted, the flames now reaching the top of the basket. She looked to the town and saw it wasn't coming fast enough. "You were there, too," she said distractedly, "as a kid. It was ... hard. It was what the Nomadiri drugs made me see."

"Finch," Jill said.

"Yeah."

"We need better friends."

"Finch is okay," Hanna said.

"How many times has he drugged us now?" Jill asked, and before Hanna could answer, Jill's leg fell broke through the basket's floor.

"Hang on," Hanna said, stepping forward, her weight combining with the fire to cause the wood to crack. Jill slipped further down. Her left leg was now trapped awkwardly at her side as Hanna jumped back to the edge. Glancing over her shoulder, Hanna could see they were still too far away from the town to reach the safety of a rooftop.

"We need to get down," she said to Jill.

"Duh," Jill said, starting to look a little panicked as she started pushing burning maggots away from her. "I don't think that's going to be a problem for me."

"I'm going to get us down," Hanna said.

"How?"

She pulled out her plasma shooter.

"That's a really bad idea!" Jill yelled.

"We've got to get down before you fall through," Hanna said. "You were right. The flames need to work faster." The Korean-American fired six pellets of hot plasma up into the balloon, causing six holes to emerge and the balloon to drop noticeably.

The flames in the basket reached the cords holding the balloon to the basket and began to crawl upwards.

"Hanna!" Jill yelled as she felt the boards around her leg begin to creak. Hanna tried to take a step forward, but the board groaned noticeably. Looking around, she acted as soon as an idea came to her. She grabbed one of the balloon cords, put the plasma blaster beneath that hand and fired, severing the rope.

The basket lilted to that side.

"What the hell?!" Jill yelled. Her body weight shifted with the basket and another crack in the wood dropped her leg all the way through the floor.

Hanna ignored her, moving to the next rope and doing the same maneuver. The basket lilted harder, putting an undue strain on the remaining cords. Hanna looked out over the edge and saw her plan was working — the basket was now careening towards town. A quick guess told her there were maybe thirty or forty buildings rushing towards them.

"Shit!" Jill yelled as her foot slammed against a chimney.

"Now or never," Hanna mumbled, jumping over Jill's head to turn on the flame full bore. The infusion of air jolted the balloon and jerked the basket, sending the cordless end rotating upwards.

"You stupid idiot!" Jill yelled.

"If you didn't like that, you're gonna hate this," Hanna said, severing two more cords with her plasma shooter. The basket dropped several feet, more wood breaking away beneath Jill.

Hanna looked down, ignoring Jill's outstretched hand. Below Jill, she could see a roof.

She slammed her boot on the floor and it gave way, sending the women falling to the roof below. Their bodies hit the thatched roof hard and burst through; they were sent crashing into the attic of a small, two-story building.

"Ouch," Hanna said.

"I hate you," Jill replied.

Their bodies sore from the fall, each woman took a few moments to catch her breath. The attic was dark, the only light coming in through the hole they made in the roof.

Hanna pushed herself to her knees, and then to her feet. Moving to the opening in the roof, she looked off to the distance in the direction of the train. Spots of orange glowed just above the tree line as the fake children kept burning. Guessing there was over a mile between them, Hanna pondered their next move. The children set on the train tracks were obviously tied to what they'd seen with Roland earlier in the day, but did that mean they should investigate here, or continue on to Mayenne?

"I just want to sleep," Jill said.

"Here?" Hanna asked, looking back at the attic.

"Sure," Jill said, shrugging. "Does it make me a bad person that I really do not want to walk back to that train?"

"We kinda have to," Hanna said.

Jill shook her head. "What the hell kind of town are we in where the kids and cops are made of maggots?"

"Sillé-le-Guillaume," a male voice in a British accent said from the roof above them. Hanna and Jill looked up to see a young, handsome black man staring back at them. "Hello," he said, giving them a hard stare.

"Yum," Jill said. "I definitely do not want to walk back to that train."

"Damn," Hanna said, scratching her head. "This is the day for hot dudes."

"Yeah," Jill said. "This must be what it's like for guys to run into us."

"True."

The man scowled, and he pulled two pistols off his hips to point them down at the women. "Who are you and why are you ruining my investigation?" he asked.

"Your investigation?" Jill asked. "Oh, nuts."

"Your Poseidon's kid?" Hanna added. "I can see it."

"Because he's black?" Jill asked. "That's so racist."

"Stop thinking between your legs."

Ignatius Poseidon shook his head. "Did my father send you?" he asked. Giving them a longer look, recognition came to him, "Are you the two Americans who stole his steam carriage?"

The Americans nodded.

Ignatius holstered his guns and a small smile came to his lips. "Then it is my supposition that we are going to get along famously," he said, and reached a hand down to offer them a way out of the attic.

*

"Here is the scene," Ignatius said as they stood in a dark kitchen of a small house at the edge of the town that he had commandeered as his headquarters. The burning balloon had crashed into an open field and was burning itself out as they formulated their next step. The young demon hunter was clad head to toe in black: boots, jeans, sleeveless shirt, and a protective, heavy vest. There was a sword on his back, a gun holster on his hips, and straps holding knives on an arm and thigh. "There are two supernatural factions in Sillé-le-Guillaume: the Krampus — these are the creatures you saw — and the Maggots, like Oudry and the children. From what I have learned, the Krampus kidnap a victim and then replace them with the Maggots."

"Maggots?" Jill asked. "Is that a professional term?"

The corner of Ignatius' mouth curled into the hint of a smile. "I don't know what to call them, but that's what they are."

"Is there any way to know the Maggots without cutting them open?" Hanna asked.

Ignatius shook his head. "Whoever is taking the original body is replacing them with a near perfect duplicate. There appears to be a limit of about a week before they falter, but between replacement and revelation, they're undetectable. Shapeshifting demons aren't dramatically uncommon, so there's no way to try to cut this problem off at the source."

"So we just have to stab them?" Jill asked.

"Yes."

Jill pulled her knife off her thigh.

Instead of looking concerned or protesting, Ignatius offered her his arm. Nodding her thanks, Jill pierced his forearm with the point of her knife, and withdrew it. There was blood on the tip.

Hanna folded her arms. "Are you sure you didn't want to get his shirt off to do that?"

Jill wiped the blood off on her pants. "The night's still young." Sheathing the knife, she pointed out the kitchen window to the pond she'd chased the Krampus to before their balloon ride. "Have you gone for a swim, yet?"

Hanna rolled her eyes. "Be serious, Jill."

"I am," she said, and her face told her partner she was. "I chased a Krampus into that pond and he jumped in but didn't come out."

Shaking her head, Hanna said, "He could have come out while we were busy in the balloon."

"If he did," Jill said, "there should be footprints."

Ignatius nodded. "Let's go check it out."

"Wait," Hanna said. "Are all the cops like Oudry?"

"I don't think so."

"But the Krampus kidnapped the original Oudry?"

Ignatius nodded. "That is my theory."

"Even though nothing in the myth suggests the Krampus comes for adults?"

Ignatius frowned.

"I know that look," Jill said, then shot Hanna a look. "Good job with all the thinking."

"Someone's got to."

Ignatius and Jill exchanged a look akin to naughty children being caught by a parent.

"Then we should split up," Hanna suggested with more indignation than she had planned on letting come out of her mouth. "You two can go check out the pond. I'm going back to the train."

"Why?" Jill asked, seeing the same look on Hanna's face that she used to give her when she was mad at Jill for flirting with some handsome young buck at a social event back in Boston.

"Because that's where our clients are," Hanna reminded her. "Once those bodies are done burning, I'd imagine the train is headed on to Mayenne. One of us needs to be on it." She looked to Ignatius. "Do you think Sillé-le-Guillaume is the epicenter of what's happening?"

Ignatius shook his head. "This is the fifth town I've been in over the last two weeks. Every town has a Krampus or five and every town has Maggots. I've been one step behind," he admitted through a frown. "That's why my father thinks I've disappeared. Better to not talk to him than get a lecture. I'm 26, not 16."

"Yeah," Jill said, poking him in his bare, muscled arm as if he were a slab of meat, "but are you, like, actually 26, or are you like your dad and look 26 until the drugs wear off and then you're all wrinkly and disgusting?"

Ignatius smiled. "I'm 26. Legitimately. I don't take drugs. Or leaf. Or drink."

Jill sighed. "Jesus, it's a good thing you're hot. You're more boring that Hanna." She turned to her partner. "Is splitting up the play you want to make? For the mission or because you're mad at me."

Stone cold, Hanna replied, "Yes."

"Okay," Jill said, "I walked into that. You go back with the Garteaus and I'll stay here with Mr. Clean Living. Let's find these missing kids, and let's hope we find them alive."

*

Though they had been friends as long as they had been alive, there were times when Hanna and Jill wanted to be apart. It wasn't because they were ex-lovers or because Hanna had always been more in love with Jill than Jill could ever be in return; it was simply that any two people who spent that much time together needed the occasional break.

At least, that's what she told herself as she walked back through the snow towards the train and the burning, crucified children.

Seeing Jill's eyes when she looked at Ignatius meant that this was one of those times for Hanna. It wasn't that she was still overtly in love with her partner, but that when Jill set her eyes on someone, she became insufferable to be around.

Or, Hanna knew, maybe it was just a matter of herself becoming too attuned to Jill's behavior and too ready to be slighted. She had not been averse to bouts of melodramatic depression over Jill's treatment of her over the years. What made it worse was that sometimes Jill didn't even know she was doing it, while at other times it was clearly on purpose.

"Ugh," she scolded herself as she made her way back through the snow-covered woods, "just stop. You're worse than a May Elizabeth Braddon novel."

Though there was no proof that all the gendarmerie were Maggots, Hanna saw no reason to risk their attention; they were either unaware that Oudry was a Maggot, in which case they would want to re-arrest Hanna, or they were aware that he was, in which case they would want her dead.

Keeping her head on a swivel, Hanna made her way quickly back through the forest along the route Jill and the Krampus had taken. Being on the ridge meant she exposed herself to peering eyes, but with the fires still blazing ahead of the train, she thought it worth the risk. The Bostonian moved off the ridge and traced the footprints back into the thick woods. She had a theory she wanted to put to the test, and she was hoping the densely-packed trees would provide an answer.

Ignoring Jill's footprints, she concentrated on those of the Krampus. At each tree those footsteps passed, Hanna would pause and look at the tree; in short order, she found what she was looking for: a tuft of the Krampus' fur.

There wasn't time to examine the evidence, as the conductor chose that moment to blow the train's whistle, signifying it's impending departing. Tucking the hair into her pants' pocket to examine later, Hanna hurried forward, reaching the tracks just as the train was starting to chug forward. She arrived in time to jump onto the steps in the second to last car, and her hand paused on the door's latch as she spied a confrontation inside the car.

Halfway down the central aisle, she saw Anar's backside, and in front of him, Sybil Garteau was standing with her back to him. Roland's mother threw up her hands, and then composed herself, bringing them down to smooth out her dress before walking away from him and into the private room she shared with her husband and Bishop Salome.

Except the bishop wasn't in that room, she saw. As Anar moved towards his cabin, the older man exited and as he and Anar both twisted their bodies to pass by each other, they paused. Salome reached out with his hand and made the sign of the cross on Anar's forehead, then reached into his robes to pull out a pendant. He kissed the pendant, then offered it to Anar, who kissed it, as well. Salome replaced the pendant and the two men continued shuffling past one another.

Hanna stepped back, out of sight, and waited in the cold until she heard Anar enter their cabin.

As she crouched in the cold, she watched the gendarmerie use snow to put out the last of the burning bodies.

It was a horrible display. Even knowing the children were actually Maggots did not make it an easy sight to see. There was something profoundly wrong with using children for such purposes, and it reinforced the question of what had happened to the real children?

*

Jill and Ignatius took opposite routes around the small pond, meeting at the point where Jill had seen the Krampus enter the water. They took their time, their breath hanging behind them in the cold night air, like ghostly reminders of a life ten seconds in the past. Jill made a point to not look across the pond to Ignatius; she knew what she was doing, of course, because she had always done it. Finding a boy to crush on and flirt with and get worked up was always how she kept herself distracted from the life of a merchant's daughter — a life she knew she was lucky to have but nonetheless found dreary. Her father — the father that had killed President Johnson and that she had killed at Kraken Moor when she discovered his treachery — had provided well for the family.

"There are no prints coming out of the water," Ignatius said, bring her out of her thoughts.

"None on my side, either," Jill said, looking quizzically at the pond. "So the Krampus went in and didn't come out. What do you know about them?"

Ignatius shook his head and kicked at the snow. "About the legend ... plenty. About the physical creatures? Not much, unfortunately. There are rumors of them in nearly every town in this part of France, but I've only seen three of them, and always from a distance. They seem to be one step ahead of me."

Jill looked at him and narrowed her eyes playfully. "Well, you do stick out."

"Because I'm devilishly handsome?"

"Because you're a black guy refusing to wear sleeves in the dead of winter, walking around with a sword, hunting demons in rural France," she said. "You tend to stick out."

"Good thing I've got a white woman to help me, then," Ignatius said. "France isn't hurting for them. You'll blend right in."

"Nobody as hot as me can blend in."

"You're physically attractive?" he asked, turning on his accented charm. "I hadn't noticed."

"Your eyes must keep going to my ass because I've got something on them, then," she said, letting him know he wasn't as cool as he thought.

Ignatius shook his head, but the smile could not be wiped. from his face. "How do you that?" he asked honestly. "You bounce back and forth between emotional states like you've got three people living in your head. I understand that it's a defensive mechanism, but are you doing it consciously or subconsciously?"

"Ugh," Jill grumbled. She could not wipe the thought aside, however. Even for her, she seemed all over the place today, like there were different emotional states inside of her taking turns being in control of the body. If she thought about it, her mind kept trying to go back to Christmases from earlier in her life, but she could remember the same moment from her childhood — her father, dressed as Santa, bringing her a box — in two different ways. In one of them the box contained a collection of dolls, and in the other memory, the box contained a key to the basement, with a note that read, "I have always been here, haven't I?"

Which was real?

Why was this happening?

"Jill?" Ignatius asked. "Are you well?"

"You sound like Hanna," Jill said, pushing past whatever she was going through. Before he could contribute further to the conversation, Jill brought his attention back to the pond before them. "Is it deep?" Jill asked.

Ignatius answered by walking forward into the pond. "Run around to the other side," he ordered. "Meet me at the center."

Jill jogged around the small pond that wasn't more than 50 feet long and 30 feet wide. By the time she'd reached the far end, Ignatius was already knee-high in the water. As cold as the night was, it had not been cold enough to freeze even a pond of this size, and the only ice on its surface clung to the edge, thin and clear. Jill stepped onto that ice, breaking it beneath her back heel, because that's the sort of thing one was supposed to do with thin, crunchy ice.

The pond water might not be frozen, but it was cold, and Jill wished she had more than her bolero for protection from the chill. If Hanna were the one walking across the pond towards her, she would have complained, but not with Ignatius. She did not know if her tongue was stilled because of who he was, who his father was, or simple because he was Not Hanna. He was certainly attractive, but that was likely to loosen, not stiffen, her tongue. Rather, it was about professionalism, she thought. Her and Hanna had decided to make this their life, and here she was walking towards someone else who had made it his life. She wanted to impress him because she wanted to be good at this.

It mattered to her, she realized all at once, that she was good at this.

That's why she was jumping moods, she realized. It wasn't just a defensive mechanism but a way to try to beat the case before it got the better of her. All these kids gone missing ...

The thought brought Timmy's image back into her mind, but this time, instead of forcing it out, she embraced it. They were stupid kids — all of them — and they did stupid things all the time. Timmy knew he wasn't supposed to climb as high as he did, but he did it, anyway, just like Jill would have done it and Hanna would have done it. Yeah, she knew, she had egged him on, but they all egged each other on.

Jill was so lost in the memory, she almost missed what was happening. Halfway to the center of the pond, she was only as deep as her knees. Across from her, Ignatius was only a little further towards the center, but the water was up to his chest.

"Stop staring at your reflection, handsome, and check me out," Jill said.

Ignatius looked up and cocked his head to the side. "Huh," he said, noticing the difference in their positions. "That is not normal. Let's take this a single step at a time," he said, taking one step forward and then waiting for her to do the same. They exchanged several steps and were now not more than five feet apart when Jill took a step forward and fell forward into the pond, splashing her way to total wetness.

Ignatius forced himself through the cold water to help her gain her balance.

"Nice catch," she said, spitting water out of her mouth.

"You'll live," he said. He was taller than her by a half-foot, so she stood deeper in the water now that they were on the same floor. Ignatius took the lead, stretching his arm out ahead of him, and where Jill had fallen into the water his hand touched a metal wall. He rapped it with his knuckles as Jill moved up beside him. They slid their hands over the surface until they found the edges, and there was only a few feet between them.

"Escape tunnel?" Jill asked, wanting it to have come out like a statement and not a question.

Ignatius nodded. "I think so, but a door ..."

Jill ran her hands over the front of the metal box and let them trail down. By her waist, the front wall disappeared. "No door," she said. "Just a tunnel."

Ignatius' hand repeated her actions until he found the opening, as well. "It can't be far," he said, "or the Krampus wouldn't be able to swim to safety."

"Oh?" Jill asked, raising an eyebrow. "Are you an expert on Krampus physiology?"

Ignatius rolled his eyes to her. "You don't really think we're chasing a Krampus, do you?"

Jill smiled. "About time you realized that, which means it's likely a short swim to wherever the one I was chasing escaped to."

"If it's such a short distance, why are you still up here instead of down there."

"I was giving you a chance to be chivalrous. What's your excuse?"

"I was giving you a chance to prove women are the equal of men."

"Pssh," Jill said. "We're totally better."

Ignatius folded his arms across his chest and beneath the water. "Okay. Prove it."

Jill opened her mouth and shut it. Scowling, she grumbled something about how his dad was way hotter, then took several deep breaths to fill her lungs with oxygen, and submerged herself in the darkness.

The young demon hunter smiled to himself as she disappeared, but his pleasure soon vanished as Jill failed to return. He did not know what kind of swimmer Jill was, and could already tell she was stubborn enough to get herself into trouble. He cursed himself for not immediately counting off the seconds she was under, guessed that it had been a minute, and started counting from 30. When he got to 60 seconds, he started to ready himself for action. At 90, he took three big gulps of air, and followed after her. The water was dark, but as he swam forward, his hands touched the side of the tunnel wall and found handles. Pulling himself forward, he wasn't more than thirty seconds into his excursion when he ran into a set of legs, and then took a smack in the back of his head.

Jill.

Standing up, he found her up to her neck in the water, and he had to slightly cock his head to the side due to the low ceiling. A low light shone in from someplace ahead of them.

"Did you forget to come get me?" he asked.

"I wanted to see how long it would take you to come rescue me."

"How did I do?"

Jill shook her head and pulled her hand out of the water to give him a thumb's down.

Ignatius smiled and turned to look ahead of them. The tunnel was rectangular and angled slightly upwards, matching the slope of the land above it. In the distance, they could see where a lamp had been lit, and they slowly started moving towards it. With each step, their bodies rose slightly higher out of the water. Ignatius pulled a thin sword off his back and handed it to Jill, then took a knife off his thigh. When they reached the lamp, they were only up to their knees in the water.

Looking at the wall in front of her, Jill pointed up to where a ladder hung down through a hole that led to darkness. "Just once," she whispered, "I'd like to fight someone in broad daylight."

"Where's the fun in that?" Ignatius asked before turning serious. "Can you reach the ladder?"

"If you give me a boost."

"If I give you a boost, that means you have to go first."

Jill rolled her eyes. "My hero," she said and raised her arms, letting him pick her up at her waist and hoist her to the ladder, his hands giving her hips an extra squeeze that she didn't mind admitting sent a warm thrill through her body. It was hard climbing with the sword in one hand, but she pulled her body up and was soon climbing the ladder with her feet, as well as her hands. The ladder was short, and in just a few steps she was standing in a perfectly normal stall inside a horse barn. As Ignatius climbed up, Jill looked at the top of the ladder and saw that it could be raised and lowered.

"Just as I thought," Ignatius said, pulling himself into the barn. "Oudry's barn."

"It doesn't count as being clever unless you say that before we're standing in Oudry's barn," Jill said. "So we've got a

Krampus climbing into the barn of a Maggot. They're connected."

Ignatius nodded. "Likely, yes."

"Are you saying 'likely' because you didn't think of it?"

Ignatius pushed past her, looking at the ground and the walls of the stall for any signs of the Krampus, but there was nothing in the barn but stalls of horses and hay. He moved across the floor and tried the main double doors. "They're locked."

"That was nice of the Krampus," Jill said, moving into one stall that had an unusual amount of disheveled hay. She began dragging her boot through it and hit something big and wet. "Monsters don't usually lock the door after they're done terrorizing the town. Of course," she added, pulling a thick coat of fur out of the hay, "they don't usually leave their costumes behind for us to find."

Ignatius moved to the stall, and drew a line in the dirt across it's opening, frowning deeply. "I really wish you hadn't found that," he said, carving a few ancient symbols through the line. "You can come out now, Oudry," Poseidon's son announced, and Jill heard the ruffling of canvas in the stall next to hers moments before Inspector Oudry moved into view, wearing only a sopping wet, white, one piece style undergarments.

"You didn't give me enough time," the gendarme officer grunted.

"I gave you plenty," Ignatius replied, pointing his sword into Oudry's gut.

Slapping the sword away from him, Oudry pointed in to Jill. "What do we do with her?"

"We leave her."

"Leave a witness?" Oudry said, crossing his arms. "You're going soft."

"And you've forgotten our mission," Ignatius replied, swiping his sword across Oudry's front, putting a huge gash in his undergarments but leaving his skin untouched. The demon hunter looked in sadly on Jill. "I would tell you to stay, but you won't. I would explain our actions, but I cannot risk you failing to see our purpose."

"Try me," Jill said, dropping the Krampus outfit and moving towards the line on the floor.

"I am afraid there isn't time to take one who we do not trust," Ignatius said, "though I promise you, when this is over, I will offer you a full explanation and put my fate in your hands. I will return for you within one day."

"The hell you will," Oudry said. "You took an oath."

"An oath that will be invalid in another twelve hours," Ignatius reminded him.

Jill took another step towards the line and the hunter put a hand up. "Do not cross that line."

"Or what?"

"Or there will be an actual Krampus in our midst this evening," he said, pointing at her, "and a nervous village looking for revenge." The young demon hunter looked at her with a sad face. "It is a damnable world we live in," he said, and left her to sit and wait.

*

Hanna entered her cabin on the train to find a dejected Anar looking out the window, his forehead touching the glass. Closing the door quietly, she sat not only on the bench opposite him, but near the door.

"Come clean with me," Hanna said in a gentle tone but a firm voice. "It's clear you're not telling us everything, just as it's clear you're in over your head."

"I cannot," Anar said, his forehead staying pressed against the glass but tilting slightly to the side so he could take in Hanna's reflection. "You would not understand."

"I travel Europe dressed as a cowboy with my ex-lover and shoot demons in the face," Hanna reminded him. "Try me."

"Very well," he said, and rose to his feet, pulling off his driver's jacket and shirt.

"Not my thing, remember?"

"I am no one's thing," Anar said, "and everyone's thing."

"Handsome, a good driver, and a philosopher," Hanna said as Anar undid his belt buckle and let his pants slide to the floor to stand naked before the American. "Seriously," she said, putting an edge of steel in her voice, "I'm not into guys and I'm not afraid to shoot them."

Anar looked at her sadly. "I wish I could get you to shoot me. It would end this nightmare," he sighed, closing his eyes. When he opened them, they had turned all white and quickly clouded over with black and then red.

Hanna's hand went to her plasma blaster, and she started to rise to her feet, but before she could straighten her body, Anar's left arm reached out to knock her upper torso through the glass portion of the cabin's door with a force his body should not have been able to generate. Hanna's head was knocked backwards and her lower back was caught on a shard of glass in the door's frame. Yanking her upper body back into the room, Anar kicked her in the stomach, knocking her completely through the door frame and into the hallway. Pulling her hands up to protect her face from falling glass and splintered wood, Hanna caught only a glimpse of Anar standing alone in the cabin, roaring like a crazed animal towards the ceiling as two dark, grey horns grew and twisted from his forehead and light, grey and white fur pushed out of his skin, covering him.

As Hanna pulled her plasma blaster up out of the small pile of debris she was buried in, Anar turned his back to her and smashed his way through the side of the train to escape into the cold, French night. Resisting the urge to shoot blindly, the Bostonian was quickly put upon by the other passengers of the train car, now pouring out of their cabins to see what was causing the noise.

Looking around, Hanna saw Leo Garteau and Bishop Salome, but not Sybil Garteau.

She was not surprised.

*

Alone in the stall of Oudry's barn, Jill stood within six inches of the line that Ignatius had drawn into the dirt and carefully moved her hands towards the invisible barrier. She half-thought (or half-wanted to believe) that Ignatius was simply bluffing and that this line with its arcane marking was nothing more than art, but as her hand moved closer to the vertical plane of the center line, she could feel her hand begin to tingle, as if her nerves were falling asleep, and so she pulled it back.

"It's always the hot ones," she muttered, kicking dirt at the carvings out of spite.

Spite led to inspiration, however, as she hypothesized she could simply kick enough dirt on Ignatius' spell to cover it, but as the dirt from her first kick settled on the carvings, a hot jet of air spiked from the ground to blow the immigrant dirt away, restoring the original design.

Stepping back, Jill looked around the stall and remembered there were three other potential exits from this trap. The two side walls of the stall extended up to the second floor, where there were half-floors, filled with hay. The stall itself had hay and a few tools, but nothing to help her climb up to the second floor. The back wall of the stall was solidly constructed.

Jill could almost here Hanna in her ear, telling her to use her sword and a knife to climb up the stall walls to the second floor, but Jill brushed the thought aside. She had a fire shooter on her hip, didn't she? Might as well burn the wall down, she thought, and if the whole barn goes up ... so be it.

She could get the horses out.

Probably.

Definitely.

Um ...

Deciding that you could talk yourself out of any half-baked idea given enough time, Jill's hand went to her hip to pull out the fire shooter and found that it was gone. "The hell?" she asked, looking down to see both her fire shooter and electric pistol were missing. "How did I lose them?" she asked herself, and her mind jumped back to when Ignatius gave her a boost to help her climb the ladder out of the tunnel. He'd given her a gentle squeeze. She'd taken that as an act of physical flirting but he must have done it when he lifted her weapons.

"Climb," Hanna's voice said in her head, and Jill moved to the wall, intending to do just that when she saw how high it was.

"Forget that," she said, held up the sword Ignatius had given her, and swung hard at the stall wall.

Thunk.

Over and over, Jill swung the sword, trying to put a big enough crack in the wood to climb through. Whenever a crack emerged from a sword strike, she'd step back and kick at the wood, trying to knock it loose. After five minutes and what seemed to Jill like a thousand swings, she'd managed to kick a hole through part of the wall, big enough for her head to poke through. Catching herself before jamming her head through without checking it out, she brought her hand to the wall as she had the invisible plane at the front of the stall. When she did not feel any tingling in her hand, she stuck her head through and found herself looking into the eyes of a barely interested brown horse, having a midnight snack of hay.

"Lot of help you are," she said.

The horse chewed the hay slowly but otherwise, did not respond.

Jill pulled back and resumed hacking at the wood, then used both her feet to kick the boards loose and her hands to rip them free. Within minutes, she had enough of the boards removed to squeeze herself through.

"Impressive, aren't I?" she asked the horse.

The horse didn't seem impressed.

"What do you say about going for a ride, eh?" she asked, looking for a saddle. Finding one, she slung it onto the horse's back, realized she had put it on backwards, and then took it off to put it on the right way.

The horse let her do her thing.

It was good hay.

"They never tell you about these parts in the stories, do they?" she asked, patting the horse as she attached the bridle. "All the grunt work. So boring. Putting the headstall right here ... the throatlatch attaches across here ... the bit goes in the mouth ... ugh, put me to sleep. This is why being a hero is so tough," she said to the still disinterested horse. "No one has the stomach to live through the moments of drudgery. Well, it's not all fun and games and shooting demons and getting wasted on hopped-up absinthe. No, it's a lot of boring-ass work."

The horse shook his head at the presence of the bit.

"Well, no, of course I don't consider myself a hero," Jill said defensively, "but others do. Sometimes. Once in a while. Remind me to tell you how much Queen Victoria likes me," she said, picking up the sword and climbing onto the horse's back. "Once we figure out where we're going, of course," she said, and dug her heels into the horse's side, easing it forward.

The horse crossed the entrance to the stall and Jill had a moment of triumph until she saw Ignatius had drawn more arcane barriers into the floor of the barn, essentially keeping them in place.

The horse whinnied.

"I know," Jill nodded. "He's kinda impressive, even when he's being evil."

Jill let herself down, jamming the sword into the hard, dirt floor. There were lines drawn across the floor one stall to the right and left of where she had been trapped. She gave a quick thought to moving back through the underground tunnel, but saw it lay on the other side of the line to her left. Looking again at the barrier, and then back to the horse, Jill openly wondered, "How bad could it be?"

Taking the horses reign, she approached the carving to her right, but as the horse came within a foot, he stopped and refused to go further.

"Come on," Jill urged, but the horse refused.

The horse whinnied.

Jill looked the horse in the eye and then made a show of looking beneath his body. "Guess you've got balls in name only," she said. "You're really just a chicken."

The horse shook his head and took two steps away from the line.

"Well, at least I know you're not possessed," Jill grumbled, looking around the barn. "Here, horses!" she called. "Maybe one of them isn't so afraid to cross a line in the dirt."

Two horses, it turned out, answered Jill's call, but as the grey horse in front of her and the white and brown horse behind her came to stand in front of each barrier. Looking back and forth between them, Jill could see that both horses were as hesitant to cross the lines as her horse was, but unlike her horse, the two new horses didn't back away from the line. Urged on by unseen riders, the two horses stepped over the barriers in unison, and yelped in pain. Their heads shook as their eyes rolled back, going all white, then all black, then all red as their bodies distended before white, spiky fur burst through the parts of their bodies that had crossed the threshold.

Dark horns grew and twisted out of their heads.

"Krampus horses?" Jill asked in disbelief, as her horse began to panic and back-stepped into his stall.

The hell horses moved towards her, their bodies transforming from normal to Krampus as they crossed over Ignatius' barrier.

With her only way out being up, Jill dashed back into the open stall and jumped up onto the nervous back of her horse, and tried to rise to her feet on the saddle, but the horse was too nervous to allow this. The two demonic horses appeared in the stall's entrance, which caused Jill's horse to go into a state of fear so intense he gave up his nervous prancing to shake in place, allowing Jill to climb to her feet on his back, and then jumped up to cling to the rafters above her.

The Krampus horses snarled their discontent, but Jill was above them now, out of their reach. With the normal horse forgotten about, the Krampus steeds raised up on their hind legs and swatted their horned heads at her as their sharp teeth snapped at her lower legs.

With no weapon on her, Jill relied on her boots to kick the horses when they came too close as she climbed, hand over hand to the edge of the stall, where she pulled herself up onto the second floor.

"Ha!" she yelled triumphantly, kicking some of the bundled hay down at them out of spite.

In response, the turned horses slammed their heads into the stall wall, attempting to knock her down. Jill backed up and looked for an escape. She reasoned Ignatius' enchantment would extend all the way to the ceiling of the barn; she could move around the extended spell wall, but not through it, so her best bet way to move outside through the barn's exterior wall, but when she started to make her way to the nearest opening, she heard the scared neighing of what she had quickly come to think of as her horse below her.

Running back to the edge, Jill saw the demonic horses had turned their attention to their unchanged barn mate. They had him pinned against the back of the stall and were taking turns huffing and stomping their feet at him, their elongated horns threatening to shred his skin.

There was a part of Jill that yelled out for her to take advantage of this and escape quickly and quietly into the night, leaving the horse behind, but there was another part of her that sat in a greater position in her mind that told her she could not leave the horse to their devices. Perhaps it was this case's focus on children, and her hatred for those who took advantage of those who could defend themselves, but Jill knew she couldn't leave the horse to fend for itself. Without any weapons on her, she wasn't sure exactly what she should do.

And then her eyes spotted the sword Ignatius had given her, sticking in the dirt back on the main floor. Leaving her vantage point to find a way down, Jill lowered her body over the ledge and then dropped to the floor, picking the sword out of the dirt as she stalked back into the stall.

Both of the Krampus horses were now fully transformed into menacing beasts of gray fur, red eyes, and spiked horns. There was no way Jill could take them both by surprise, but with their backs to her as they focused on the normal horse, Jill quietly slipped between them and shoved her sword straight through the horse's front rib cage, stabbing its heart.

The horse reared in pain and raised its front hooves into the air. Jill hung onto the sword, pulling down at the horse raised up, and slicing deep through its ventricle. Yanking the sword free, she turned on the other horse just as one of its horns jammed towards her. Spinning to the side, Jill's arm was still scratched as the horse trapped her between it's horns, but she kept her body spinning in a tight circle until she was facing the horse.

Dropping to the earth, Jill shot the tip of the sword upward, puncturing the lower jaw and tongue before jamming into the top of the horse's mouth.

The first horse's body fell hard to the floor, spurting blood out of the gash Jill had caused. It wouldn't be a problem, but the second horse was still jerking its head around dangerously. Jill ducked out of the way, trying and failing to reclaim her sword.

The normal horse wanted to escape and kicked its legs hard to jump forward, but the Krampus horses blocked his path, and his hooves connected instead with the wall of the barn, sending a swift crack running up one board.

"Do that again!" Jill yelled, but the horse was too far gone to understand her command, even if he could understand her command. Diving beneath the one remaining upright Krampus horse, Jill positioned herself in the rear of the stall and slapped at the normal horse's back legs, causing him to kick back hard again. Consumed with panic and the flight response raging hard within him, the horse kicked again and again, feeling the wall start to give way.

The second Krampus horse slumped to the floor, and Jill quickly ascended to the saddle of her horse, calming him just long enough to urge him to jump past the two demonic horses. Once out of the stall, her horse remembered the lines in the dirt and reared up, almost sending Jill to the dirt.

"Back the way we came, big fella," Jill said, aiming the horse back into its stall, where two Krampus horses lay in the dirt, one dying quietly and the other dying violently. The wall behind them was cracked through in multiple spots. "It's the only way," she said, patting the horse on the side.

The horse dug its hooves into the dirt and lurched forward. When his front hooves hit the dirt in front of the

Krampus horses, it jumped forward, slamming into the wall of the barn and crashing through.

It didn't need Jill's urge to run as fast as he could into the night, happy to put Oudry's barn behind him. And it didn't need to ask the question that Jill was asking herself ... where were they headed?

*

The train kept hurtling through the night towards Mayenne, the passengers put back into their private cabins, on edge and ill at east. The images of the burning children were fresh in everyone's mind, and now there was a cabin with the wall blown out. The conductor had decided they were close enough to power through the remaining thirty minutes of the trip, and those in the cabins near Hanna's who complained about the cold were allowed to move to other rooms.

There were plenty of complaints.

Leo Garteau had tried to bring his wife to another car, but Sybil was near inconsolable and refused to move. Wanting to cut off a fight before it started, Hanna suggested to Leo that he go in search of brandy and blankets to help his wife make it home without catching cold; when Sybil's husband hesitated, Bishop Salome stepped in and suggested they both go forward, and Leo agreed.

Hanna stood in the doorway of the Garteau's cabin until Leo and Salome were off their car, leaving Hanna and Sybil alone.

"Spill it," Hanna ordered.

"I don't—"

Hanna clicked the hammer on her electric pistol to get Sybil's attention, then let it glide back slowly, letting the charge dissipate on its own. These fancy weapons Lady Carashire had paid for were hard to wrap one's head around, but easy to get used to.

Sybil wiped tears from her cheeks and sniffled loudly, sucking snot back up her nostrils in a most un-ladylike manner. "What do you want to know?" she relented.

"Did you know your boy had been replaced?"

Sybil shook her head.

"How could a mother not know?"

The young American snapped her head around, her eyes flashing with fire at having her parenting called into question, but it was a reflex response of an aggrieved mother and the fire put itself out. "He's not even my child," she said weakly.

"The whole truth, please, not just the half of it," Hanna said, glancing down the aisle to where Leo and Salome had exited. "Before your husband gets back. You were having an affair with Anar?"

Sybil choked down a sob and nodded, her thin fingers playing with the hem of her dress. "It is more complicated than that," she whispered, "but ... but Leo ... when I met him, I knew he wasn't a perfect man, but he promised me Europe and wealth. Do you know what I did back in the States?" she asked, looking up through swollen eyes. "I was a tobacco girl at a bar in Nebraska. Leo was my ticket out. I don't apologize for that."

"I'm not asking you to," Hanna said, and as Sybil attempted to get control of her emotions Hanna decided to share her own history with the girl that was younger than she was. "I was a servant, too, back in Boston," Hanna said, entering the cabin to sit on the bench opposite the blonde woman. "I was Jill's servant, in fact. We headed west a few months ago and ended up being rather good at shooting weird and dangerous things. Over here, it's easier to treat each other as equals, but I can't lie about how that past never lets me go. If you're brought up in one part of the house, it's hard to transition into living in the other part, isn't it?"

Sybil nodded, and offered a small smile. "I understood those men who came into our hotel. They liked to pinch and grab, thinking a piece of me came with the cigarettes and cigars I sold them from my tray. I didn't like it," she added, her hands balling into fists, "but I understood it. But this ... Leo expects me to be the dignified woman we both pretend that I am." The blonde woman balled her hands into fists. "What kind of woman am I that I prefer dealing with men who want me to be less than I am versus a man who wants me to be something more?"

In the distance, Hanna could hear the far door open, and wanted Sybil to get to the point. "How does this relate to the kidnapping? Did you know what Anar is?"

Sybil shifted on her bench, trying to find the words. "When a cowboy or miner took a handful of my ass instead of a pinch, I could turn and give him a little whack. He knew he went to far and didn't protest. Usually, at least. And if he didn't, I had a few security toughs I could call on. But here," she said, dropping her voice as Leo and Salome could be heard entering the far end of the car, "there is no recourse when it's your husband's ... stern gaze and cutting words. You can't give him a slap. You can't call on someone for help. He owns you. All you can do," she said, her voice quickening, "is find ways to distract yourself. Anar was ..."

Sybil hung her head, ashamed, and Hanna put the pieces together.

"You weren't having an affair with Anar, at all, were you?" She asked. "Not the version of him that was human, anyway."

Shutting her eyes tight, Sybil's head turned to the window, her thoughts reaching out to the monster in the countryside. "I know Anar would never hurt Roland," she said quietly but with total conviction, "so long as I kept the monster satisfied." The Nebraska girl looked up with haunted eyes. "Make no mistake, Miss Pak, there is a monster in my house, but it was not my lover."

"But who took Roland?" Hanna asked, still not fully understanding.

"What I realize now," she said, the tears coming back, "is that Roland was the distraction I should have been paying attention to, not Anar's cursed self. Maybe if Leo saw that I loved his son, that I could be the mother he needed, his hands would find me with the same gentleness they did in Nebraska and not with the rebuke of Europe. Leo would spend hours with that boy ... hours that I would spend with the creature only a scant few rooms away ..."

Leo and Salome were only a cabin or two away now, so Hanna dropped to one knee and grabbed Sybil's hand. "Listen to me carefully, Sybil. Who was hurting Roland? Or," she asked, thinking of what she'd witnessed that afternoon, "did anyone ever hurt the real him? Did the bruises start after the kidnapping? Or before?"

Sybil turned to the door, refusing to answer the question. "Leo, dear," she said, wiping away tears and turning cold, "I want to sit in another cabin. I am tired. Please, do keep the help away from me until morning, and please make it clear to them that you will do whatever it takes to get your son back."

"Of course, my dear," Leo said, stepping into the car and putting a rough hand on Hanna's shoulder. "Away, away," he demanded. "Come now, you heard my wife."

Hanna rose to her feet. "Yes," she said, meeting his eye. "I did, indeed."

Mr. Garteau led his second wife away from the cabin, leaving Hanna with Bishop Salome, who held a tray with brandy and glasses in one hand and a blanket in the other.

"Well," the Bishop said, "I suppose we shouldn't let the brandy go to waste."

With slumped shoulders, Hanna reached for the decanter and poured an inch worth of the brown liquid into two glasses, then took the bottle and left the bishop with the glasses. "I'm less civilized," she said, taking a swig straight from the bottle.

Salome nodded, dropping the blankets onto the bench on one side of him, and then placing the tray on the other. "What is troubling you?"

Pulling one boot up to the bench, Hanna looked past her knee to the old man. "How much of this do you know?" he asked.

"Of what part?"

"Of all of it," Hanna said. "The bruises to Roland. The kidnapping. The monster in our midst?"

"I don't know what you're talking about," he said, his face turning cold.

Wincing, Hanna ran a hand through her hair, pausing to scratch her head. "You see, Bishop, I know you're lying. I saw you, earlier, offering Anar the sign of the cross, so I know you know more than you're telling me."

"I don't—"

Hanna pulled her plasma blaster off her hip and pointed it at the older man.

"You wouldn't!" he insisted

"I'm an atheist."

"Heathen!"

Hanna's thumb worked the gun's intensity to its lowest setting and fired one shot across the short distance, the hot pellet slamming into Salome's black robes, just below his neck. As he jumped back in shock, Hanna moved onto him, straddling his waist. The tray of glasses was knocked to the floor as she held the blaster in one hand and the decanter of brandy in the other.

"I bet it's flammable," she said, looking down to where the plasma pellet had hit Salome's clothes, leaving a small burn mark.

"You're crazy!"

Hanna took a pull from the decanter and spit it onto the burn mark on Salome's robes and then cocked her gun. "Show me the pendant," she said, "or I fire. And before you ask, 'which pendant?', just assume I mean all of them."

"Fine! Fine!" Salome said, pulling out the pendant with nervous hands. When it was free, Hanna snapped it from his neck and rose to her feet, then sat back on her own bench.

Looking at the silver, oval-shaped pendant caused her to frown; she was expecting something demonic, but it was an image of a human stabbing a dragon. "Michael?" she asked, trying to recall the catechism she was forced to learn in the Masters' home as she turned the pendant over. There was an inscription: "Daniel 12.1." She held the inscription up to Salome.

The nervous bishop swallowed and wiped sweat off his forehead, and said, "You don't understand!"

Hanna cocked back the hammer on the plasma shooter.

"Okay!" Salome said, holding up his hands. "It won't matter. You're too late. You're far too late!"

"Then tell me what Daniel 12.1 says," Hanna insisted, firing a shot of plasma into the leather bench, burning a hole through leather, cushion, and wood.

Bishop Salome nodded nervously. "And at that time shall Michael stand up," he said in a haunted voice, "the great prince which standeth for the children of thy people: and there shall be a time of trouble, such as never was since there was a nation even to that same time: and at that time thy people shall be delivered, every one that shall be found written in the book."

Hanna's brow furrowed. "The great prince," she repeated, "which standeth for the children. You're in on this." She shook her head. "How does this work? You send Anar to steal the kids away from their parents? Or does he find them and come to you for permission?"

"Anar finds the children and alerts us," he explained quickly, "but it is Oudry who steals them away. He is a good boy but a cursed one. Anar lets the demon out to help spread rumors about the presence of the Krampus, and our agents wear costumes to do the same."

"You bastard."

Salome righted himself. "I trust in my God to judge my actions, not yours," he said. "And not that bastard Garteau and his American wife! If Poseidon were here ..."

"He's not," Hanna said, her mind giving Jill and Ignatius a quick thought. "Tell me where they're taking the kids."

Salome was indignant. "If you cannot figure that out," he said, his eyes darting to the pendant, "then you are not worthy of the answer."

Seeing his glance, Hanna looked down to the pendant, and the answer came to her almost instantly. "Of course," she grumbled, "St. Michael. You're taking the kids to Mont Saint-Michel."

*

Jill slowed the winded horse down a mile outside of Oudry's cabin, at the edge of a narrow road, lined with tall ash trees on either side. At the end of the half-mile long road that rose slightly in the country hills was a series of larger estates. The village was behind her, and behind that were the forest and train tracks that had brought her to Sillé-le-Guillaume. Patting the horse on his neck, Jill forced herself to do the thing she hated most: think.

There were fake Krampus and real Maggots. Except ... the horses suggested there were real Krampus, too. The Krampus — either real ones or humans in costumes — were clearly behind the kidnapping of children. She surmised the adult Maggots, like Oudry, were probably the people in the Krampus costumes doing the kidnapping, and while they took the children to wherever they were taking them, they left a Maggot behind to fulfill their duties so no one would suspect them.

Poseidon had mentioned hearing of something called the Krampus Society, and it wasn't hard to reason Oudry was among them.

And so, apparently, was Poseidon's kid, Ignatius.

Jill swore at herself, her breath visible in the night. Did her flirtations blind her to something she should have seen?

A woman's scream cut through the night behind them in the village, and Jill knew it was time to make a decision. The

Krampus horses had been uncovered, she thought, given how her horse began prancing nervously. Ignatius hadn't given her a clue as to where he was headed, so her next best option was to either stay here and look for clues or head to Mayenne and reconnoiter with Hanna.

Looking back to the village, she did not think Ignatius fool enough to leave an obvious clue, so Mayenne it was. She didn't think this horse could make it all the way in its present condition, and she doubted another train was coming until morning. Glancing up the road lined with ash trees, a smile crept across Jill's face as she took in the larger estates.

Three estates, in close proximity ... one of them must be desperate to outdo the other.

"Let's go, boy," she encouraged.

The horse wasn't thrilled with the idea of moving down the snow-crusted dark lane, and he moved ahead at a forced trot. Jill wanted him to go faster, but she could sense his tense muscles and didn't want to spook him.

A Krampus was there to do it for him.

Emerging out of the trees ahead of them, the tall, gray-furred "demon" snarled as it stood in the lane, motioning for Jill and her horse to come to him.

"That will not be a problem," Jill said, feeling smug at knowing the Krampus' secret. "Let's run him over, boy," she said, digging her heels in.

The horse didn't move.

"Come on," Jill urged. "Let's go get him!"

The horse refused to budge.

"It's just a guy in a suit!" Jill said, looking up the road to the Krampus and instantly losing some of her confidence as the Krampus started to run towards them. It ran not like a human but more like a gorilla, using its hands to assist in its forward progress. Letting out a chilling roar, Jill's horse bucked wildly, sending her flying into the snow.

The horse bolted, and in doing so, bought Jill time. Pushing herself to her knees and drawing her fire shooter, Jill saw the horse slam straight into the charging Krampus and get knocked back in her direction. The demon and horse rolled one over the other, the Krampus digging his sharp claws into the horse's side and his teeth into the horse's neck. Blood spurted off, its warmth splitting the cold air and nearly sizzling as it splattered against the snow's crust. Jill dove towards the trees to her right, taking cover just in time for the horse and Krampus to roll past.

Hating herself for abandoning the horse before all hope had been vanquished, Jill jumped back onto the road and headed for the large houses. Pumping her legs as fast as she could, the houses weren't getting closer as quickly as she wanted them to, the snow causing her to slip every few feet and the gentle rise of the road adding another level of difficulty. She was damn cold already from the trip in the pond, but now that she had to move instead of the horse, Jill understood just how tired her limbs had become. Pocketing her shooter, she sacrificed the weapon for balance. Even through the loud thumping of her heart in her ears, she could hear the horse screaming in pain behind her as the Krampus growled and snapped and feasted on the still breathing body. With her legs and lungs screaming, she finally neared the end of the ash tree lane. Stealing another glance behind her, Jill saw the Krampus' blood-soaked face turn to face her.

Perhaps if she hadn't chosen that moment to look back the Krampus would have continued its feasting on the horse, but in this moment, across the nearly half-mile distance, woman and beast locked eyes.

The horse was forgotten.

With a demonic yell that cut the night in half, the Krampus was on his feet and bounding after Jill. The Bostonian swore at herself and turned back to concentrate on running. Nearing the end of the ash trees, Jill pulled out her fire shooter and torched the last two trees on her right as she ran past, then did a quick 360-degree spin and blasted the trees on the other side.

Lamps began to turn on inside the houses, and Jill looked for a sign to tell her which one to ransack. Her goal wasn't the house, but the barn behind the houses, and as she looked at the three of them, she saw fire pouring out of the left two houses and steam emerging from the newer house on the right.

Steam.

Jill split the difference between them, the trampled snow between them telling her the two houses shared a road to their respective garages. When she was between them, she glanced to the windows on her right and saw a wide-eyed kid looking out at her.

Jill stuck her tongue out at him, causing the kids eyes to go even bigger before he burst out giggling.

Slipping in the snow, Jill hit her knee hard and bounced forward, losing her fire shooter. The kid laughed at her, so Jill flipped him off, then motioned for him to get out of the window, just as a loud, beastly exclamation behind her brought the Krampus bursting through the burning trees. When he was clear of them, he looked around for Jill, who forgot about her fire shooter in favor of reaching the barn. Clearing the back of the house, she pulled out her plasma shooter and blasted four shots at the furthest garage, hoping to draw the Krampus' attention in that direction, both for her benefit and that of the kid who, if he was a real kid and not a Maggot, was certainly too stupid to do the right thing and hide from the monster.

Jill quickly entered the barn by the side door, immediately banging her leg into something hard and metal. Swearing, she gave herself a few moments to let her eyes adjust to the lower light, then quickly paced down the center aisle, looking for a mode of transportation. The whinnying of several agitated horses told her she had an out no matter what, but she was looking for something else.

Something quicker.

Something like she'd stolen from Charles Francis Poseidon only a few weeks earlier.

A steam carriage.

Far to her left, Jill heard a loud crash and knew her attempt to draw the Krampus away was successful. With a horse to her immediate left and an empty stall to her right, Jill stopped in the middle of the large barn and just looked through the darkness.

Her heart jumped when she spotted the large, boxy frame of a carriage sticking out from one of the final stalls on the right, and as she sped across the floor to it, she desperately looked for any sign of any kind of steam mechanism.

Nothing ... nothing ... nothing ...

She rounded the corner of the stall and saw a set of iron pipes moving from beneath the carriage to curl up to rest against the side of the dark green car and then snake towards the rear, where it ended after it passed the large, wooden wheels.

"Let's hope it's loaded with water," she mumbled, trying not to dizzy herself with the rush of excitement that exploded inside of her when she caught sight of the pipes.

Stepping on the foot ladder, Jill moved up to the open driver's bench. The wheel sat dead center and a set of controls were set in a small dash on either side of the wheel. Having driven Poseidon's steam carriage, she knew what to look for, and hit the largest button to fire the steam engine. Beneath the carriage, the engine pppppppppsssssssshhhhhhhhhhhhhhhed to life, and she released the hand brake. Two pedals at her feet handled the acceleration and deceleration. Pressing down on the accelerator, the carriage did little more than dribble forward, so she reset the handbrake and waited for the engine to come to life.

A thunderous explosion from next door told her the Krampus was approaching. Jill could hear shouts coming from the houses now and she knew she couldn't just sit here. With the steam carriage not yet ready to move, she hopped down off the seat and pulled free her plasma shooter. Running back to the entrance door, Jill ducked outside and saw two men in their long johns coming out of the first house, yelling and waving their arms.

"Get back inside!" she yelled, but the men paid her no attention.

So she fired plasma pellets in their direction, the small, orange balls sizzling the snow by their feet.

"Do you know who I am!?" one of the men yelled.

"A guy who's going to die in his underwear!" Jill shouted back, just before the Krampus smashed through the front doors of the middle barn, red eyes blazing in the night. The beast saw the men first and started off in their direction, and Jill wished she had loose enough morals to let the Krampus go after them.

Firing several shots at the monster's back, one hit him just behind his left ear. He turned instantly around, and Jill fired several more rounds at his face as she backed towards the door to the third barn. The Krampus roared and came after her, so she stopped firing and ran inside. Holstering the blaster just as she jumped up onto the driver's bench, Jill released the handbrake and hit the accelerator. The carriage lurched forward and she turned hard to the left to be able to drive down the middle of the barn. With the accelerator pressed to the floor, Jill didn't lift when the Krampus smashed through the double barn doors and stepped inside.

Just in time to get hit by the steam carriage.

The Krampus was too strong to get knocked aside, and as the beast dug his claws into the front of the carriage, his face was mere inches from Jill's.

He roared.

She sent three plasma pellets into the back of his mouth.

The Krampus sent his hands to his burning throat, putting him in a precarious situation of holding on only by his feet. Jill leaned back in the bench and brought both of her feet up, above the steering wheel, and kicked the Krampus with both of them square in the chest. The beast leaned back, waving his arms for balance. His right hand connected with the front of the car, but before he could get a grip with the other hand, Jill used the road to her advantage. She needed to turn to the right then to the left to shoot between the houses, then right again to move to the ash-lined road, then left to exit down the straight lane. Pushing the steam carriage as hard as it would go and keeping her plasma blaster in her left hand, Jill jerked the wheel to the right with her right hand, causing the Krampus to miss connecting with his left, then fired two more rounds into his face, sizzling his left eyeball.

The Krampus swiped at her with his free left hand, but she leaned back out of the way, then jerked the wheel hard to the left, causing the Krampus to lose his grip with his right hand. Before Jill could knock him free, his left hand connected, though his body swung beyond the right edge of the carriage.

Firing three shots into his chest, the fur and skin beneath sizzling as the pellets exploded, Jill drove towards the edge of the middle house, intending to hit him with the building. Taking the corner tight, she succeeded in clipping the Krampus' arm, but failed to dislodge him as she plowed through thick snow to head towards the burning ash trees.

The Krampus snarled and snapped at her and Jill had no intention to take him to Mayenne with her, so instead of aiming the steam carriage for the road between the ash trees, Jill sent the car hurting straight for the burning tree on the left side of the lane.

Regaining his balance, the Krampus dropped his head, intending to gore Jill with his twisted horns. One connected with her left shoulder so she tossed the blaster to her right hand and moved the gun beneath his face, and pointed it straight up, smashing his face with plasma from close range. Her own hand, wrist, and arm burned from the plasma that sloshed off his face.

He raised his head.

She jumped off the carriage, rolling in the snow with a heavy thud, and looking up just in time to see the back of the Krampus slam into the burning ash tree. Branches, leaves, and fire rained down on the demon and his fur flashed orange and red as it caught fire. Trapped between the carriage and the tree, the demon could not push himself free fast enough to escape.

Members of all three houses poured down to Jill, watching in terrified awe as the Krampus was burned alive, his fur twisting and crackling until it drifted away in the French night, revealing a man beneath the fur.

Anar.

The horns were the last parts of the Krampus to fall away, dropping onto the burning steam carriage just before the smaller human body fell into the snow.

Jill moved to the unconscious, smoldering body, and kicked snow over the young man's back. She watched the steaming body for signs of life, intending to drive the remaining plasma in her blaster through his back to his heart, but when she saw the subtle rise and fall of the body ceased, signifying his death, she didn't have the heart to put another round into him to make sure.

The American stood there, simply watching, her soul a mix of emotions until one of the villagers was standing beside her with a pitchfork in his hand. He raised the tool, clearly intending to drive it through Anar's heart.

Jill put the plasma blaster in the man's face. "Find me another steam carriage," she ordered without turning her head to look at him. "This man's souls has already gone back to Hell."

*

Hanna couldn't wait for Jill, so instead of debarking the train in Mayenne, she made her way to the engine car. "Where are you headed?" she asked the conductor.

"Nowhere tonight," the older man said in a heavy French accent, scratching his bald head and not bothering to stifle a yawn. "The company wants the train to stay here for repairs."

Hanna frowned.

"What's the matter, miss?" the conductor asked. "No place to stay for the night? I'm sure the company would put you up at a hotel 'til the morning."

Rubbing her face with both hands, Hanna leveled with the man. "I need to get to Mont Saint-Michel. I need to get there right now."

"Why?" the conductor asked. "After all you've seen tonight, don't you think a sniff of brandy and a comfortable bed are what you need?"

"After what we seen," she asked in a hard voice, "don't you want to catch the bastards responsible?"

The man's thin face instantly hardened. "Let me disconnect the engine from the passenger cars," he said, and in five minutes, Hanna and the conductor were blasting through the night in a northwesterly direction, headed for Mont Saint-Michel. Despite the noise, the heat from the engine, the flask of brandy they shared, and the task in front of her, Hanna dozed off somewhere along the way.

When she awoke, she found herself laying on the deck of a ship, looking up into the concerned face of Ignatius Poseidon. The morning sky was an icy blue that matched the crispness in the air.

From her back, she could hear the sounds of children playing.

Children.

Bolting upright, she saw twenty ... thirty kids running around the merchant ship, playing with wooden swords and plush dolls. Ignatius offered her a hand up as Hanna searched the children's faces until she found Roland Garteau standing off to the side, playing Noughts and Crosses on the deck of the ship with pieces of white chalk with a middle-aged woman.

"Is that ...?"

"Roland's mother," Ignatius nodded. "Associates in America helped her fake her death. They had intended to fake Roland's death there, as well, but not everything works according to plan. Leo Garteau quickly moved on to the young Miss Sybil and kept Roland under 24-hour protection. We didn't have a chance to grab him until he returned to Mayenne."

"But ... who are these kids?" Hanna asked, not seeing enough parents to come close to matching the number of children. "Why kidnap them? And, for that matter, where's Jill?"

"If Jill is smart, she's stuck in Officer Oudry's barn in Sillé-le-Guillaume," Ignatius said.

"She's not very smart."

"Then you'd best run back to get her," Ignatius said, a hint of regret in his voice.

"Not until you explain all of this," Hanna insisted.

"Leo Garteau beat his son and beat him hard," Ignatius explained, not needing to elaborate. "All of these children come from bad situations. Kidnapped? The Krampus Society rescued them. Oudry is a member. So is Anar."

"But Anar is actually a Krampus," Hanna said.

"He is," Ignatius acknowledged. "Cursed, with no control over that half of his persona. He feels terribly guilty about it, which is why Salome introduced him to the Society. He helps keep nervous townsfolk focused on the possibility of a demon in their midst while Oudry orchestrates to steal the abused children away, and Oudry works some dark magic to animate look-alike shells with the maggots and slugs while we make our escape. Playing up the Krampus legend helps provide cover for parents who, truth be told, adjust rather quickly to not having their child around."

"Where are you taking these kids?" she asked, trying to wrap her head around a very complicated cover for a very simple motivation. "Do the kids have any say in this?"

"America," he said, "and they do. If they don't want to go, I make sure the KS puts them back. But they're good at what they do and they only take the ones that want to leave."

Hanna moved to the deck of the ship and saw nothing but the ocean around them. "Am I going to America, too?" she asked, her heart jumping back to Jill and hating herself for it.

"No," Ignatius said, "you're going back to rescue Jill, remember?"

"Hell," Hanna said, shaking her head, "you left her there. You should go rescue her."

"She's probably really mad at me," he frowned. "I couldn't risk her coming along and disagreeing with what we are attempting to do. Oudry wanted to kill her."

"You couldn't take Oudry in a fight?"

Ignatius shook his head. "I can do spells, but Oudry can do dark, dark stuff with his magic. Trapping Jill was the best compromise I could come up with in the moment. No, better you go back to rescue your friend."

Hanna looked at Ignatius over her shoulder. "You fight demons for a living but you're afraid of Jill Masters?"

Ignatius shrugged. "We all have our weaknesses," he admitted.

Hanna rolled her eyes. "Fine, tough guy, I'll handle Jill," she said, shivering as a gust of wind swept across the deck, "and you go deal with your father. We've got a line on a ship full of vampire seamen set to dock at Brest for our next case.

You can catch us there. Now, how do we get off this ship and back to France?"

"There's a hot air balloon below deck," Ignatius said, "if you're not afraid to get back in one."

"Not me," she said, and Ignatius headed off to get the basket and corresponding balloon, leaving the Bostonian alone with her thoughts.

"He didn't even crack a joke about 'vampire seamen' and 'Brest' even though I totally set him up for it," Hanna remarked to herself. "He'll never last with Jill."

Hanna looked across the ship to where Roland hugged his mother tightly. She wondered what she could have told him to explain all of this to help him understand, but then her mind drifted back to her own childhood, of her parents explaining to her about the Colony and the world that existed alongside our world, active but mostly unseen.

Childhood, Hanna understood, was the best time to tell someone about the existence of ghosts and werewolves and aliens. Kids were adaptable. Kids weren't bitter. Kids believed there could be magic in the world and that it could be a good and majestic thing.

Twenty years ago, Hanna believed that.

Jill believed that.

Timmy believed that.

And then Timmy was gone and they saw the world for what it was.

Around her, kids played and singed and jumped and ran around. If the Krampus Society stealing them away from abusive situations delayed their own Timmy moments by a few years, Hanna's only desire was to wish them well on their journey.

THE MAN IN THE RED COAT

INTERSTITIAL
MORNING EGGNOG

1866, December
Three Days After the Man in the Red Coat Left Hell

"I'm sorry," Camille Renoir said to the American investigator, Hanna Pak, as she quickly hurried up the street. "I have not even heard of the ... what did you call her?"

"The Mistletoe Queen," Hanna answered, showing the Frenchwoman an illustration. I

Camille shook her head, barely glancing at the drawing, and apologized aa second time before continuing on her way.

She was running late because she was perpetually running late. Her entire life, from the moment she made her mother spend three entire days in labor until this very morning's trek to work, was lived in a world that moved ahead of her. By the time she would ingest breakfast, others were digesting lunch. By the time she realized a boy was interested in her, he was walking down the aisle with some tramp from Le Mans or Lyon or Limoges. Her friends would joke that any day now, Camille would be caught up in the Revolution, some 70 years after it soaked their country in blood and paranoia.

It was somewhat surprising, then, that she was running behind this Friday morning because she had thought it was Saturday. Even when her mind placed her in the future, it seemed, it was done only at the expense of falling behind the present, and it was lucky for her that her boss had sent a runner to make sure she reported for work.

Rushing through the frosted maritime streets of Brest in her black and white servant's garb, Camille ignored the catcalls from the sailors that were responsible for the city's continued existence. There were two main paths she could take that would bring her to work, and this run down the docks was the quicker, but less preferred option.

So naturally, she was forced to take it almost every day.

It was a cold December morning because all December mornings in the bay were cold. The sea on her left was cloaked in a dark, gray fog that sent a ghostly pall over the hundreds of docked ships. The sun lay somewhere beyond the veil of its density. Masts and riggings emerged from the fog only in glimpses and shadows, and every creak of wood or sailor's muttering seemed to her to be coming from a place of evil.

"Place of evil?' she laughed to herself. "I will have to work on that," she muttered, running both hands through her shoulder-length blonde hair.

"Work on what, dear?" an old woman said from a nearby doorway.

"On my turning of a phrase, Mrs. Fitzwallace," Camille smiled broadly.

The old woman scowled and puffed on a cigarette in a long, thin holder. "Writing ain't a proper life for a lady, Miss Renoir," the properly attired madam insisted, clinging as she always did to the doorway. She wore the most fashionable dress the working part of the docks were likely to see all day, and the gold chains that hung around her think, pallid neck attracted the attention of any and all who caught a glimpse of it. "When you want to make a real living, come see me. There will always be a bed for you to ply my trade on at the Willing Mermaid."

"Thank you, again, for the offer," Camille smiled, giving Mrs. Fitzwallace a small bow, "but I am happy to deliver my pleasure to our city's fine workmen in the kind of pies that come on a plate."

"I can arrange that," the old madam promised, taking another drag off her cigarette.

From down the street, a rough, male voice called, "Move yer tits, girl! We're understaffed and overbooked!"

Camille and Mrs. Fitzwallace smiled politely at one another.

"You'd better hurry, dear," the Scotswoman said with a glance down the street. "My husband can't seem to run his establishment without you." She winked. "Even if you are always ten minutes late."

The young Frenchwoman smiled, and ran her hands through her hair for a second time. "How do I look?"

"Too good to get your cheeks pinched without being paid for it," Mrs. Fitzwallace said, "but the old bastard might have a point today. There was something going on his way this morning that caused quite an eruption. Or maybe it was nothing," she shrugged, noticing a few sailors stumbling down the ramp of their ship and automatically straightening out her dress and rearranging her golden necklaces to look as presentable as she needed to. "My lesser half fumbles through a crisis worse than he does our bedroom."

Nodding her goodbye, Camille walked briskly down the street to Tasse de Café, taking momentary note of a strange sight on the ships where the stumbling sailors had just come from: a woman in a stylish red dress and green mask standing on the bow of the ship.

Was this the, what was she called? The Mistletoe Queen?

There was a man with her, too, in a red British military jacket. His arms were wrapped around the stylish woman, and he appeared to be whispering in her ear. This odd woman was staring at the cafe, yet as Camille's stare linger, the woman turned her attention to the young Frenchwoman, causing

Camille to stumble in the street. Hastily, she turned her attention back to her place of employment, where Mr. Fitzwallace's ever-expanding gut brought him as much attention as his wife's jewelry. He was waiting for her one storefront before his own shop, and the smell of baking bread and simmering soup had her regretting for not the first time which shop she toiled away at each day.

"You are late," he scolded, before quickly telling her, "but never mind that. There has been ... well, the two women say we were infested with Baobhan Sith!"

Camille blinked. "We were infested with Scottish vampire women?"

"Yes!" Mr. Fitzwallace said, running his hands over his belly-stretched white shirt. "At least, that's what the women said!"

"The women? What women?"

"Two Americans," Mr. Fitzwallace said, grabbing Camille's arms tightly. "Oh, they are very good with the violence." The shop owner looked around nervously. "Quickly," he said, his Scottish accent thick, "we must go inside."

Camille nodded dumbly and let Fitzwallace usher her past him and towards the shop. She was surprised to find the front windows pulled down to keep people from looking in the windows and the CLOSED sign hung on the door. He pulled open the door for her and she entered to find a room of ... of ...

"Well, something that means 'nightmares,'" she mumbled, "without being so tacky as to say 'nightmares'."

The room had been laid to waste. The Tasse de Café was a small shop, but there was room for fifteen circular tables spread across its uneven, wooden floor. All but one of the tables had been destroyed. Dead bodies lay amidst the broken wood, consisting of sailors and women in black robes that Camille took for the Baobhan Sith.

In both back doorways — the one on the right that led to the kitchen and the one on the left that led downstairs to the cellar — there were horses standing placidly, munching on straw that had been placed on the bar top that ran between the doors. A part of Camille's brain buzzed something about how the Baobhan Sith were notoriously twitchy about the presence of horses.

"Focus, girl," Fitzwallace sighed, accustomed to Miss Renoir's flights of fancy. He pointed to the center of the room, where an American woman was dressed much like the woman she'd engaged on the street: blouse, vest, jeans, boots, and guns. This woman was white and slurped eggnog while munching on bread brought in from next door.

As she was watching, the door opened and Hanna Pak stumbled in to join her partner at the table. Her walk across the floor was full of starts and stops.

"Go to them, go to them!" Mr. Fitzwallace urged.

Camille looked at him over her shoulder. "I'm not picking up all these bodies."

"You don't have to," he said, patting her shoulders with more familiarity than Camille appreciated. "Once the sun breaks through the fog, we can top the blinds and the sunlight will kill all of them like this!" he said, snapping his fingers. "You'll have to sweep up, of course," he added quickly.

Looking past him, Camille wondered aloud, "Why not open them now?" She moved to the window and peered behind the dingy, green blind. The sun was not yet shining through the morning's weather, but its presence could now be felt in the lightening of one circular patch of fog. Her thin hand went to the thin bit of twine that hung off the thin bottom of the blind when the fat fingers of Mr. Fitzwallace grabbed her harder than was necessary.

"We don't want the customers seeing this, do we?" he asked, his breath washing over her face like ... like ...

"Like the ass of a sailor?" she asked, mumbling to herself.

"What?"

"Nothing."

"You live in your own head too much, girl," Fitzwallace grumbled. "Lucky for you I sent that runner."

"Lucky for me?" Camille asked, yanking her hand away to motion around the room. "Yes, I am so lucky that I almost missed all of this Scottish vampire nonsense. Were they after you?" she asked pointedly.

"Do not be stupid!"

"You and the wife are the only two Scots in Brest."

"That's not true."

"It sounds true."

Mr. Fitzwallace folded his arms on top of his bulbous gut and his mouth pantomimed chewing a cigar that wasn't there. "You're always on about wanting to be like them fancy writers Stendil and Flubber, aren't you? Well, I bet they haven't seen anything like this, have they?"

"I'm not sure what Stendhal and Flaubert would do with something like this," she mused, moving over and around various dead bodies to get to the two American women. She looked at the pair and could see they were tired. Camille did think it a bit rude that neither of the women had said anything since she entered, but they were probably typically rude Americans who thought servants were beneath them.

Looking down on them, she saw the white woman to her left looked the worse for wear. Blood oozed out of the corner of her mouth and nose, and there were heavy scratches on her neck. Her yellow blouse was torn in several places and her right hand — the hand she used to numbly sip the eggnog before her — had a large gash from the index knuckle back to the wrist. The Asian woman had a black eye, but looked equally pale. The left sleeve of her green shirt was torn down to her elbow and tears ran intermittently from her eyes down her brown cheeks.

"Well," she said, a burst of excitement pumping to life within her, "you two had a fascinating morning, it appears."

The Asian woman said nothing, but the white woman took a sip of a nearly empty eggnog cup.

Undeterred, Camille pressed forward. She was quite certain she had not plumbed the full depths of Mr. Fitzwallace's ignorance, but he was right that these two Americans would make a fine topic for a story. Her mind raced to put all of the room's various elements together as she announced, "Let me get you two another cup."

"Nnnnnnno," the Asian whispered. "Nnnnnnnnooooooo nnnnng noooogggg...."

"Do not be godiche, ma'am," Camille said, patting her shoulder. "You two look like the living dead, and the living dead would not look so ... living deadish, let us say, pretending this is a first draft, if they ingested a firm cup of Mr. Fitzwallace's eggnog. The old man might be a creep, but his drinks are to die for."

She moved around more prone bodies to get behind the bar, her mind already away from this room to think up plausible ways for the horses to get into the room. And what of the sailors? Did the Baobhan Sith target these men? Were they all from the same ship? Camille imagined a dangerous encounter in the savage South Pacific, where ... where ...

"Where Scottish vampire women were hanging out?" she asked herself. "That's dumb."

"Just pour the eggnog, dear," Mr. Fitzwallace said in an agitated fashion from across the room, moving away from the blinds as the sunlight brightened the room a small, but noticeable amount.

"Why can't you do this yourself, eh?" she asked, reaching for the pot on the stove. "Ugh, someone left garlic all over it," she said, making a face as she tossed it aside.

Mr. Fitzwallace smiled at her back.

Camille's mind created a back story for how the women came to be together. Maybe their husbands had abandoned them? Or maybe, she thought, feeling a salacious thrill devour her spine, they were lovers, on the run from bad men. "Oh!" she yelled to herself, deciding that yes, they were lovers on the run from bad men who also happened to be sailors that had docked at Brest with a cargo of ... of ...

Sighing, she took the pot off the stove and noticed there were four cups already laid. Absently, she remembered the Asian woman slurring "no eggnog," so thinking she might already be drunk, Camille filled two cups with eggnog and two cups with just water.

"I'll have to create something sensible for the Scottish women," she murmured, and then realized it was her story and she could turn the vampires into Pacific Islanders or Africans or something particularly devious, like Australians.

"Today, Miss Renoir!"

"Hold your stomach together," she replied dreamily, bringing the women their eggnog. Noticing the growing brightness of the room, Camille told her boss to open the blinds, but he ignored her, as was typical of him. She removed the old cups and placed the new cups on the table, giving the eggnog to the white woman and the water to the Asian.

"Taaaakkkeeeee iiiittttttttt awwwaaaayyy ..." the white woman whispered, but Camille placed a finger on her lips and kissed her cheek.

"You just hush now, beautiful," she said, the real woman before her already less interesting that the fantasy woman Camille was turning her into inside of her head, "and drink the eggnog. It warms the bones. Trust me, I'm a doctor," she said, and then whispered, "But not really."

Turning back to the room, she saw her impatient boss looking out the window. "Quickly, quickly," he called to her, "get the horses from the room."

"You get them from the room."

"None of your lip today, girl!" Fitzwallace roared as he spun around. "You get those horses out of here right now!" he ordered, gripping the door handle. "You know how I dislike them! Filthy beasts!"

Sighing, Camille did as he asked. He was the boss, after all, so if he wanted to pay her to move a couple horses out of a coffee shop, she would move a couple of horses out of a coffee shop. The horse on the right of the bar was her first target, so she took the reigns of the big, black horse and led him over the dead bodies. When she neared the door, Mr. Fitzwallace opened the door and jumped back, moving away from them.

"It's just a horse, boss," she said, bringing it out onto the street and tying it to a post. The sun was nearly through the fog and she thought Fitzwallace might as well pull the blinds and let it in. It's not like their clientele was the picky sort. Turning back to the door, she saw Mrs. Fitzwallace and several of her prostitutes moving towards them from the Willing Mermaid.

"You probably want to stay back!" she called to the madam, and then moved back inside the Tasse de Café. "Excuse me," she said as a robed woman bumped into her.

Camille Renoir froze in place. Around her, sailors and Baobhan Sith rose to their feet, though they were cautious to stay away from the side of the room with the remaining horse. The Asian woman slurped her hot water, the liquid spilling down the side of her mouth, and reached slowly for the second cup.

"Um ..."

Mr. Fitzwallace put an arm around her. "I would so dearly love to thank you, girlie," he smiled in her ear. "The Americans proved themselves very worthy adversaries, putting the garlic on the eggnog pot once they realized it was laced with a poisonous sedative and leaving their horses inside the room, knowing the Baobhan Sith do dislike the four-legged beasts. The same applies to the men, like me, who serve them. We needed an ordinary human like you to assist us, and only one as space-addled as you would do." He touched her ear with his lips, "Though you may want to leave that out of your story. It does not make you look very good, if I am being honest."

Camille had no words. Behind her, the door opened and Mrs. Fitzwallace entered.

"I am going to devour your neck," she said, moving behind, "and then you will work for me. This is the price you will pay for having your head in the fantasies of children. Of course," Mrs. Fitzwallace said, licking the stunned Camille's neck, "maybe you will live long enough for lady writers to become fashionable."

Mrs. Fitzwallace opened her mouth to bite down on the pale neck, but the only item that passed her lips was a bullet shot from the gun of Hanna Pak.

Camille screamed and her hand went to her neck, where blood flowed quickly. "You shot me!" she yelled at Hanna.

The partially paralyzed American sent another bullet whizzing across the room to crack Mrs. Fitzwallace's face. "I'll ap-ap-apologize later," she said, her hand dropping the gun with bullets to slowly reach for another gun at her hip. The roused vampires, of both male and female varieties, bore down on her, but they were too late to stop her.

Hanna slowly raised a fire shooter into the air, and fired, coating the nearest vampires first, and then sending burning arcs of gasoline to the blinds, which quickly caught fire.

Camille felt her legs give way beneath her as she tumbled to the floor and then into darkness.

On the way to the end, she saw the burning blinds fall to the floor and sunlight smash into the room.

Everyone but her and the Americans burst into flame.

ACT TWO
EXALTED WATERS

1866, December
Seven Days After the Man in the Red Coat Left Hell

"It's a fake name," Jill Masters said from her position behind the bar of a socially upscale fraternal club in Lille, France. Gunshots slammed into bottles of alcohol above her, raining shards of glass and drops of vodka, brandy, whiskey, and wine down onto her and her partner.

"What's a fake name?" Haneul Pak asked. Unlike Jill, who sat with her back against the bar and her feet extended towards the wall, Hanna crouched low, facing the room, with two energy blasters in her hands.

"Sinterklaas," Jill sighed, showing Hanna a small, four-page pamphlet. "No one names their kid Sinterklaas."

Hanna shook her head, peaking between the wooden slats of the bar. What was happening on the other side wasn't their fight, but the bullets, electricity, fire, and steam pellets that were zipping around didn't care who they hit.

"Sinterklaas is a Dutch version of Saint Nicholas," Hanna told Jill. "I think. Probably. This is boring," she said as a blast of energy sizzled the bar near her head. "I want to shoot someone."

"We can't," Jill said, studying the pamphlet. "Nobody weird out there to shoot."

"Speaking of that," Hanna said, ducking back to safety. "Our business card says, 'We Shoot the Weird in the Face,' but that's not entirely true."

"It's not?" Jill asked, putting the pamphlet down on her thigh to take a coffee cup off a shelf beneath the bar. Looking around, she saw vodka spilling down from a broken bottle

above them and reached her hand out to gather the clear
liquid in the cup.

"We don't shoot any old weird person," Hanna said above
the sound of tables crashing and bones breaking just a few
short feet away. "They've got to be weird and evil."

Sipping vodka out of the cup, Jill asked, "How many weird
and nice people have we met?"

Hanna furrowed her brow and peeked back out at the
room on the side of the bar. "That guy at La Boutique des
Merveilles au Rebut down the street seemed nice."

Jill blinked. "You actually remembered all that? Worst
name for a store ever."

"I thought Monsieur Inconnu was ... interesting."

"The dude in the bright yellow suit? Well, nice, sure, but
he was weird because he kept asking us if either of us was
'The Partridge'," Jill said, "not because he was a half-elephant
demon trying to impregnate rocks or something."

"Looked like he had a hot air balloon behind the shop,"
Hanna said as a chair was thrown over the top of the bar to
land on her right. "We should rent it."

"Why?" Jill asked. "Don't you remember what happened
the last time we got in a hot air balloon? Like, a week ago? We
crashed it into a house."

"Yeah," Hanna chided, "and you ended up with a new
crush out of it. We should really figure out how to fly one."

Jill waved the thought aside. "What are the odds we're
going to be in a hot air balloon, again, anytime soon?"

Hanna said nothing. She didn't want to complain too hard
about their business cards given that her name came first; if
she pushed it, Jill would probably agree to buy new cards and
turn them into "Jill & Hanna" instead of "Hanna & Jill."

"Should we get involved?" Jill asked, flicking the pamphlet off her thigh, where it landed amidst alcohol, glass, and the blood of the very dead barkeep.

Hanna didn't know if Jill was being serious. "Are you asking if we should get involved for the good of the public?" she asked.

"I'm getting wet in all the wrong ways," Jill grumbled at the blood and liquor on her jeans and blouse.

"So ... we should join in?"

Jill gulped down the rest of her cup of vodka. "Alcohol is so much better in Europe, even if it was probably made by some crazy-ass botanist trying to rip an ancient demon out of Hell to terrorize the world." Jill wrinkled her nose. "Where do you want to spend Christmas?"

"Dunno," Hanna said. "You want to spend it with Ignatius on top of you?"

"Thinking about it."

"Do you think your mom would be angrier that you slept with me or with a black guy?"

"I'm bored," Jill pouted.

"Then grab some steel and let's end this."

Jill hopped up onto her haunches and removed a fire shooter and steam pistol from her gun belt, thinking she had to figure out a way to sneak these back to the United States. "He shouldn't even be here," she said.

"Who?"

"Sinterklaas," Jill said, nodding to the pamphlet. "In this part of the world, it should be Saint Nicholas."

"Leave you to be an expert on quasi-religious figures dedicated to giving people things."

"Someone has to."

The two women jumped to their feet, guns drawn, and watched the last socialite fall to the ground. The upscale room was a broken mess, but one man remained untouched, sitting at a table in the middle of the room, sipping coffee with shaky hands. Dressed in a dark, maroon suit, the thin man looked to be in his late sixties, or even early seventies. He had hollow eyes, and thin cheeks hidden beneath a wispy, white beard. His thin, spotted hands kept touching his face, as if needing assurance it was still present.

"Lyon is nice this time of year," he said, after a few moments. When he spoke, his body shook slightly, caught between ecstasy and loss. "And yes," he added, turning to Jill, "Sinterklaas is not my real name name. It's Milton. I think. Perhaps. Maybe once upon a holiday past." Milton gave a half-smile, but his body quickly forced it from his face, sending his eyes to find answers in his white cup of coffee. "You should call me Milton," he said weakly. "My reputation has suffered since I failed to deliver my gifts to the children."

Hanna and Jill shot each other a look, their eyes going to the other's guns. A sense of foolishness came over both of them, and then dropped their weapons back into their belts.

"So ...?" Jill started to ask.

Milton took another shaking sip of brown and let the empty cup fall from his lips to the table. "Revelation," he said, his eyes on the wobbling cup as the remnants of his coffee soaked into the white tablecloth. "Acceptance. Transformation. Revalation. These are the Exalted Waters of Minister Sinterklaas, and they are my gift to the world." He looked to the women, his lips quavering. "They were, at least. I want to hire you to help me get them back."

"Um ..."

"What my partner means," Hanna said, coming out from behind the bar, "is that we don't come cheap, and we specialize in cases where there's a spot of weird. We are not repossession agents or mercenaries." She looked around the bar. "I see a bunch of drunk, rich idiots, and one minister who's lost his church. Why should—?"

Milton snapped his fingers. "Rise," he ordered in a voice with more than a glint of power in it, and the roomful of dead and dying gentlemen picked themselves up and stood waiting for additional instructions. "Transformation," he explained, "was their water of choice." Milton rose to his feet, taking a white cane off his knee. "They wanted to be a part of something bigger than themselves," he explained, his voice growing in confidence, "and so they became my undying flock of sheep."

The minister ran his thin hands down the front of his suit and licked his thin lips.

"A train comes to town at 10:50 this evening. The man who recommended you to me is on it. If you want this case, you will meet him on the platform and he will lead you to the exalted waters and that will lead, I sincerely hope, to my reclamation of my church." Milton stepped away from the table, his legs appearing brittle beneath the thin pants. "If I reclaim my church, I may finally deliver the gifts to the poor children of this region. Gifts I was not allowed to deliver on the 5th," he seethed, "which is my day of delivery. My day!" he yelled, his face glowing red with such intense passion that his thin frame could hold it for only a moment before descending into a hacking cough. One of his flock, a middle-aged man with a half-severed neck which did not bleed, moved to steady his minister. Milton accepted the help, and with a dismissive wave of his hand, ordered his flock, "Pay the women."

One by one, each of the blank-faced gentlemen walked to the table where their minister had sat and placed a small piece of gold or silver on its surface, and then left without a word.

The last member of Sinterklaas' flock put a canteen on the table and said, "For the man who recommended you, and no one else."

*

It was 10:46. Hanna and Jill waited on the platform of the one-story, rectangular train station with a handful of other locals, visions of the Kansas City platform where their new life had really started dancing through Hanna's mind. It was hard not to reassess their journey from then to now, though she knew Jill's refusal to look backwards probably had her thinking of a future rendezvous with Ignatius Poseidon, who had failed to meet them in Brest.

The winter night was pleasantly warm, though they still wore coats to protect themselves from the chill: Hanna wore a long, brown duster, while Jill chose a long, black, leather coat. Beneath the coats, Hanna wore blue jeans, a green shirt, and a black leather vest, while Jill was dressed in a black shirt and pants. Hanna's cowboy hat was brown; Jill's was black.

"Did you run out of other colors?" Hanna asked, staring down the track in the eastward direction, as the train was coming in from Belgium.

"It's night," Jill said. "I've dressed for the occasion."

"You couldn't find anyone to do your laundry, could you? I told you — go to McAff's, ask for one of the girls."

"I did that. He sent me one of his whores." Jill wrinkled her nose and changed the subject. "Who do you think is stepping off that train?"

Hanna shook her head. "We've been doing this for a few months now. Lots of folks could have passed our name along. Probably Poseidon," Hanna said, "though I don't know if it'll be Daddy or Junior."

"If our name was passed along in a positive manner," Jill said, a grin coming to her face, "it's probably Ignatius."

"Why?" Hanna asked. "You think he thinks you're that good in the sack?"

"I couldn't use a night with him," she added in a disgruntled mumble.

"He did trap you with two demonic horses," Hanna reminded her.

Jill shook her head. "They weren't demonic when Ignatius and Oudry left me there," she reminded Hanna.

"Still," Hanna said sharply, "it wasn't smart of him to do."

Jill jammed her hands into her coat pockets. "That's better than the things Dotson did."

"And that's the problem getting coerced into agreeing to marry a dirtbag like Dotson Winters," Hanna said sharply. "Everyone else doesn't seem so bad. Even if they threaten to turn you into a monster."

"Bellingham locked me in a room, too," Jill reminded her.

"And you ended up dead."

"And then I came back to life," Jill shrugged. "It all evens out."

"You came back to life but you're like a magnet for Hell demons," Hanna reminded her.

"Which keeps us busy," Jill said, staring hard at the approaching steam train. "She's coming in hot."

Hanna leaned to the side to look around Jill's head. Less than a half-mile from the station, the black train was hurtling towards the station at full speed, no signs of stopping. A string of lights on this side of the tracks combined revealed two men locked in hand-to-hand combat on the top of the train cars.

"Is that ...?" Jill asked, pointing to the men as she turned her head sideways to try to get a clearer view.

"Yeah," Hanna said, "it is."

Jill pulled out an electric shooter, and when the combatant's car reached them, she knocked both men off the train and into the snow opposite them with a wide burst of yellow energy. The two Americans watched the train continue west, waiting for it to clear them so they could walk across the tracks and pick the men up. As the caboose roared past, a little dark-haired girl with a freckles, pigtails, and a lollipop nearly as wide as her head tugged on Jill's coat.

"Excuse me," the little girl said politely. "Do you think it's coming back? My cat is on that train."

*

Jill came back with the drinks as Plummer was examining the canteen he'd been left.

"Beer," she said, putting the first glass down in front of Hanna, and then announced, "brandy, beer, brandy" in turn as she placed the drinks in front of Plummer, Ignatius, and herself. Taking her seat on Hanna's right, she asked, "Why don't you tell us what and why you boys were fighting."

American Special Agent Plummer and British demon hunter Ignatius Poseidon refused to look at each other, and offered no answer. Plummer was in his early '40s and hardened by a career as a soldier and special agent, both times at the side of Ulysses S. Grant. He sipped on his beer as he looked around the hotel's restaurant, the pure personification of what people wanted in a cowboy.

The tables were clean and made of lacquered wood, and water-powered lamps were strung around the room, their energy derived from the man-made waterfall on the wall opposite the bar. It was late enough for the kitchen to be closed, but not so late they couldn't get drinks. A handful of locals and travelers were seated around the room, but the rear corner of the room was theirs.

Hanna shook her head. "Are you men or children?"

Ignatius grunted and pushed his beer away from him. "I told you before I don't drink," he said to Jill, and then crooked his thumb at Plummer, "and I don't trust this man, or any of the American soldiers working with him responsible for shooting up our train," he said in a calm voice that seemed to be a accented with a mix of British and African dialects. The demon hunter was in his mid-20s, but carried himself with a confidence beyond his years. Running a hand through hair several inches thick, Ignatius looked completely miserable.

"That's because you're perceptive," Jill said.

"I don't trust him, either," Plummer added, drumming his fingers on the canteen.

"That's because you're racist," Jill said.

"I don't have time for this," Plummer grumbled, standing up.

"Sit down," Hanna ordered. "Neither one of you is as trustworthy as a cow's piss. You work for the government. Ignatius locked Jill in a barn with demon horses."

"To be fair," Ignatius mumbled, "they were not demon horses when I left. I, um, I might have improperly drawn one of the magic symbols in the dirt. The spell was only supposed to work on humans."

Plummer caught quick, but powerful glances between Ignatius and Jill and a knowing smile came to his face. He sat back down, and said, "Alright, let's do business. Being in Europe makes my skin crawl." Taking a swig of his beer, he said, "I recommended you to Minister Sinterklaas. He's a good man in a bad spot. Sinterklaas—"

"Milton," Hanna and Jill said in unison.

"Milton," Plummer acknowledged, "was a once-wealthy American who'd come to Europe because he had nothing left in the States. His wife was killed in an Apache raid and his children stole his business out from under him, so he came to Europe just to wander around. This must have been in '58 or '59. He was looking for himself, is what he told us, and when he found a set of three pools in the forest to the southeast of Lille ... well, he found what he was looking for."

"Pools?" Jill asked.

"Himself," Hanna corrected without looking away from Plummer. "Where did you meet him?"

"He didn't have enough money with him to buy the land, so he came back to the States to try to convince his kids to give him his own money," Plummer answered, sipping his beer, "and then the Civil War broke out."

Ignatius glanced to his left to look at Plummer without turning his head. "Sounds like you two have a history."

Plummer took a big gulp of beer. "We do," he admitted, wiping his lips with the back of his hand. "We crossed paths with him in Paducah, Kentucky in September, 1861. Grant seized the town and we found Milton hiding in a church. He told us his story and said that now that he was here he wanted to do his part for the good of the country. What can he do, right? A sixty year old stick figure? He had passion, though. Grant took pity on him, I think. Milton tried telling us he was a minister but he didn't know the good book from a cook book." Plummer knocked off his beer and then reached for Ignatius' discarded glass. Halfway there, his hand paused as his face grew dark. "He stayed with us through April 7, 1862."

"How can you remember that?" Ignatius asked.

When Plummer didn't answer, his thoughts drifting back to those days in southwestern Tennessee, Hanna answered for him.

"Because that's the day of the Battle of Shiloh," she said softly.

"Bloodiest damn day in American history," Plummer said, letting his memory have one last soak before he pushed Tennessee away and came back to Lille. Grabbing Ignatius' beer, he took two big, slow gulps before continuing. "I hadn't heard from Milton since he walked out of camp that night," Plummer informed them. "Then, two weeks ago," he said, reaching into a pocket of his brown vest, pulled out a telegram, and tossed it on the table, "I received this."

Jill and Hanna both reached for it, but Jill won out. She read, "I need you. Exalted waters stolen. Men in Confed coats. Please."

"Confederates?" Hanna asked. "In France?"

"There were some Confederate sympathizers in France during the war," Plummer explained. "The Union blockade cut France off from receiving Southern cotton and some businesses suffered. I suppose it's possible the Gray could be here, looking for funds to continue the Lost Cause."

Jill shook her head and leaned back in her chair. "You don't believe that, though."

Plummer shrugged. "My guess is that some Confederate prisoner we had in camp heard Milton talking about the exalted waters and made his way here after the war, after times got desperate."

"Milton said the exalted waters had some kind of supernatural power to them," Hanna said. "Was he on about that back then, too?"

"Yes," Plummer acknowledged. "But most people didn't think he was being literal."

"You did?" Ignatius asked skeptically.

Plummer had just about had it with the younger man. "When Jill's tucking you in tonight, she can tell you what I do," he grumbled. "After you thank her for saving you from me kicking your ass on top of the train."

In a flash, Ignatius had a dagger jammed under Plummer's jaw and the federal agent had a fire shooter pressed against the demon hunter's skull.

"Okay, okay," Jill said, putting up her hands. "Let's take a deep breath and relax. This is a little too homoerotic even for Plummer. Put the weapons away."

While Jill calmed the two men, Hanna's eyes scanned the room. The burst of action had caught the attention of several locals, and while the hotel restaurant was not a place local ruffians were invited to imbibe, there were more than a few men in the room who looked like they could handle the steel at their waists just fine.

"Put your weapons away," Hanna ordered in a harsh whisper, and at last, the men relented. "Why are you two at each other's throats, anyway?"

Plummer's brow furrowed. "Kid got in my way."

"Old Man America here was wearing a gray coat," Ignatius countered.

"I was undercover!" Plummer snapped, and then scowled at himself for getting flustered. "There's a contingent of Grays on that train," he explained. "Our spies in Amsterdam let us know there were some southern boys making trouble in Flanders. I tracked them to Brussels and when I found out they were connected to the exalted waters, I convinced them I was a like-mined sympathizer."

"Beating up a black guy on the train probably didn't do anything to change their mind, then," Jill pointed out.

Hanna put her hand in the middle of the table. "Enough. We're not going to do any good with us at each other's throats." She looked to Plummer. "We've already received payment from Milton's army of sheep so we're committed to getting him his waters back, exalted or not." She looked to Ignatius. "We wouldn't say no if you wanted to help. We'll cut you in on the payment."

Ignatius pushed back his chair and rose to his feet. "My purpose here is on that train, and has nothing to do with exalted waters or American racists. I wish you well, but I have my own mission," he said, and with one final glance at Jill, left the table.

Plummer folded his arms across his chest and smiled at Jill. "Think your mom would be more upset at the fact you slept with a Korean woman or a black guy?"

Disgusted, Jill drained the remaining half of her brandy, slammed the glass on the table, and stood up. "You and Hanna hiring the same joke writers, now?"

*

"I need a horse."

"I don't rent to your kind."

"Then sell it to me."

"I don't sell to your kind."

Ignatius chuckled and shook his head. "My kind?" he asked before leveling his gaze at the night watchman, an elderly man with dirty everything and a missing right leg. Ignatius leaned in close and made a show of sniffing around the man's chest. "What about your kind, huh? You've got the stink of zombie on you. Were you at the pit fights tonight? Huh?" he asked, slapping the man in the face. "How popular do you think you'll be if I call in my palls, the Lafayette twins? The normal vamp might be content to watch zombies tear each other apart for your sport, but Remy does have such a streak of morality about him, doesn't he?"

The watchman's eyes went wide and he spat on the ground. "Damn you all!"

"You're gonna sell me a horse, even if I have to beat you senseless and stick my money in your rotted mouth."

The watchman coughed and took a step backwards, inviting Ignatius into the barn.

"Better," he said, running his hands down the front of his dark green coat, and then stepped inside, where Jill Masters was waiting for him. "What do you think you're doing, woman?"

"Drop the tough guy act," Jill said. "I'm coming with."

"No."

The watchman coughed. "Would you like to know the prices of our horses?"

"Get out," Jill ordered, and the watchmen did as he was told.

Jill and Ignatius stood five feet apart. The only light in the barn came in slivers of moonlight piercing the barn's exterior. To one side of them, the outer wall. To the other, seven horses in stalls.

"I don't want you," Ignatius said.

Jill cocked her head. "We both know that ain't true."

Ignatius corrected himself. "I don't want you to come on this mission."

"If you're hunting demons, you could use my help."

"Americans," he repeated. "I have trained with each of the Seven Tribes. I have studied in the secret libraries of Alexandria. The monks of Tibet, the samurai of Japan, and the Warrior Kings of Mongolia all know the cut of my blade. You have done none of these things. All you have done," he said, "is prove to me that you are too stupid to stay where you're told."

Jill flashed a snark, taking a step towards him. "And all you've done is prove to me you think I like being told what to do."

"You are sloppy," he replied, taking a step towards her, "given to running your mouth when you should be running your feet, and your primary method of attack is to shoot wildly and blindly in the direction of your opponent." Ignatius threw up his hands. "You almost burned three houses down to stop the Krampus!"

"Total exaggeration," Jill replied. "And I already paid for two horses, so pick one and saddle up," she said, turning to the individual stables and crossing her arms.

Ignatius gently grabbed her arm. "This is not wise," he said, stepping into her.

Jill leaned back into him, her hand reaching to rub his leg. "You still owe me an apology for Sillé-le-Guillaume."

"I do," he said, his voice choking slightly as her hand traveled higher. He couldn't stop his body from giving a slight shiver as he murmured, "Your apology is on the train."

"All the more reason for me to come with," she said, stepping away from him as he grunted in the loss of her hand. "I guess I'll take the grey horse. We need to be back by sunrise."

*

"I heard you almost blew up London."

"An exaggeration."

"That's not what Queen Vic told Grant."

Hanna waved the thought aside and sipped on the beer Plummer had just bought her. He wanted to sleep more than he wanted another drink, but after Jill had chased after Ignatius, Hanna had told him about how Jill had shot her father after learning he was the man responsible for the assassination of President Johnson, leaving out the part that Jill really did it because of what her father had said about her sister. Plummer didn't need to know that. As is, it was a lot for him to take in, and he could see the look of anguish that Hanna tried to keep off her face that neither of the two women had properly digested what Jill had done, yet.

"Yuck," she said, looking at the light amber liquid. "Beer is awful. Who comes to France and buys beer?"

Plummer shifted in his seat and coughed, making sure he had Hanna's attention. He placed his hand in the middle of the table near Hanna's, and leaned in. "Why don't you slide over next to me?"

Hanna raised an eyebrow. "Even if you're into ladies now, I'm not into dudes."

Plummer smiled, but his voice had an edge to it. "Pretend," he whispered, "or you're going to get shot in the back. We're drawing a crowd."

Nodding, the lithe Korean-American gave Plummer a charming smile and slid over into Jill's abandoned seat. Her eyes took in the room in the quickest of glances, and then her brain processed what she saw when her eyes went back to Plummer. "Ten men," she whispered.

"Seven of them interested in us," Plummer nuanced. "Three on their feet. Four looking to them for instructions. Which means, if I'm correct, that the three who are still sitting are about to slap gray hoods on their head."

"Gray hoods?"

"They're called the Prophets of Gray," Plummer informed her, revealing he knew more than he'd let on with Ignatius, "and they're why Grant let me come all the way across the ocean to investigate old Milton. We don't know exactly what they are or what they're after, but the connections to the Klan are obvious. We suspect they're trying to refashion the Lost Cause as a religion."

"Why are they in Europe?" Hanna asked quickly.

Plummer shook his head. "That's what I'm here to find out. Grant is worried they're pulling a Brigham Young and looking to create their own private kingdom somewhere."

"Grant's worried about that," Hanna asked, "or hopeful of that. Be nice to get rid of the Confeds, wouldn't it?"

"If we wanted to get rid of them, we'd have let the bastards secede," Plummer snapped. "Now, get ready."

Seven men were now on their feet. They had moved around the room, blocking Plummer and Hanna into the corner. All of them were well-dressed. When they were in position, the three men who remained seated proved

Plummer correct as they reached down into their laps for gray hoods.

"I'm blaming this on you," Hanna mumbled, her hands going to the gun belt on her waist.

The Prophets of Gray rose to their feet and spread out behind the seven mask-less men. Their hoods looked like burlap painted gray, with rough eye holes cut out. Mouth holes had been cut, but purposely sewn shut with heavy, black cord, forming an 'XXXXX' pattern.

The three Prophets spoke in unison. "Do not interfere," they said, their voices raspy, and pockmarked with electric snaps and pops.

"Okay," Hanna said. "We'll just be going, then."

The Prophets each raised their right arm and pointed it at her. "You are not our concern, jezebel." Their fingers rotated to Plummer. "Revelation. Acceptance. Transformation. The exalted waters await you."

Hanna frowned. "They await you?" she asked Plummer, keeping her eyes on the Prophets. "What do they mean?"

"Sorry, kid," he said, stepping behind her and shoving one hand into her lower back. The move unbalanced Hanna, and as she was forced to fall back into Plummer, his other hand moved in front of her nose and popped the cap on a small, bronze cylinder. A red steam whistled free, and Hanna fell unconscious to the floor.

*

Jill and Ignatius tied their horses to trees a couple miles outside of town, and found a small hill to lay on to look down at the train. It was a steam train, long and green, and its steam-powered engine was cooling but not extinguished, letting white smoke waft into the night.

"Plummer's cavalry," Ignatius said, pointing to the men in gray uniforms that surrounded the train.

"Golly, thanks, mister," Jill deadpanned. "Is that why they're wearing those gray uniforms? Could you count them for me next, please?"

Ignatius continued on without acknowledging Jill's retort. "There's something on that train," he said, "and I don't know what it is, but two stops back, they made everyone get off, no matter what their ticket said. No one was allowed to take anything off. The Gray just stood up, pulled out some rifles, and forced everyone off. That's why I was fighting with Plummer. I got out of the train and hid out on the roof. I was crawling forward to get–"

"Zzzzzzzzzzzzzzz. Who do we shoot?"

Ignatius stifled his reply. The things that he hated about Jill were the same things that attracted him to her. "I had the sword with me in the fourth car from the caboose. We will need to—"

"The caboose plus four cars?" Jill asked. "Or the fourth car all by itself? Oh hell," she spat, "it doesn't matter. You're getting it," she said, and without as much as a glance in his direction, Jill stood up and walked down the rise towards the train. "Hey!" she called towards the cavalry when she had given Ignatius enough time to hide himself. "Hey, soldier boys! When can I get my stuff off the train?"

Ignatius watched, feeling twisted around inside. Whether he agreed or disagreed with Jill was immaterial now that she had acted and determined their course. When he saw how the soldiers were moving, he quickly slid off to his right and circled towards the caboose. Soldiers had been stationed at either side of the car, but the left soldier had left his post to help deal with Jill and the right soldier had slid to his right to stand guard in the center of the caboose's rear. Ignatius had already decided his best route was to move on the top of the train, even though he risked detection thanks to the rich moonlight.

Jill's flirtations with the soldiers was drawing plenty of attention, and the rear guard kept inching closer to his right to peek around the corner of the train to get a look at her.

Circling around to stand on the tracks, Ignatius removed his coat and checked his gear. He wore a black and gold samurai armor that the weapon master of the Fourth Hidden Tribe had modified to make it lighter and stronger. Constructed of metal cloaked in black leather with flecks of golden highlights, the outfit consisted of a vest-like do top and six-paneled kusazuri bottom to protect his groin, buttocks, and upper legs. Beneath the kusazuri, longer panels hung to protect his upper legs. Beneath them were baggy, black pants, and lower were metal armor plates strapped to his lower legs and thick black boots on his feet. He wore a black shirt and had only small metal plates strapped to his upper arms near the shoulder for protection.

He waited until the soldier at the caboose had an eyeful of Jill and then ran hand towards him. His right hand went to his waist and removed a Roman pugio from its scabbard, and his left removed a four-pointed throwing star.

It would be up to the fates to determine which weapon he would use to take out the American soldier.

At twenty feet, the Gray soldier turned away from Jill and looked back down the tracks. His eyes went wide as he saw a black man in samurai armor with a Roman dagger rushing towards him, but not so shocked that his hands didn't move to raise his rifle. He was a young man from Georgia guarding a train in France and preparing to go steal some magic water, after all, so an appearance of a black samurai wasn't all that impossible to believe.

Ignatius didn't hesitate, and sent the throwing star spinning through the air to rip into the wrist of the soldier's firing arm. Grunting in pain and surprise, the soldier's arm began to shake as he tried to aim the gun. Too late, he realized he should call for help. His mouth had no time to open before Ignatius was on him, slamming him back against the caboose and holding the dagger to his throat.

The soldier was not inexperienced to the ways of war, and he understood the serious assailant was putting him at the crossroad of life and death and letting him choose the path he would walk. He dropped the rifle and held up his hands. His whole body was shaking.

Ignatius nodded at their agreement and whispered, "The star is poisoned. You will fall asleep, but you will not die."

The American nodded and the two soldiers remained in that embrace until darkness claimed the cavalryman. Ignatius picked him up and placed him on the caboose's landing, then pulled the shooting star from his wrist, wiped the blood off on the American's shirt, and slid it into its sheath in the kusazuri.

Moving quickly, Ignatius easily moved up the stairs, jumped to grab the roof's ledge, and pulled himself onto the roof. He was tempted to try the rear door, but the caboose had been occupied by military earlier and Ignatius saw no reason why it would now be empty. Giving the flirtatious Jill a quick look, which she acknowledged by making an even greater show of herself for the soldiers, the African moved quickly and silently across the roof of the caboose and the next three cars. Silently lowering himself before the fourth car, Ignatius quickly stepped inside. He had been expecting either an empty car or one populated with soldiers.

He had not been expecting a tiger.

The demon hunter was, to some degree, in luck. He quickly recognized the tiger by its relative smaller stature, deeper orange fur, and fewer black stripes as a Bali, the smallest of all tigers.

That still made it the size of a leopard.

The tiger growled at Ignatius from halfway up the aisle. The seats in this car were padded benches, and the tiger was winding its way back and forth, skipping over the central walkway as it sized Ignatius up.

The young man had plenty of weapons on him that had helped him kill bigger cats than this, but never inside a train and never when he wanted to be a ghost. The soldiers had clearly taken the cat from storage and placed it in the main section as a warning system. He glanced out both windows and on either side saw one soldier, their backs turned to the car, as the tiger had yet to make a noticeable noise.

The tiger growled and hopped two benches in one leap, putting him three away from Ignatius.

Man and beast readied themselves, their eyes locked together. Ignatius lightly tossed his pugio back and forth, back and forth, looking to draw the tiger's eyes in and mesmerize him.

It didn't work.

The tiger leaped.

Ignatius dropped backwards to the floor and the tiger's jump carried him over Ignatius' chest. The demon hunter dropped the pugio and reached for two throwing stars, which he shot up into the tiger's underside. The cat yelped in pain, but landed softly on the floor. Flipping over onto his stomach, the British demon hunter watched the tiger spin on him. The move caused the cat to lurch slightly to the side. Regaining its balance, the cat shook its head to clear cobwebs that weren't going anywhere.

Crawling closer, Ignatius picked up his weapon and extended his hands towards the tiger. He held the pugio aloft, catching the animal's eye. Repeating his earlier move, Ignatius gently tossed the blade back and forth, from one hand to the other. This time, with the poison from the stars working their way through its system, the tiger found the blade fascinating, and it watched the gentle sway of metal until it closed its eyes and fell asleep.

Ignatius let his body relax and the night come back to him. His heart and breathing slowed and his ears reached out to take in the voice of Jill Masters flirting with the soldiers. She was going on about the Parthenon and how her souvenirs were on board and she needed them to give to her father so he wouldn't try to fix her up with some dandy from the east when really she preferred a man who knew how to whistle "Dixie," if they caught her mean—

Boom.

Everything stopped.

The soldiers began shouting, asking if anyone saw anything.

Boom.

Louder. Closer.

The train shook, slightly but more significantly than last time.

Boom.

"Do you see it?"

"No!"

"Look north! North!"

"I don't-!"

"Look at the moon!"

"Dear God! What is ...?"

BOOM.

The door to the train car opened and Jill appeared on the other side of the tiger.

"One," she asked, "is that a tiger? Two, if you killed it, I will never have sex with you. Three, can I keep it? And four, are you gonna keep laying there until I get the sword?"

"Yes," Ignatius said, pushing himself to his feet and turning away from Jill. "I didn't. No. No." He moved to the bench where he'd been sitting, knelt down, and removed a sword just over two feet in length.

BOOM.

"Huh," Jill said, stepping over the tiger as the train shook. "I thought it would be bigger."

"It is called wakizashi," he said. "It is a smaller blade than the katana."

"You didn't think I was worth the katana?" she asked. "You are lousy at apologizing."

"I didn't want to get you a blade that could kill you when you forgot you were holding it."

Jill crossed her arms. "Your superiority complex is-whoah! Look!"

Ignatius turned to follow Jill's arm in time to see a handful of naked men, covered in snow and ice crystals as if it had been tarred-and-feathered on, falling to the ground as if they had been dropped from the sky. "Deviltry," he said, frowning.

Jill shook her head. "We should follow this lead. Men falling from the sky is a new one. Well," she remembered, "minus the zeppelin episode."

"No," he said seriously, pointing to the panicked state of the Gray's soldiers as they ran around, firing stun rifles into the sky. "Let us take advantage of this distraction and return to town. There are too many Gray soldiers here for us to fight if things turn sour."

"You just want to try to get in my pants," she teased.

Ignatius' eyes burned brightly. "Yes," he said, "I do."

"We should bring the cat," Jill said absently as the demon hunter moved to her. "I think I know who it belongs to."

Ignatius pulled her forward. They did not take the tiger with them.

*

Plummer entered Jill's room at the hotel, a bronze cylinder in his hand. A scowl hit his face as he saw her empty bed. "Just once," he grumbled, "could you be where you're supposed to be?"

*

An hour later, the door to Jill's room opened again and the speculation about falling men was absent from the minds of the room's newest occupants. Her mind wanted to protest against the desire of the body, but Jill put all thoughts of Hanna and her father and demons and Kraken Moor and Dotson Winters and Lady Carashire and absinthe aside and with the "click" of the closed door, she let her physical needs take over.

Clothes were quickly and roughly pulled off as lips and tongues and flesh became acquainted.

"The hotness of that samurai outfit loses something when it takes forever to get you out of it."

"Patience," Ignatius said.

"I'm fresh out," she murmured, smothering him with a passionate kiss.

*

Morning.

"Get up."

Jill smiled and kept her eyes closed. Reaching for Ignatius, she groaned, "You get up. Oh hell," she mumbled, her hands not finding him, "you're already up. Why on Earth are you not in this bed?"

"Hanna's gone."

Jill snapped awake, pushing herself into a sitting position. "How do you—?" she started to ask, but stopped when the demon hunter handed her a piece of scrap paper.

It read: "This is Plummer. I have Hanna. Do not come for her by land. Trust me. TRUST ME."

Jill crumpled up the paper and tossed it off the bed. "We're going."

"I know," Ignatius said. He'd discarded the samurai outfit for black pants and a dull, blue shirt, and and he tossed Jill a pair of jeans, white shirt, black vest, and black cowboy hat. "I'll get the horses," he said.

"No," Jill said, swinging her legs off the bed and running her hands through her tousled, black hair. Ignatius felt a deep and powerful desire to take her again, but knew that his desire was born out of its impossibility; when the issue at hand was saving Hanna, Jill became a hardened, focused version of herself. Without looking at him, she continued her order. "You will not get the horses."

"You're not really going to tell me not to come with you, are you?" Ignatius asked, crossing his arms in annoyance.

"Don't be daft," Jill snapped. "But forget the horses. Get to the roof and prep the weapons. I need to see a man in a yellow coat."

*

"Are we ever going to be able to trust you, Plummer?" Hanna asked. Her body was pressed against a large yew tree at the edge of a clearing. Both arms and neck were held in place by thick, half-circle metal bands that had been hammered into the trunk. Plummer, now clad in a gray Confederate jacket, stood between her and three round pools of water. In the water, the three Prophets of Gray were submerged up to their necks, their gray hoods touching the top of the pool, and there were several other soldiers milling about on the opposite side of the pools, setting up cameras on tripods. The pools were no more than six or seven feet across, with only a foot between them, and the impression the mostly submerged Prophets gave them was that the pools sat in the ground like self-contained jars.

The entire clearing was like a forest's version of a cul-de-sac, roughly 100, 120 feet across, surrounded by a single line of tall trees, which were in turn surrounded by mountain. A thick, fluffy snow lay on the ground and encumbered trees. Gray rock of various shades comprised the mountainous barrier, which rose nearly straight into the air, and much like the pools, Hanna got the distinct impression the cul-de-sac was a man-made construct. Hanna looked to the sky, abut the high walls prevented her from seeing the morning sun, then back to the cul-de-sac, looking carefully around the grass, trees, and gray walls before she realized what she should have seen straight away:

There was no path leading in or out of the area.

Plummer unscrewed the cap of the canteen Milton had left for him and turned to her. "Thirsty?" he asked, moving through the heavy snow to offer her a pull from his canteen.

"Blow yourself."

The government agent's face flashed anger at her and he jerked the canteen at her face, dousing her with water. "Don't be so goddamned foolish," he said through gritted. "Drink the damn water. The Prophets are submerged in the water and deep in mediation. The rest of the Gray are off getting supplies."

Plummer pushed the canteen to her lips and Hanna took several long pulls from it. Hanna could see that his eyes were bloodshot and his face haggard. Whatever Plummer was going through, it was intense.

And personal.

"You're welcome," he said when she was finished.

"You drugged me, kidnapped me, and nailed me to the wall of a canyon populated by crazy water and crazier hooded men," she said. "Thank you so much. Is this why you wanted us here?"

"I wanted you here because I can trust you."

"Fat chance of that happening again."

"Don't presume you know everything, girl," he whispered, grabbing her chin for effect, "and don't struggle too hard against your restraints or you might pop them free."

Hanna sighed. "More games," she mumbled. "Why didn't you just tell me this was some crazy plan?"

"Wasn't time," he said. "Between Poseidon's boy jumping me and the presence of the Gray in Lille before the train even arrived, I couldn't risk being heard."

"Then tell me now."

"I'll tell you this," he said, pointing to the pools. "They really work. Revelation. Acceptance. Transformation," he said, his finger moving from left to right. "What do you think—?"

Hanna kicked him in the shin. "I am not in the damned mood for a pop quiz, company man," she sneered. "So tell me or bugger off."

"Ow!"

"Appearances," she whispered, flashing a snotty look that substituted for an apology.

Plummer shook his head, then let his chin sag to his chest. He turned away from Hanna and began walking around the edge of the trees. She watched him go slowly in the heavy snow, watched him taking several deep breaths, letting them out slowly as he moved around the perimeter. With his breath rising into the air, he moved like a fading steam engine ... every step matched by a puff of white escaping his mouth. Hanna was disappointed, hoping he would have expounded more on this story instead of walking away, but she supposed it wouldn't look good for him to be chatting up a prisoner. She was surprised, then, when his voice arrived in her ear. When he spoke, his voice suggested he was no longer here in the present, but somewhere in the past.

"Milton hadn't returned to the States empty handed," he admitted. If Hanna was at the "6" on a clock, Plummer was standing where the "2" would have been, and made a show at checking some provisions the Gray had already delivered. He'd pulled the collar of his coat up to hide his mouth, but made a show out of rubbing his hands, giving the impression he was cold. "The guys either ignored him or teased him, at first, but I liked talking to him," he continued. "They didn't really understand why Grant allowed him to stick around, but we were doing good in the battles and Milton proved to be a good listener. That's important in war, you know, having someone to talk to, and we could go to Milton with our troubles, whether we were struggling with injuries of a physical or emotional kind. We could tell him anything.

"Anything.

"And some of us told him things we couldn't bring ourselves to tell anyone else."

Hanna recognized the pain from her teenage years with Jill. "Was that when ...?"

"Revelation," Plummer said, though Hanna couldn't tell if he was responding to her directly or not. "I knew what I was, of course, even if I couldn't admit it to myself, and as we steamed south as part of Foote's naval flotilla, I wandered down to Milton's room. The old man sensed I was struggling with something dark, something I couldn't bring into the light, so he pulled a small vial out of a metal case he kept on him at all times, and told me to drink it, that it would give me some 'liquid courage,' as it were to give voice to who I was. I thought it was vodka. It wasn't."

"Revelation," Hanna said.

"Revelation," Plummer said. "I spilled my guts, and when I was done, Milton had a kind smile on his face, and told me I should talk to another one of the boys in our unit, a kid from Kentucky. Ricky Senton. Handsome lad. Strong and with a bright smile not yet crushed by battle. He had a big scar on his neck from a farming accident when he was a kid. Well, it took a week or so to find him as we were getting ready to attack Fort Henry, but Milton must have said something to him because every time our paths crossed we'd look at each other and just connect, you know. Connect, like we had a secret no one else knew about, and when we encamped around Fort Donelson, I went and found him in his tent. And we did talk, and more. Plenty of alcohol flowed, of course. We were celebrating Buckner's surrender to Grant that night. That's the victory that gave Grant the 'Unconditional Surrender' nickname. Anyway, you understand what Ricky and I did," Plummer said, spitting in the snow, and Hanna did understand, because she'd been through all of these emotions with Jill a decade ago. "The next morning we couldn't even look at each other, but after a few days of both me and Ricky being the two most miserable bastards in the whole company, and flat refusing to look one another in the eye, Milton slips us both another vial."

Hanna knew the second vial contained water from the Acceptance pool, but kept her mouth shut. She still didn't know if Plummer could hear her or not, but the man was on a roll and she wasn't inclined to stop him. Instead, she concentrated on the three gray hoods resting on the top of the water in each of the three pools. Plummer was talking about drinking the water, but these so-called Prophets were submerged in it. What effect would that have? Heck, how did Milton figure all of this out, anyway? And why take on the guise of Sinterklaas? Was he giving kids in the surrounding villages gifts of this water?

"This new vial was Acceptance, of course. The feeling it gave me was incredible. It didn't hide my conflict, you understand, but sort of ... rearranged all of the emotions raging inside me, so while I still felt shame and joy at what Ricky and I were doing, I was able to feel the happiness more than I did the guilt. Sneaking around became a game for us, and while we weren't ready to flaunt what we were doing, getting what we could when we could made it more fun, more thrilling.

"Secrets," Plummer spoke truthfully to Hanna's ears, "are better when you have one other person to share it with, aren't they?"

Hanna's frowned and nodded, her own memories of Jill threatening to boil up and over.

"But then Shiloh happened," Plummer continued, his voice cracking as he leaned his shoulder into the tree beyond the provisions, "and when it was over, I couldn't find Ricky anywhere. Do you know how many men we lost over those two days?

"Twenty-four thousand.

"That's 24,000 men who were killed, captured, maimed, or missing. I must have looked at every dead body I could find, but I never found him. I hoped he was captured, feared he was dead, and contemplated something worse. When the reports came in from our spies in Amsterdam about a strong, handsome man with a scar on his neck making noise about finding the exalted waters ..."

Plummer let his thoughts remain his own after that, and in a few moments he pulled down his collar and moved away from the trees and towards the edge of the pools. Hanna thought story time was over, but Plummer had one last comment for her.

"I never did try Transformation," he said, looking as if diving into the third pool was his option. "Milton had promised the third and final pool would bring us feel like one of the world's greatest wonders, but I didn't need any fancy water to do that so long as I had Ricky."

*

"I have need of your hot air balloon," Jill said to the man in the yellow suit before the door to *La Boutique des Merveilles au Rebut* had closed.

"Of course, Mademoiselle Masters," the man smiled. He was a small, round, bald, pleasant man in a garishly bright suit of yellow: shoes, pants, jacket, shirt, and tie. Around him, his shop wound through aisles that were shaped like pretzels instead of straight lines, and all matter of weird and interesting objects were available for purpose: instruments, books, toys, tapestries, clothes, dead animals in jars, dead animals on plaques, dead animals positioned to look like they were dancing a tango on the deck of an impossibly large ship called Titanic, and a picture frame that promised to play moving paintings when connected to something called a VCR. "Monsieur Inconnu will be happy to serve you. Por favor, give me just a moment I will be with you," he said, motioning to a little girl who stood nearby, looking at a collection of wooden toys.

"She doesn't look like she's ready to buy anything," Jill said, "and I want the balloon. So, let's deal."

Monsieur Inconnu tsk-tsk'd Jill with a wag of a chubby finger that had an oval-shaped yellow gemstone on a gold ring. "Please, mademoiselle, there is no need to hurry. Monsieur Inconnu gives full attention to all his customers. Take a moment to look around and perhaps— mon Dieu! Put that away!"

Jill did not put her H2O pistol away.

"I have a friend in jeopardy and I need that hot air balloon," Jill said.

"Mademoiselle!" Monsieur Inconnu snapped, stomping his foot onto the ground. The balloon you see behind my establishment is simply for show! You cannot make it fly!" Monsieur Inconnu was adamant on this point, stomping his foot several times. "Unless," he said hopefully, turning charming, "you are the Partridge? Are you the Partridge?"

"I'm going to shoot you if you don't get me a balloon," Jill said, growing tired of Inconnu's fascination with birds who lived in pear trees.

With Inconnu growing too flustered to talk, the little girl interjected herself into the conversation. "Hey, lady, I'm not impressed with your little water gun," she said, baring her fangs.

Jill pulled a fire shooter off her other hip. "How's this one work for you?"

The girl growled.

"Mon Dieu!" Inconnu yelled, stepping between them. "I will not have violence in my shop! You will stop this confrontation this instant or I will have you both removed from my business!"

The little girl hissed at Inconnu, and lunged forward, prepared to bite him in the hand.

Jill shot her with steam pellets from the H2o pistol, burning her face.

"I will kill you for that!" the vampire yelled, lunging for Jill.

It was Monsieur Inconnu's turn to do the saving, reaching out and grabbing the little girl by the back of her shirt and hoisting her up into the air. "You will wait outside!" he proclaimed, walking the vampire past Jill to toss her outside into the thick blanket of snow. "And if I hear of you attempting any form of retribution against either myself or

Miss Masters," he called to her from inside his shop, "I will personally inform the Vampire Council of Europe about your proclivity for baring your fangs in public. I bid you ... adieu!"

Inconnu slammed the door shut, took one second to regain his composure, and then reopened the door. In a chipper voice, he called out in a calm voice, "I hope to do business with you, again!" And then, in a whisper, confided, "Come back in ten minutes, please."

When Inconnu turned around, Jill had holstered her weapons. "Can you please overcharge me for a damn balloon now?"

Monsieur Inconnu smiled as if none of what had just transpired had actually happened. He was the essence of entrepreneurial cool. "But of course, Miss Masters. Right this way."

*

Hanna wanted to ask Plummer what happened next, but before she could raise the issue, men began walking through a small crack in the wall of the carved-out mountain over at the "10" position. When the first man walked through wearing the grays of the Confederate army, Hanna's heart sank. There were two factions out there seeking to control these waters, Milton's men and the Confederates, and she was hoping for the former.

She hoped for that right up until the moment she got it.

Mixed in with the twenty or so members of the Gray were Milton's men from last night, gentlemen instead of soldiers, wearing beautiful winter coats of either red or green and with their hands bound behind their backs. Upon entering, the Gray moved the followers of Sinterklaas to their right, closer to Hanna. Glancing over to her fellow American, Hanna saw that the government agent wasn't expecting or desiring this, either, but he could do little but stand near the third pool and watch as Milton, still dressed in his finely pressed maroon suit, entered on the arm of a handsome man with a scar on his neck that was clearly Ricky Senton.

"Hello, Plum," Senton smiled. "Old Milt and I have been chatting after his unwise attempt to attack my men on the train last night."

"Ricky," Plummer breathed, feeling the interceding years from Shiloh to France drop away. "What ... what are you doing here?" he asked, even though he knew he would be.

Senton smiled and motioned around to the mountainous cul-de-sac. "I'm here being a good imperial, of course. General Forrest is always looking for new and interesting weapons for the Gray to utilize."

Plummer spat in the snow and looked to Milton. "And you, of all people, are okay with this?" he asked.

Milton shook his head, looking old and frail in the cold morning. "I make the best choice for my flock, not myself," he said weakly. "If Ricky wants to take some of the water back to General Forrest, I'm alright with that, so long as he leaves me in charge of my ministry."

Plummer shook his head. "You can't be that dumb, Milt, not after everything you saw in the Civil. You know he's going to try to take all of the water."

"I know that both sides of the Civil were anything but," Milton said, his passions rising. "I learned that at Shiloh, and I would have thought you did, too. There were over 100,000 men in that battle and nearly a quarter of them became casualties! Now," he said, trying to calm himself, "if you want to say that the Union cause was more just, well, I will stand with you on that, but you know damn well as I that in most instances the only difference between the men wearing blue and the men wearing gray were their place of birth!"

Plummer nodded towards Senton, "He fights for Forrest now. Nathan Bedford Forrest. And fighting under the leadership of that man is a far cry than fighting under Lee."

"Is it?" Milton asked pointedly. "What makes you any different than Ricky here? You're aiming to take these waters back to Grant every bit as much as Ricky has designs on taking them back to Forrest. Neither one of you sees these exalted waters for what they are, for what they can bring. All you see in them are weapons!"

Milton turned away from both Senton and Plummer and walked in the direction of his men. "Ricky comes crashing in here, taking ownership of what isn't his, and so I send you a letter to come, too, but I'm not expecting you to save me, Plummer." Milton's face turned sad, the wrinkles on his face seeming to grow deeper. "I was hoping you'd bring men of your own so the two of you could kill each other off, but you didn't, and that's why I asked about finding reinforcements."

Milton looked across the ponds to where Hanna was bolted to the tree, the three hoods belonging to the Prophets of Gray so still it was as if they had removed themselves from consideration. "For your involvement," he said to the American woman, not caring that his voice would be barely audible, "I am truly sorry."

He looked to Ricky and then to Plummer, and then to the heavens. "I am doing good here," he said. "I am using the gifts of the pools in a manner of which I think God would approve. Revelation. Acceptance. Transformation," he said reverentially, his thoughts drifting away from him and threatening to leave his old body without anything of substance inside of it.

Ricky laughed. "Well, thank you for that Sinter-Milt," he said, "but your time playing dress-up has come to an end. It's time for the men to do what men do." He looked to Plummer and cocked his head, as his right hand went to an electric shooter on his hip. "You should've brought an army. You still would've lost, but at least Milt would get a show. Do you want to surrender or do you want to die? Your choice." Ricky patted his heart. "It's the least I can do for my old lover. After all, I do owe you for all that information you gave me about Grant's battle plans. I owe at least two of my promotions to what came out of your mouth."

Plummer said nothing, but looked around, calculating the odds of every potential play. There were twenty men under Milton's command and maybe a few more than that among the Gray. Maybe if Hanna and Poseidon's kid were here they'd have something of a shot, but as it was, he was going to get nothing out of this.

"Boys," Ricky announced loudly, "let's capture Mr. Plummer and Milt here and then get to transporting this water back to the General. If you have to kill Plummer," he said, staring daggers at his ex-lover, "do it, but don't kill the old man. No one knows more about these waters than he does, and General Forrest will be wanting him to advise us on their powers. Get this done, and the drinks and the whores are on me tonight!"

The Gray troopers yelled their approval and started to take guns off hips and rifles off shoulders. One of the soldiers grabbed Milton's arm, and the physicality of the act shook Milton out of his pondering and back to the present.

"Oh, Ricky," Milton said, trying and failing to pull his arm away from the Gray that held it. "You always were rash and impatient. Pity for the world that you are like that, and pity for you that I remembered it." Milton tapped the side of his head. "You're right to want me captured and not killed," he said. "If you drink these waters without knowing the power they possess, they ain't nothing but water. But if you have someone who understands them, someone like me, for instance, who can manipulate those with water in their system ... well, then ... then you have something."

"What are you prattling on about?" Ricky snapped.

"My men," he said, finally pulling his arm free and pointing it at his flock, "are willing to die for me and die to protect these exalted waters. Are your men willing to do the same?"

"My men believe in the Cause," Ricky said confidently.

Milton narrowed his eyes. "That's what we're going to find out," he said with a slight sneer on his weathered face. "How'd that water taste, Plummer? Let us find out, shall we? Let your true nature come into the world at the command of Sinterklaas!"

Milton looked expectantly across the three pools to Plummer.

Nothing happened.

"You talking about the water from the canteen?" Plummer flashed a smile. "You don't think I'm that dumb, do you, Milton? I've already tasted from Revelation and Acceptance. You filled that canteen with Transformation, didn't ya? Yeah, I know you did. Ain't no way in hell I'm finishing off the trilogy. No, I remember what you said — you have to take them in order or they're useless."

"You're a damned fool!" Milton yelled. "Did you not taste from it?"

Plummer shook his head. "I did not," he said with a smile.

Sinterklaas pointed behind the American government agent to Hanna. "She did, though, didn't she?"

Plummer's face went from victory to confusion in the turn of a head. "You said the waters had to be taken in order!"

"You don't think I learned more about the waters in the intervening years?" the old man asked. "No, I suppose lapdogs like yourself never do think about what more they can learn when it's so easy to have the world explained to you by the man on the other end of your leash."

All eyes turned to the Korean-American who was bolted to a tree in the far corner. Hanna gasped, and looked like she was about to vomit. "No," she said, her body doubling up in pain as she pulled herself free from Plummer's loosely-applied bondage.

"If you hurt her," Plummer warned, sending Milton one last glance as he began his trek through the heavy snow to Hanna's side. The thick, wetness of the snow left the threat unfinished as he needed all his strength to get to the hurting woman.

Seemingly all traces of the frail old man had left Milton. Perhaps, Plummer and Senton both reasoned, it was the close proximity to the exalted waters that gave Milton a full supply of spit and vigor. The aged American's spine straightened and his wobbly legs turned to steel. He moved effortlessly through the same heavy snow that caused the others to struggle, as if the frozen water around the pools bent to his will. His maroon suit now seemed to bulge instead of hanging off his slender frame, and his wispy beard appeared thicker.

"I am called Sinterklaas," Milton said, his voice hard, "and you are trespassers in my domain. You," he said to Senton, "blocked my access to these waters with the intent to steal. The other one," he pointed to Plummer, who was nearly at Hanna, "is no better, and would gladly claim these waters for his master, as well. With thievery in your heart, I command you to death!"

Ricky laughed. "Have you lost both legs of your rocker, Milt?" The Confederate looked around and saw one foe running towards a sickly woman, and his other opponents already defeated and certainly no match for the men in gray jackets guarding them. "Is there an army hidden somewhere I haven't seen?"

"Oh, no," Sinterklaas smiled. "You have seen my army."

"And we defeated them," Senton replied, motioning to the defeated gentlemen in red and green coats with their arms secured behind their backs.

Sinterklaas smiled, and Senton was man enough to not ignore the sinking feeling developing deep in his gut.

"Guns out!" he yelled as the gentlemen of Sinterklaas snapped their bonds and rose to their feet. They pulled off their coats, revealing naked torsos, just as Senton ordered his men to "Fire!" The Confederate bullets hit their targets, they drew no blood.

"The power of Transformation!" Sinterklaas proclaimed. "Men who wanted nothing more than to believe in something bigger than themselves and make the world a better place! Become, my men, become!"

The gentlemen followers of Sinterklaas moved towards one another, hugging and locking their nearly naked bodies together as they fell to the ground. Watching from a distance, Senton at first thought this was an odd time for an orgy, but he soon realized that Sinterklaas's sheep were not lost to lust, but were arranging themselves in a specific set of positions ... a set of positions that led the twenty-odd individuals to merge into the form of a headless giant. When all the bodies locked and intertwined together and completed the formation, the giant sat up, and then rose to his feet, causing some among the Gray to drop their rifles and scream for their God to help them.

"Bind yourself!" Sinterklaas commanded, and as the men who comprised the giant struggled to keep their positions, the giant raised his hand-less arms to a 45-degree angle. Senton's men resumed firing, but the wind in the cul-de-sac was suddenly harsher and wilder, swirling snow from the ground around their bodies and stinging their eyes. Senton's men were not the target of the storm, only a happy victim from Sinterklaas' perspective. The wind created a whirlwind effect, and the snow started to cling to the giant.

Across the way, Plummer glanced at the proceedings, glad to see that Milton and Senton were busy with each other. Hanna was in bad shape, completely doubled over in the snow and holding her stomach. Plummer knew she was in pain and respected her toughness, but the screams of anguish still came. "I'm burning!" she yelled, sitting back against the tree and pulling up her blouse to show that her skin was scorching red. Plummer set his jaw and started grabbing snow to put on the burning skin, but no sooner would the contact occur than the snow would melt.

Plummer needed help, and there was only person who could give it to them: Milton. Looking back over to the old man, he saw the giant was now covered in ice and snow, creating a terrifying, monstrous, abomination.

All that was missing was a head.

And as Plummer called for Milton to come and assist Hanna, the giant turned to its master, reached down, and picked Sinterklaas up, depositing him into the neck and giving itself a head.

"Protect the exalted waters!" Sinterklaas roared. "Kill them all!"

*

Jill Masters had the large red balloon in the air and was attempting to pilot it over the city of Lille. Never a great student, Jill nonetheless had learned her lesson with the hot air balloon ride she and Hanna had taken in their Krampus adventure. While Inconnu's employees had raised the balloon for her, Jill paid careful attention to what the shopkeeper had told her about piloting the craft, and now that she was in the air she was absolutely certain she remembered at least half of what he'd said.

Her goal was the roof of their hotel, where she could see Ignatius waiting for her on the roof with a large, black bag of weapons in his hand. The balloon wasn't moving fast enough to keep her thoughts focused on the mission, and they kept drifting back to the previous night. Was this her fault? Had she let Hanna down by taking Ignatius to bed?

For that matter, why had she taken Ignatius to bed? Was this a fling or something more?

As she lowered a secured rope off the side of the casket, the reality of Lille gave way to the horrors of Hell. A new vision rose up around her, transposing her to the fiery underworld. Hanna was there, resplendent with black wings to carry her over the rivers of lava. Her eyes sought Ignatius, but standing there instead was the Man in the Red Coat.

"Come to me," he whispered across the distance.

Jill's mind exploded, and the vision of Hell was replaced with memories that were both real and not real, yet all somehow hers. Images rushed past her mind's eye too fast to comprehend, except in glimpses of staircases and cellars and her bedroom where the wardrobe ... the wardrobe ... the wardrobe ...

Hands on ears, Jill started screaming at memories that she had lived but somehow not remembered.

The Man in the Red Coat smiled.

"Did you think I had forgotten about you?" he asked.

*

Richard Collard Senton had not risen through the ranks of the Confederate Army by being either stupid or cowardly, and he quickly assessed the situation. His mission was to bring the exalted waters back to the Gray to help further the Cause. He saw that slipping away and knew one did not continue to rise by failing in their mission. It was a big risk to take 25 men to Europe to search for magical water, and General Forrest would not look kindly at an empty-handed return.

Looking at the pools, he saw the Prophets were still submerged, still seemingly unaware of the chaos around them. These had been ordinary soldiers two weeks ago, but every day they bathed in the waters and everyday they lost a bit more of their humanity. They were the prize he'd return to Forrest, even if he did not know the exact nature of this prize.

"Men!" he yelled as the snow giant began reaching down to slug and squeeze his soldiers. "Drink from the third pool! Transform yourselves!"

With their bullets failing to do anything to slow down their foe, the men followed their commander's order and ran to the third pool. There was less snow in the cul-de-sac now, and the men made good time, despite slipping in the increasingly slushy slop at their feet. They reached the edge of the pool and dropped to their knees. Cupped hands dipped into the warm water, and eager lips sucked the liquid into mouths.

The giant roared, Sinterklaas' voice now louder and deeper, speaking with the strength of all the men beneath him. He reached one soldier on his way to the pool and picked him up in the air with hands made of ice. The soldier screamed as the giant ripped him in half, splattering the monster's icy body with Alabaman blood.

"You can do nothing, Ricky!" Sinterklaas roared from on high. "Transformation takes time unless I choose to prod it along and I do not! I had hoped not to risk my men but the failings of Plummer have forced my hand and now we will eliminate you, Ricky, you and all your men! Give my regards to Forrest when he joins you in Hell!"

Senton's thoughts were given pause. This damned Milton might just be right. He looked to Plummer, wondering if his one-time lover had any card tucked away up his sleeve, but it was the Asian woman with him that caught his eye.

Hanna screamed in pain as her body convulsed towards the center. Blood ran out of her eyes and her body began to glow a bright red. When she screamed, a white light poured from her mouth and eyes.

The seated Plummer was forced back from the heat. He wanted to help her, but he was smart enough to know he needed help. Turning around to see if there was anything to catch his eye, he was greeted with his ex-lover pointing a fire shooter down into his face.

"Lot of good that's going to do," Plummer grumbled.

Senton pulled the gun away. "Temporary truce?" he suggested.

"Go to Hell."

Senton shook his head and brought the gun back around, but Plummer was ready for him, punching his ex-lover in the groin. As Ricky doubled over, Plummer grabbed his gray coat and pulled him down into the snow. The two men who once rolled together in a different kind of battle now punched and kicked and tore at each other in the French snow. So personal was their battle that there did not seem a force on Earth that could separate them.

Perhaps, then, it was good Hanna was no longer a force from this Earth.

The Bostonian screamed with such an intensity that both men turned to her in time to see the transformed woman rise to her feet. Her entire body was now glowing with a silvery-white light save for her eyes, which glowed with the fire of Hell that had previously consumed her body. Stepping away from the tree that she had been bound to, two large, gray wings unfolded from her back. With one powerful flap, they lifted her several feet off the ground.

"Hanna!" Plummer called.

Looking down at the government men with nothing but contempt in her eyes, Hanna let loose an ungodly, sonic scream that knocked both men through the snow, stopping only when they ran into the Gray soldiers that had tasted of

Transformation. While still herself, she felt a greater connection to the universe, and as she looked down on the men beneath her, she could look right through the world, too, down to the bowels of Hell, itself. There was joy, too. Looking up, she could see a glittering city of gold connected to Earth by a rainbow bridge.

Across from her, Sinterklaas roared in expected triumph. "You will all be dead before your transformed selves can come to be! You will— wait! What madness is this?"

The madness was that it was in this moment that the three Prophets of Gray decided to enter the fray, rising on their own out of the water to float above the surface. Their hoods remained dry, but the rest of their robes and bodies were soaked with the exalted waters. Seeing them, Plummer punched Senton hard in the jaw, knocking him out. Pulling his electric shooter off his hip, Grant's right hand man fired at the Prophets.

Yellow electricity sizzled in the cold air, only to stop in mid-air a few feet from their target.

The Prophets laughed, low and rumbling, almost with the collective sound of a swarm of bees. "The North may have stolen the Civil," they said in unison, the buzzing of their joined voices growing in intensity but not volume, "but thanks to the exalted waters of Minister Sinterklaas, the South will rise again!"

In front of the Prophets, the soldiers of the Confederate military who had refused to recognize the call from General Robert E. Lee to put down their weapons and rejoin their nation, refused to accept defeat. Like Hanna, they, too began to transform into something beyond human, but this was a deeper, more sadistic transformation. They burned too, bright and intense enough for their clothes to catch fire and burn away. The men began to claw at their own bodies, and bright bursts of light shot out with each rip and tear in their skin.

Chunks of flesh dropped into the snow, sizzling their way to the grass beneath. As their bodies fell away, what remained were transparent images of the men they had been.

"Ghosts," Senton chuckled from his knees beside Plummer. "Eternal warriors of the Cause."

"Balls," Plummer grumbled.

"Kill them all," the Prophets ordered, sending the Risen South into the conflict.

Plummer glanced back to Hanna, who was levitating thirty feet above the floor, watching these new transformations intently as her own clothes now fell away, revealing a leather bodice and thigh high boots. She had been content to simply watch the play below her, but as the ghosts and the snow giant began to fight with one another, a new change came to Hanna, one that sent deeper shills through Plummer's body than the cold, French snow.

She was smiling.

*

"You okay?" Ignatius asked, climbing into the balloon's basket.

"I'm fine," Jill said, wiping tears off her face.

"What were you screaming about?"

"Just drive the damn balloon," Jill said, zipping open the bag of weapons. She wasn't refusing to answer Ignatius' question because she was being rude, but because the Man in the Red Coat seemed to be staring back at her through time and did not want her opening her mouth.

"Monsters!" Sinterklaas yelled gleefully from above the floor of the canyon, rising to the challenge as his negative thoughts about the military men were brought into being. "It is not a surprising, is it, Plummer?" he asked, reaching for the spy. "The military does make monsters of us all!"

Plummer had a different take on the ghost army; he thought their existence was far more dangerous for the fate of the United States than the Civil War had been because they ingested Transformation and became some kind of ultimate version of what they wanted out of themselves, and what they revealed themselves to be were true believers. These were not simply disgruntled men with a grudge against the North because their pride was wounded by the loss in battle. No, these were men who believed passionately and deeply about the Cause, whatever that nebulous concept meant to each of them.

Looking around, Plummer could see he was the forgotten man on the battlefield. Ghosts, the snow giant, and Hanna fought indiscriminately, fighting whomever was in their path. A flaming sword had appeared in Hanna's hands, and she swung it at the ghosts, carving effortlessly through the wispy bodies, but doing no permanent damage as the ghosts simply reformed themselves. The Gray ghosts were not having much more luck against her, their bullets seeming to either miss Hanna or connect with her sword or leather armor, bouncing harmlessly aside.

It was Sinterklaas and his followers that were taking the brunt of the battle, as the Confederate ghosts were passing through the giant, chipping off chunks of snow and ice and revealing the human men beneath the snow giant's surface. Sinterklass still stood in the neck, commanding the giant's movements, but he'd been forced to go from offense to defense.

Plummer's military mind could see that if the ghosts concentrated their attack solely on the snow giant, they could bring Sinterklaas to his knees, but half of them were still fighting with Hanna, who swooped and dove and slashed her way through their ranks. Why wasn't Ricky having them concentrate on the snow giant?

He was blindsided by his former lover, and the two men returned to trading blows in the snow.

"I never loved you!" Senton roared as he punched Plummer in the side.

"I wasn't interested in your love, Ricky," Plummer shot back, both of them lying and both of them knowing it. He tried an overhand shot, but his feet slipped in the snow, and Senton was on him in an instant, kicking Plummer in the side of the head with his boot. Collapsing in the snow, Plummer felt a shadow move over him and thought it was Ricky, but when he opened his eyes and looked skyward, he saw not Ricky blocking out the sun, but a hot air balloon.

"I'll be damned," he said.

*

In the balloon's basket, Ignatius steered as Jill gripped her samurai sword as hard as she could.

"Take us down," she said. There was something in her head that she thought she should be thinking about, but she couldn't remember what that was; she remembered freaking out but that must have been because of Hanna being in jeopardy. It must have been that because she couldn't remember anything else about her meltdown.

"Are you sure?" Ignatius asked. "Are you okay?"

"Ugh," Jill snapped, banging the sword against the basket. "I don't need sensitive right now. Take us down. Now," she said, peering over the edge. "Our first goal is finding Hanna."

"Then you best look behind you," a voice that sounded like Hanna said, causing Jill and Ignatius to turn around to see the angelic Hanna floating in the air. She looked regal and menacing, and Jill's heart jumped and sank at once because this was and was not her partner.

"The devil is inside of her," Ignatius said, reaching for a weapon.

"I told you," Jill said, her heart racing at the sight of her friend matching those of Hanna from her visions, "she's not into dudes."

Ignatius looked at the powerfully beautiful creature — for that is what he saw when he looked at Hanna now — and mumbled, "A shame at that."

"I heard that," Jill snapped, moving to the edge nearest Hanna. "Hey," she said, looking into her friend's blood-red eyes. "What's going on?"

Hanna slowly flapped her wings to hover in the air. "Everyone must die," she said, "so that I may bring them to eternity." She let loose another sonic scream that knocked Jill back into Ignatius. Her scream roared a second time, and the ropes connecting the balloon to the basket began to snap.

"You're gonna kill us!" Jill roared, rising to her feet as the basket and balloon began jerking and twisting.

"I have spent my life in your shadow!" Hanna yelled, her eyes radiating red energy. "But when I have delivered you to the land of the dead, my obligation will be complete!"

Jill reached for the samurai sword leaning against the wall of the basket. "You ungrateful tramp!" she roared. "I brought you an awesome sword and you're gonna kill me?"

Winged Hanna scoffed at that and flashed her own, flaming sword. "Mine is bigger," she sneered.

"Yeah, well, mine's sharper," Jill said, tossing it to Hanna, who caught it and half-unsheathed the blade from his onyx scabbard. "It's ... it's ..."

"Beautiful," Ignatius prodded, as the basket began to stabilize.

Hanna looked at him. "It's smaller than I thought it would be. Are you sure it's a samurai sword?"

Jill drilled her elbow into Ignatius' ribs. "Told you," she muttered as she moved past him to the ledge.

"If I had known you were going to give the sword to Haneul," Ignatius said, "I would have acquired the larger blade."

Jill wrinkled her nose and turned back to her now winged friend, "Well, what do you think?"

Hanna looked to the ground and fired her flaming sword down towards the reeling snow giant. She didn't bother to watch the blade's path, and pulled the whole samurai sword free. As it touched the air, the blade flashed in her hands, the silvery energy that covered her body now covering the sword.

"Okay, I admit it, she's pretty damn hot, at the moment," Jill said.

Hanna grinned wickedly and slid to the basket, where she grabbed Jill's head and kissed her ex-lover passionately. Jill felt a whole cauldron of swirling emotions mix together as her body burned at the touch of Hanna's lips and tongue and hands. When Hanna pulled away, Jill groaned at the loss.

"This ends now," Hanna promised, and Jill could see the red energy had drained from Hanna's eyes and her beautiful browns were back and cognizant.

Ignatius and Jill moved quickly to the opposite edge of the basket as Hanna dropped back down into the battle. Their actions sent the entire balloon jerking and twisting again, and they began to plummet towards the ground below.

Jill let Ignatius worry about that; her eyes were locked on Hanna, who dove towards two waiting ghosts. She flew hard between them, her body rocking to the side. When she passed them, the ghosts looked at each other, astonished looks on their transparent faces. Hanna had cut them straight through and their bodies began to slide apart, and this time, when they tried to reform themselves, their bodies burst into silver flame and wafted away in the cold morning light.

As Hanna was sweeping way the ghosts focused on her, the remaining ghosts of the Cause were engaged with the giant, who was weakened by Hanna's first sword that was now imbedded in his chest. The giant's locked-together bodies were struggling to stay upright, and nearly half of the snow and ice that helped bind them had been broken off by the ghosts.

Plummer tried to rise to his feet, but Senton kicked him in the jaw and Plummer saw stars. He tried to push himself into a sitting position, but his equilibrium was shot. The government man had not felt this lost since before he'd first tasted the exalted waters back during the war. He was here because Milton had called for him and because he had dutifully passed that request onto Grant and because the President wanted these waters under his control, likely for the exact same reason the Prophets wanted it.

He looked for the Prophets but they had disappeared.

He turned his attention to Ricky, but the Confederate leader was busy running through the snow to get back to the crack in the wall to escape. Part of Plummer wanted to catch him, but a greater part just didn't care anymore. His biggest fear had been realized when it came to Ricky - Plummer had been used and no doubt Union boys and died because of it.

Letting the hurt come and blur his vision, Plummer pulled out a Colt revolver and fired.

Senton fell against a tree, then slid to the snow.

He did not arise.

Wiping the tears away, Plummer's eyes found Hanna, flying with righteous vengeance across the field of battle, single-handedly ending the fight as no one could stand against her blade. The snow giant finally broke, the gentlemen followers of Sinterklaas falling into the snow.

Sinterklaas fell, too, and when his body hit the ground with a wet thud, it seemed to Plummer as if Milton had returned, and all his frailty with him.

Plummer laid back down.

Everything seemed so pointless.

The cul-de-sac was full of dead bodies but it was also full of people who knew what they were and embraced the ultimate expression of that idea. His eyes stopped following Hanna run her sword through ghosts and found that one of the Prophets of Gray now stood over him.

"Transformation," he said, pointing to the third pool. The Prophet was right. It was time to complete his relationship with the exalted waters and become something more, something that was a heightened version of who he was and what he wanted, to become something more than a loyal foot soldier. Plummer walked slowly through the remnants of battle. Ghosts burned in the air around him, but he gave them no mind, and they did not bother with him. His eyes were locked on the pool. A hot air balloon swooped past as it crashed into the trees to his right and he didn't bother to turn in its direction.

He should have.

"Hey!" Jill called to him as she rushed to him.

"Go away," Plummer said numbly.

"Have you see Hanna?" Jill replied, putting two electric blasters between them. "Drinking that water is a mistake," she said and unloaded both barrels on Plummer, sending him to darkness.

Across the cul-de-sac, Hanna had finished killing ghosts and turned her attention to Sinterklaas, only her eyes didn't find the strong-willed man who'd orchestrated this chaos, but the weak man who'd asked for her help. Seeing him like this, a primal tiredness enveloped her and she landed in the snow. Her wings became slightly unresponsive and the silver flame on her samurai sword burned itself out.

Hanna began to walk towards Milton, her wings dropping off her back. She intended to kill the old man, but when she reached him, she found she had no heart to do any more killing this morning.

"Sleep," Sinterklaas commanded.

"Okay," Hanna said, and collapsed into the snow, joining Plummer in darkness.

*

When Hanna awoke, she was lying on a small hill away from the exalted waters. Around her, Ignatius and Jill were hauling the last alive humans out of the cul-de-sac with the repaired balloon. These survivors quickly moved to join their fellow men as they hurried away from the ledge and towards the interior of the woods. Below her, the dead bodies were laid out on the ground together. More than half of the men who had fought were now dead, and most of them at Hanna's blade.

"Of course you wake up when the lifting is done," Jill chided, jumping out of the basket to give Hanna a hand to her feet. "You lost the wings. Too bad. They were hot."

Hanna shook her head, trying to remember just how many different worlds she had seen. Seven? Eight? Nine? "The Prophets?"

"Gone," Jill answered.

Hanna looked down into the cul-de-sac. "What happens with this place?"

Ignatius answered for her. "We're going to destroy it," he said, holding up a string of hand grenades.

"The hell you are," Plummer said, moving to them to grab the grenades from the demon hunter. "We leave it be. The Prophets of Gray, if my reasoning is sound, have immersed themselves in the waters to the point they can revelate, accept, and transform on their own. We need these waters," he said, pointing to Milton, "and besides, look at him."

The old man had his back against a tree and tears were streaming down his face.

"It's the kids," he mumbled to himself. "It's the kids who will suffer."

"Let him go back to doing what he was doing," Plummer said, turning to leave. "The kids in this area deserves the gifts of Sinterklaas. I've got a zeppelin waiting for me in Paris. Anyone wants to hitch a ride back to the United States, you've got three days to get there."

"You okay?" Hanna asked him.

"I'm fine," he grunted, turning away from them and patting his jacket, where three glass jars filled with exalted waters rested comfortably.

Mission complete.

INTERSTITIAL
THE SHOP OF DISCARDED
WONDERS

1866, December
Two Days After Hanna Lost Her Wings

The bell above the door in La Boutique des Merveilles au Rebut jingled, and Monsieur Inconnu replaced the hand-sized snow globe containing a solitary tree back onto its shelf, between a snow globe of the Acropolis and a snow globe of a snow globe. Of all the sections of his ever-expanding store, it was the clock section that made him the happiest. There was something soothing to the middle-aged, slightly plump man in the yellow suit about standing in a place where time could be whatever you wanted it to be, simply by changing the hands of a machine.

One could not literally alter time in this manner, of course, Monsieur Inconnu understood, but if you could ... now that would be a clock to own!

"Un moment!" he called out to the store's newest guest as he made his way through the winding aisles, past the Poetry section and the Wooden Toys section and back through the Poetry section before emerging at the entrance area to his place of business to find a woman in highly fashionable green corset and dress, highlighted with red, and wearing a green mask that appeared cut from a single emerald.

"Mademoiselle!" Monsieur Inconnu gasped with delight, moving around the counter to stand in the small greeting area. Trinkets and objects and treasures of all kinds surrounded them. The middle-aged Belgian took great pride in arranging his items by a value beyond money, so a tin toy of simplistic design and half-destroyed paint that sold for a minuscule amount sat beside an architectural sketch from Da Vinci that was worth millions. To visitors, this sometimes seemed odd, but to Monsieur Inconnu, it was the most rational thing in the world.

"Monsieur Inconnu," the woman said, bowing almost imperceptibly.

"Are you, at long last, La Partridge?" he asked.

"I am not," the woman said apologetically.

"Ah," Inconnu shrugged, his disappointment obvious for only a moment before he brightened. "Your voice, it is American in origin, yes? I sense a touch of the Queen's English in your voice, making me think you have lived on Arthur's Island for a very long time, but down at the bottom of it ... American, yes?"

"Very perceptive of you," the woman nodded.

"Then perhaps you know of La Partridge by her American name, where she is called ... The Partridge?"

"I am afraid not," the woman said.

"Or by her British name ... The Partridge?"

"I am the Mistletoe Queen, and it is very nice to meet you, Monsieur Inconnu," the woman said, a thin edge now appearing in her voice.

Sensing he had pushed the question too far, Monsieur Inconnu turned away from personal pursuits and to professional concerns. "The pleasure is all mine, mademoiselle!" he said, giving a dramatic bow. "Now, merci, tell me what Monsieur Inconnu can do for you? My shop has sights and delights one can find nowhere else!"

"Yes, it does," the Mistletoe Queen said approvingly. "The Shop of Discarded Wonders, if my French is correct."

"It is! It is!"

"And you purchase items, too, do you not?" the Mistletoe Queen asked, reaching into a pocket to remove a green sack far bigger than the pocket it was removed from.

Inconnu's eyes went wide at that, and he pointed eagerly at the coat. "Your ... your coat, mademoiselle," he said, drumming the tips of his fingers together. "It is ..."

"It is not for sale," she said, "though all of the contents of this sack are."

Monsieur Inconnu clapped his hands together before taking the sack. "Let us see what treasures we have here!" Moving to the counter, the Frenchman opened the three-foot high sack on the counter and his already high interest grew to dizzying heights. There were goggles the likes of which he had never seen, a bracelet with a red gem on it, a samurai sword, and dozens of weapons of a Steampunk design. Monsieur Inconnu did love the emerging fashion trend of Steampunk and though he abhorred weapons, he understood that weaponization was an important part of a niche trend becoming a cultural phenomenon. Guns like the H2O pistol, the electric shooter, the plasma blaster would fetch a high return, if he could get them for the right price.

Not that Monsieur Inconnu was motivated by money, of course, but he did believe in bartering, and the nicer the object, the higher the return.

"Tell me, mademoiselle," he said without pulling his head away from the beautiful bracelet, "where did you get such wonderful objects?"

"Why," the Mistletoe Queen laughed, "let us agree that they are mine to part with."

Monsieur Inconnu spun around quickly. "Mademoiselle Mistletoe, I have a reputation, and I cannot purchase items that are stolen!"

The Mistletoe Queen smiled beneath her mask. "Who said anything about you purchasing them?" she asked. "They are a gift."

"A gift?"

"It is the Christmas season, non?" she asked. "I am not unaware of you, Monsieur Inconnu, or your shop. I know you buy and sell, but I also know that the Shop of Discarded Wonders serves as a way station for items of interest without a home. These weapons were owned by acquaintances of mine who are no longer in need of them. That's what those items behind you on the counter are, monsieur ... items looking for someone who needs them. Items looking for a purpose."

Inconnu licked his upper lip, and then ran his sweaty palms down the front of his yellow suit coat. "And, to be clear, you do not want anything for these items?"

"I do want one thing," the Mistletoe Queen said, her eyes dancing around the store. Inconnu's eyes tries to mimic hers, looking everywhere the woman's eyes looked, growing ecstatic when those eyes lingered on a child's toy and fearful when they lingered on a large painting from Sandro Botticelli. The items the Mistletoe Queen had brought him were fantastic — he believed the goggles might even be alien — but there was a limit to their value.

"Yes, mademoiselle?" Inconnu pressed. "What would you like in exchange?"

"I want only one thing, and I am afraid it is non-negotiable, Monsieur Inconnu."

"Yes?"

"I want the Partridge."

Inconnu's eyes went wide with surprise. "But ... mademoiselle! I do not know the Partridge. That is why I am endlessly seeking her, oui? A man in a red coat was in here just last week, promising me ... ah," he said touching his nose. "You and he."

"Me and him."

The lights in the shop darkened and the Mistletoe Queen's mask began to pulse with light until soon it was the only light in the shop. Monsieur Inconnu, who was used to dealing with shady characters of ill-repute, would later admit he had never been more confused in all his dealings.

The Mistletoe Queen extended her arm and opened her palm. From somewhere back in the store, a ball of light slowly wound its way through the snakelike aisles, sending streaks of light through shelves and cabinets and display cases.

"I will take the Partridge now," she announced

"But ... I have no such person here by that name!" Monsieur Inconnu insisted.

The Queen said nothing as the ball of light floated into her palm. On contact the light from the ball was extinguished and the light in the room returned. Monsiuer Inconnu could not believe what he saw, for it was the snow globe containing nothing but an anonymous tree.

"If that is all you want ..." he started to say when the Mistletoe Queen shook the snow globe, sending the little white pellets inside swirling around the water that filled the glass. As the snow circulated wildly, Inconnu lost sight of the tree, but as the snow began to settle at the bottom, the Frenchman could not believe what he saw standing by the tree:

A woman in a white cloak highlighted with light green markings.

The Partridge.

"But ... but ..."

The Mistletoe Queen dropped the snow globe into the same pocket from which she had removed the sack of gifts.

"How is this possible?" Inconnu asked.

Beneath her mask, the Mistletoe Queen smiled. "Thank you for holding her for me, Monsieur Inconnu. Do have yourself a Merry little Christmas, won't you?"

THE MAN IN THE RED COAT

ACT THREE
FIVE GOLDEN RINGS

1866, December
Two Weeks After Hanna Lost Her Wings

Less than a week before Christmas, and Hanna and Jill were undeniably lost and tired. France had been an exhausting run around the country, and with Christmas approaching they simply wanted to get to Paris or Toulouse or back to blessed London to sit in a fancy hotel and do nothing.

"I'm not buying you a gift," Jill said from atop her horse.

"You never do."

"I'm not having one of my other servants buy you a gift."

"Touché," Hanna smiled as she paused in the saddle to look around. It was dark and cold despite their thick coats, and the moon's light seemed to remind them of both of these facts more than it lit the way forward. "Where are we?" she asked.

"Was I supposed to be paying attention?"

"Yes."

"Oh. Well. We're in southern France."

A smart retort formed in Hanna's brain but it came out only as an easy laugh. They'd left Toulouse this morning, heading east after Ignatius had given them a lead on a wealthy potential client in the village of Saint Elle. All of the weapons had been stolen, and they needed to make a quick buck and restock.

And, eventually, get back to America.

Jill had a mother and a sister and a half-sister that deserved to hear about what had happened to the family patriarch.

Pushing thoughts of her family aside, Jill tried to warm herself with thoughts of Ignatius Poseidon. This current adventure had started with him. Riding in horseback through the snow, it seemed almost hard to believe it was only a week ago that Ignatius had risen up from the bed they share to push open the bedroom window, letting in the cold December air to help cool down their bodies.

"I'm sorry about your guns," he said.

"Hanna's fuming," Jill sighed. "We need a quick job to get some money in our pockets and weapons in our holsters."

Ignatius nodded, sliding back into bed. "I might have something. There's a woman who knows my father from the old days and has been begging him to come take a look at strange goings on in her town."

"Why hasn't he?"

"Asking someone to explain the machinations of Charles Francis Poseidon—"

"Too much talking," Jill said. "We'll take it."

"You haven't even heard what the job is, yet?"

"Can she pay us?"

Ignatius nodded.

"Then anything else is just an unnecessary complication," Jill smiled. Meet us in Paris in a week. We're going to Christmas there."

"We are?"

"We are," Jill said.

And that was that. The women had ridden east, searching for a small village tucked somewhere in the forests between Toulouse and Montpelier, and had yet to find it.

"Let's stop at the next village and get shelter for the night," Hanna suggested. "I'm cold, and we still don't have any weapons. I don't know why you wouldn't let us take some from Ignatius."

Her partner was unusually quiet and contemplative, and Hanna let the silence linger until Jill broke it a few minutes later.

"I don't know how long this whole 'Gunfighter Gothic' thing is going to last," Jill admitted, "but whether we do this forever or we break up tomorrow, I care about you, Hanna."

Hanna wasn't sure she heard Jill right. What came next was even more confusion.

"I know I was never the best friend in the world, but I will always be in your debt. It was you, after all, who helped me destroy the wardrobe."

Hanna glanced over with a sense of confusion. "The wardrobe? What wardrobe?"

"We never talk about the wardrobe," Jill said, feeling overwhelmed by the sudden eruption of emotion threatening to burst to the surface. "Ever. But I want to talk about it now. I want to talk about the Man in the Red Coat."

"Jill," Hanna said quietly, seeing the obvious turmoil Jill was in, "I don't remember any wardrobe."

"But you do remember Red Coat," Jill whispered, her words an accusation.

"From Muerte?" Hanna asked, referencing their adventure with the Universe Cutter.

"From before Muerte," Jill said.

"But we didn't know him before Muerte," Hanna insisted, thinking Jill was being funny right up until she saw the haunted look on her friend's face. What the hell was Jill talking about? Muerte was the first time they'd met him.

Right?

Hanna scowled. Jill was making her doubt herself, so she searched her memory for something she knew she wasn't going to find.

And then she found it.

A cold deeper than the French night gripped her spine and held it tight.

Muerte was the first time they'd met the Man in the Red Coat, she was sure of it, yet know she had a very clear memory of a very young Jill talking about the Man in the Red Coat that would come to see her that no one else saw. It was one of the primary reasons Jill's parents had agreed to let the two girls become friends, as they reasoned Jill being friends with a servant was better than Jill being friends with an imaginary man, who not coincidentally seemed to be around mostly at Christmas.

What the hell was this memory? Was it something she'd repressed? Why would she do that?

Cautiously, Hanna asked Jill if she wanted to talk about it.

"What I want to talk about is that thing behind you," Jill said pointing over Hanna's left shoulder.

Hanna turned, expecting to see something trivial that Jill had brought up to back out of the conversation she had created, or perhaps, given their line of work, something horrific in the forest, but she did not expect to see something bright and large and festive.

"Is that ...?" she asked, but of course it was.

"A candy cane," Jill said, looking above the trees. "It must be eight thousand feet high."

"More like 100 ... 120 feet," Hanna corrected. "But what's it doing out here?"

"Let's go find out," Jill said, and urged her horse forward to look for a path through the woods that would take them there. Behind her, Hanna followed along, thinking something was wrong with Jill and maybe wrong with herself, too. It was this wardrobe business. The harder she thought, the more she seemed to remember a wardrobe in Jill's room, but she didn't remember anything about destroying it, and if she didn't destroy it with Jill, who would?

In less than a mile, Hanna had pushed thoughts of wardrobes and men in red coats out of her mind and Jill had found a path that moved to the right, through the trees and in the direction of the giant candy cane. As they approached, a second giant candy cane could be seen off to the left, and in short order they reached a wide tree with a door in it that resided in the middle of the two candy canes, which stood a half-mile through the forest in either direction.

"I don't know what's stranger," Jill grumbled, "two giant candy canes or a path that leads to a door on a giant tree."

Hanna pointed off to their left. "It's probably the satyr dressed as Santa Claus or Sinterklaas or Saint Nicholas or whatever the hell name they use in France."

"Greetings, greetings, and a Merry Christmas, and a Ho-ho-ho!" the satyr called to them. He wore a blue coat with a white scarf, embroidered with crosses instead of a red coat with white fur, and it was too large for his thin frame; his beard was black instead of white, and full-grown without being bushy; his feet were hooves naked to the world instead of being inside black boots; and he had small horns on his head instead of a large hat, yet there was no doubting who he was supposed to be. "I am afraid we are not yet open for the season," he smiled absently. "It's a common mistake that people make, thinking the twelve days of Christmas end on Christmas, when in fact they begin on that day. A very common ... mistake," he said, his voice trailing off as his eyes lit up bright and wide. "Unless, of course, could it be, it must be, you must be, yes, yes, yes, ho, ho, ho, of course—"

"If you say, 'of course' three times in a row I'm going to shoot you," Jill promised.

"Of course!" he said, dancing around the horses as he stared up at the women. "You must be here to audition for one of the dancing ladies," he said to Jill, "and you," he turned to Hanna," will make a most delightful milking maid."

Hanna and Jill looked at each other. "Do you have any idea?" Jill asked.

"Not a one."

The satyr clapped his hands together, "Oh, you would be perfect. Both of you would be so perfect. You must come inside, come inside, come inside!"

"Look," Hanna said, holding up her hand, "we're just travelers looking for the village of Saint Elle. We're tired and hungry and just need to secure lodgings for the night."

"Oh, I'm terribly sorry," the satyr said, frowning almost comically, "but Saint Elle is at least an hour's ride to the north, and it is getting so very late. Please, do come inside," he offered, "and be our guest for the night. You many call me Nikolaos the Wonderworker," he said, bowing low.

The women exchanged tired glances, both wanting to hear the other one suggest stopping for the night. It was Hanna who finally gave their voice desire.

"I don't know," Jill answered, looking down at the satyr. "If we go inside, he's just going to try to get us involved in some weird Christmas orgy. Think what he said - ladies dancing, maids milking ... I bet the Wonderworker here has a Wonderpenis or something."

Nikolaos looked horrified. "Heavens, no!" he yelled, pointing at the crosses on the scarf. "I have taken a vow of abstinence! Further, I find the suggestion that all satyrs are led through the world by the desires of their libido to be highly offensive! Not all satyrs fit that stereotype," he insisted.

"All the ones we've met fit that stereotype," Jill countered.

"How many have you met?"

"Like ... three or four," she said, looking to Hanna for help. "Remember, when we were underground in London?"

"London!" Nikolaos gasped dramatically. "Well, of course the British satyrs are hedonistic beings to the nth degree! Why do you think their skin is so red? It's all the wine in their system and the blood rushing around, looking for the proper head to fill!"

Hanna had enough. "Okay, just ... " she pinched the bridge of her nose. "Do you have a place for us to sleep tonight? We're happy to pay, of course."

Nikolaos' good cheer returned. "But of course!" he said, waving them forward. He snapped his fingers and a swarm of tiny fairies appeared. "The women will take the horses to the stables," he assured them. "Now, come, come, come," he said, putting his hand on the doorknob, "and let me welcome you to the Candy Cane Lane!"

As the Americans dismounted their horses and turned the rains over to the six-inch-tall fairies wearing very unattractive sweaters with Christmas-themed designs on them, Jill remarked, "Yeah, there was nothing sexual about that last statement. At all. Not a bit."

"Shush."

"I'm telling you," Jill said, "before this is over ... orgy. Goddamn Europe should never bother to get dressed," she grumbled, moving past the smiling Nikolaos to enter the hollowed out interior of the yew tree. Moving through the dark, but relatively short hallway, Jill was thankful for the warm steam that was pumped in through vents in the ceiling.

"That's quite nice," she said, turning to watch Hanna get her steam bath. "But still," she scowled back to the satyr, "no orgies."

"Of course not, ma'am," he promised.

Jill exited through the other side of the yew tree and her eyes lit up with an almost childlike awe. "Whoah," she gasped. "This place is incredible!"

"That's one word for it," Hanna said, no less impressed by the sight before them, but much less appreciative of it.

"Welcome to the Candy Cane Lane!" Nikolaos said loudly and proudly.

The Candy Cane Lane was a traveling carnival, but unlike one the two women had ever seen. Directly in front of them was a massive glass ball resting on a wooden pedestal. By itself, the pedestal was quite impressive. The wooden frame was tall enough for a person to stand in. Looking up at the glass ball, they could see big white balls that gave the cumulative appearance of snow across the bottom, and a large tree with hanging green fruit grew up out of the snow.

"It's a pear tree," Nikolaos explained, "and that is where the final performance will take place. It's quite impressive." He winked at Hanna. "You would make such a fine maid-a-milking."

"God," Jill teased, "you have no idea how wrong you are."

It was on the main ground around the stage pit that truly made the Candy Cane Lane unique. Moving out away from the door in a circular pattern was a series of twelve stations, each one dedicated to one of the gifts given in the holiday song, "Twelve Days of Christmas," but hidden behind a closed tent flap. In between each station was a place to buy food, play carnival games, or buy merchandise. On the opposite end of the carnival from where they stood by the main door was a square, canvas-covered stage "for a most unique set of performances," Nik assured them.

"We — that is, my employers and I — have a vision for Christmas that goes beyond the boundaries of praying to gods," Nikolaos explained. "Our vision is to turn Christmas into a festival for all people, not just this Christian sect or that Jewish tribe. We want to encourage people to give gifts and celebrate family, not send empty prayers to disinterested higher beings. And if we can be the ones to profit by that, all the better. Look there," he said, pointing to one of the massive candy canes, "a symbol we seek to associate with Christmas. It's sweet and bouncy and a delight! Despite it's shape as a shepherd's staff, we think children can look past that to the joy of confectionary delights! My employers believe in making this a better world!"

"That's great," Jill said, exaggerating a big yawn, "but right now, I'm only interested in sleep."

"Of course, of course, of course!" he beamed. "Sugar plum fairies do need to dance and whatnot holiday cheer mistletoe decking the halls with bulls and hollies! Come, come, come, there is room for you all to yourself in Tent 2." Nikolaos positively beamed at them, "Such lovely turtle doves you will make!"

*

Nikolaos the Wonderworker led the two Americans to the square, light-blue tent, and then bid them adieu for the evening. Stepping outside, the satyr looked around at the Candy Cane Lane, feeling satisfied. He was responsible for this plan, and, he thought, looking to the yellow, Tent 5, when the events of this operation were over, his reward would be great and mighty.

The satyr's thoughts were interrupted by the clapping of hands, and he looked to the snow globe's base to see the smiling face of his employer. At 34, Grande Veracroix was the oldest Progenitor of Steam, a group of scientists seeking to rise to prominence by developing the next phase of the global revolution via the use of steam. Only the Russian horologist, Emil Vozhov, had been older than Grande, but Vozhov had died due to the interference of the same two Americans that the satyr had just captured.

"Monsieur Veracroix," Nikolaus greeted warmly. "We make a wonderful, wonderful, wonderful team, non? You drive the women to me, and I put them to bed."

Dressed in a refined black suit with a stylish purple shirt beneath, Veracroix bowed to the hired help in a display of mock fraternity. "Have I ever told you my area of expertise, Monsieur Wonderworker? I am engineer of a social kind. Where other engineers might seek to build ships or buildings or great and powerful engines, Grande Veracroix builds societies, Monsieur Nikolaos. Societies. It was but a simple task to manipulate the Poseidons with the endgame being our acquisition of Madam Masters and Madam Pak. And now that we have them, we shall put them to a very specific purpose."

"I cannot wait, Monsieur Veracroix!"

"I tell you what does disappoint me, though," he said, lowering his voice as he put the end of his walking cane into the satyr's chest. "The lack of orgies."

"Ah!" Nikolaos beamed. "You were listening to my conversation! No worries on that account, Monsieur Veracroix. Now, you must tell me," he charmed, snapping his fingers and making a host of fairies appear, "if you have ever known the pleasure of laying amidst the swarming fairies?"

Grande smiled at the seven … eight … ten fairies that buzzed around his face. "I have not, Monsieur Nikolaos."

"Then come, let us retreat to my private tent," Nikolaos grinned, "and you shall experience the full service the clients of the Wonderworker have come to expect!"

*

Morning.

Hanna and Jill awoke in their tent without acknowledging the heavy presence of steam being pumped into the tent from above. There were two beds in the tent, and a long bench between them, containing clothes. The floor was grass, cleared of snow. The only light came in through a small hole in the ceiling of the tent. Both Americans sat up in bed, and pushed off the thick, wool blankets, and swiveled their bodies to put their feet in the dirt. They stood up, without acknowledging or even looking at each other, and removed the clothes they wore the night before. Moving to the clothes that had been laid out for them, they seemed to know which clothes were for who, though it hardly mattered given both outfits were exactly the same: knee-high white boots, short light-blue skirts, and a shirt with white sleeves and a light-blue torso. In the middle of their shirts were black silhouettes of a bird that their minds recognized as turtle doves. There were white belts to strap on, and two H_2O pistols to fill the belt's empty holsters. The guns were brass, containing large cylinders to hold the light blue pellets that would be superheated when the gun's safety was clicked off.

When they were dressed and ready, they sat back on the bed.

Over the course of the next hour, Hanna and Jill slowly awoke. They became aware of a dim roar taking place outside of the tent, like hearing the ocean in a shell at the beach. The fuzz slowly coalesced into something festive, and they knew there were people milling about outside.

They wanted to join them.

Hanna rose from the bed and looked for water, but the tent had nothing but the beds, the bench, and the now-discarded clothes. Looking down at herself, Hanna didn't recognize the outfit or have any memory of how the clothes had been placed on her body. Shaking her head to clear the cobwebs, she checked the room again for water, but the only thing different about the tent this time was that steam was being pumped into the room from above.

There was a peculiar smell in the air, some kind of scent she couldn't quite place, so she sniffed the air, bringing more of the steam into her lungs.

Hanna sat back on her bed and a blank look returned to her face.

She was still sitting there several hours later when the flap to the tent's door was pulled back, and Grande Veracroix and a dozen fairies in shimmering purple dresses entered the tent. The Frenchman smiled at the sight of the two Americans sitting placidly on their beds; he did not particularly care for either Oliver or Emil, but he could not let transgressions against another Progenitor pass by without enacting revenge. And when they became aware of the powerful the Mistletoe Queen ... their opportunity for retribution came quicker than any of them could have anticipated.

Grande stood to the side of the entrance, at the bottom of Jill's bed, and motioned for his assistants to enter. Wearing a full body, white rubber suit with a glass faceplate above twin canister gas masks, one of the two female assistants moved in front of Jill while the other took her place in front of Hanna. They handed Hanna and Jill a questionnaire, and without instruction, both women calmly filled out their names, birth dates, and preferred weapons.

When the questionnaires were completed, the assistants handed them to Grande and left. The Frenchman felt a stirring in his manhood at the two docile women before him and the temptation to treat them like the harlots they were tempted him, but that was not the mission, and Grande would rather repeat the previous night's proceedings with the highly energetic fairies and the satyr.

"Prepare yourselves, ladies," Veracroix announced. "We begin at sundown."

*

"Unnngh," Jill groaned, rubbing her head. "I feel like I slept the day away."

On the bed opposite her, Hanna struggled awake, too, but was on her feet first. "What the hell are you wearing?" she asked, seeing Jill's knee-high white boots, short light-blue skirt, and a shirt with white sleeves, a light-blue torso, and a silhouette of a bird on her chest. "For that matter, what the hell am I wearing?" she asked, seeing herself dressed in the same uniform.

Jill rubbed the sleep out of her eyes and moved to the table. A glass pitcher of ice water, flavored with orange, lime, and lemon wedges, sat on the table between them. On either side of the round pitcher was a small, square glass and a domino mask. Jill's was light blue, matching their skirt, and Hanna's was white, matching their boots.

"What are these?" she asked, picking up her mask.

"No idea," Hanna said.

"I'm going to put it on."

"What? No," Hanna said. "Jill, this is ... strange, wrong, and all kinds of ... who put us in these clothes? That damned satyr? We shouldn't put the masks on, we should take these clothes off and get back into our own!"

"You're absolutely right," Jill said, and pressed the domino mask onto her face.

"It's about time you listen to me," Hanna said, and put on her own white mask.

The two women looked at each other and shook their head.

"Why did we do that?" Jill asked.

"I don't know," Hanna said. "Take yours off."

"Right," Jill said. "I'll do that."

She didn't do that.

Jill shook her head, feeling slightly sluggish. "We should get out of here," she said and moved to the tent door. Pulling aside the tent flap and stepping forward, Jill slammed her face into a glass wall and bounced back.

"Ouch," she said, rubbing her forehead.

"What did you see?" Hanna asked, moving towards her.

"Stars," Jill grumbled, pointing to her reddened forehead. "Any idea what's happening?" she asked. "Besides, of course, this all being some fancy satyr-conspired trick to get us into an orgy."

"Stop."

"Seriously," Jill said, "look at these outfits ... someone wants us to look damn sexy."

"We always look sexy," Hanna said, pulling back the tent flap and reaching her hand out to find the glass. Looking to the other side, Hanna could see a large and ordinary crowd milling about, enjoying the carnival and completely uninterested in what was happening in this tent.

"Hey!" Hanna yelled to the crowd, but no one turned around. She tried again, banging on the glass, and encouraged Jill to join her. After some rigorous pounding, the two women finally caught the attention of a woman in a long, stylish red coat with her back to them. The woman turned around and Hanna & Jill got their closest look at the Mistletoe Queen.

"You!" Hanna yelled, slamming her fist into the glass.

"Damn," Jill grunted, staring into the eyes beneath the emerald mask. "What the hell do you want with us, lady?"

The woman pointed behind them, and the two Americans turned to see steam being pumped into the tent via the vent in the ceiling.

"The Progenitors," Jill grumbled. "You'll get yours, lady," she promised.

The Queen gave them a small bow, pointed towards the far end of the fair, and walked away in the other direction.

"Welcome, one and all, to Candy Cane Lane!" Nikolaos the Wonderworker shouted. Hanna and Jill could not see the satyr from their pulled-back flap, but they could here his strong voice. The satyr had mesmerized the crowd with his presence.

"What do you think of the Man in the Red Coat?" Jill asked.

"What man?"

"The woman, I mean," Jill said quickly, feeling a nauseous wave roll through her. "The woman in the red coat. What do you think of her?"

"Shush," Hanna ordered. "We'll figure her out later."

Nikolaos continued, heard but not yet seen, and then Hanna realized she could see him because he was not on the stage at the far end where she assumed he would be, but rather was standing on top of the giant snow globe right in the middle of the fair. "It is my hope and the hope of my business associates that you are enjoying yourselves at our traveling carnival!" The crowd roared wildly. "We have food and games and now ... now we have the real reason you are here! We have the entertainment! We have the War for Christmas!"

The sound of a cable disconnecting came down to Hanna and Jill and the entire square tent that surrounded them was jerked into the air. Large, steam-powered spotlights sent bright shafts of yellow light pouring down into their glass cage and they had to squint to see the impressive sight around them. There were eleven tents in the air, swaying high above the ground on the end of heavy ropes, and the large snow globe remained large and menacing in the center of the activity.

"Eleven glass cages," Jill grumbled, pointing across the way to where twelve men in outfits fit for an Elizabethan court looked just as confused as Hanna and Jill. "How does that damn song go?" she asked.

"Depends which version they're using," Hanna explained, "but given it looks like those twelve across from us at the lords a leaping, I'd say Nikolaos is using the original version of the song, from the Mirth Without Mischief book."

Jill blinked. "How the hell do you know that?"

Hanna smiled, and pointed to a leaflet that had blown against the cube's wall that contained all the information she had just relayed.

"I hate you."

Hanna moved to the left of their cage to look through a stand selling baked cinnamon dough. "We're the two turtle doves, which makes these ladies next to us in the loose one-piece outfits the three french hens."

"Look around, my good folk!" Nikolaos instructed from atop the snow globe, "and you will see ten square cages ringing the perimeter of Candy Cane Lane filled with our contestants. Starting by the entrance," he called, and the crowd turned towards the Americans, "we have two tenacious turtle doves, three feisty french hens, four carnivorous colly birds, and then, ah then, look one and all at the cage to my right, where five golden rings have been placed on ice pedestals. Yes, yes," the satyr promised, "I shall come back to them in a moment for they lay at the heart of this holiday battle."

"If we're going to fight," Jill said, "I'd rather be with the eleven dancing ladies than just the two turtle doves. No offense."

"None taken, but we don't know what the rules are, yet," Hanna reminded her. She was studying Nikolaos, and saw he was standing alone on the stage in an ornate blue robe with a white scarf hanging off both shoulders.

"Continuing on," he said, controlling the crowd, "six geese, seven swans, eight maids, nine drummers, ten pipers, eleven ladies, and twelve very handsome - if I do say - lords that will soon be leaping for your benefit!"

The crowd roared their approval in the cold night as Nikolaos worked them into a frenzy.

"The rules are simple," he said, the crowd instantly falling silent. "A spotlight will fall upon the cube containing a combatant."

Nikolaos motioned to someone in the trees by the giant candy canes, and the spotlights hitting all of the cages save for cages six and nine shut off. "The contestants inside the cubes will need to select one among their number to participate. When they do, the participant must then exit the holding area and come to the stage where they will engage their chosen opponent in hand-to-hand combat!"

The crowd thought this delightful.

"When one fighter has knocked has knocked the other to the canvas for a ten count, two things will happen," he explained and the crowd hung on his every word. "The first is that the loser will be eliminated. The second is that a new opponent will be chosen. This repeats itself until a contestant has won five fights in a row." Nikolaos winked to the crowd. "What do you think happens then?"

Various voices shouted, "Golden rings!"

"Ah, one cannot get anything past the fine folks of France!" Nikolaos laughed and the crowd laughed along with him. Claim a golden ring and you advance to the final round. You can take a seat in that cage and simply rest. Are you ready to start?"

"Like they're going to say no," Jill said. "What's the plan?"

"Escape if we can, fight if we have to," Hanna said.

"There is no doubt," Nikolaos continued, "that what you are about to see will be violent, and perhaps one of our contestants - who are all here willingly, I assure you - will decide they don't want to be here."

For the first time, the crowd booed.

"Do not despair!" he assured them. "If a contestant tries to escape ..."

Nikolaos opened his arms wide and a flash of fire and smoke exploded on top of each cage. When the smoke cleared, demons of various forms were standing on top of the glass cubes. Above the Bostonians, a giant white and silver snake coiled and uncoiled as it hissed with the aid of a devilishly black tongue. "And if that is not enough to satisfy you," Nikolaos continued, "look behind the cages."

Turning around, Hanna and Jill saw a heavy suit of armor walk out of the woods.

"Steam men," Hanna remarked.

Jill nodded. "Emil's design."

"This is really not good," Hanna said. "Demons and Progenitors working together."

"Makes you wonder why," Jill said. "What's the endgame here?"

"Let me assure you," Nikolaos said to the crowd, "that none of us, even with our wild appearances, are not evil. In our hypothetical, a drummer and a goose fight. Let us say the drummer loses. What happens to him? If he dies in combat, we will celebrate his memory. If he is simply knocked unconscious, he is given medical attention and held in custody until the end of the competition. And what of the fairness of that winning goose not getting a chance to recover? Ah, that is the wrinkle. After every victory, a combatant may choose to return to the safety of their cage in order to recover and await their next opportunity in the ring, if they so choose. But enough of the rules and regulations," Nikolaos said. "Who wants to see a fight?"

The crowd went wild, some of them coming to Hanna and Jill's glass cage to pound their fists on its surface.

"There are three rounds to the War for Christmas!" Nikolaos said. "In round one, we determine the five holders of the rings! In round two, the five ring bearers will fight one another in a single battle! And in round three," Nikolaos stomped on the snow globe, "in round three, that winner will face the Patrtidge in the Pear Tree inside this very globe! Ah, but the Wondermaker knows what you are thinking, my new friends! If our champion can best the Partridge, what do they win? It is a glorious prize, I assure you, a prize I will reveal only after we have our five ring winners! But now ... now let us begin. Master of the lights, find us two combatants!"

The spotlights were turned back on and each cage was relit. The crowd hushed and waited, and one by one, the lights above each cage were turned off and on, teasing the crowd and the combatants about who would be chosen. Hanna and Jill's spotlight was turned off and on six separate times, until Nikolaos called out, "Choose!"

The lights went out over nine of the eleven cages, leaving lights shining down on the french hens and the pipers. Hanna and Jill looked through the baked bread stand to see the three women in the french hens cage looking at one another as they tried to decide who would go first. They were dressed in an unusual uniform, a loose-fitting outfit that looked something like a scuba diver's gear, though without the bulk or the helmets. The uniform was white, with brown coloring around the feet. One of the women backed out immediately, but the wicked smile on her face told the Bostonians she was not surrendering the spot out of a lack of confidence.

"She's no dummy," Hanna said. "Fighting against a fresh opponent is the toughest opponent. Better to fight someone who's been through a few rounds."

One of the other hens (without names, Hanna and Jill fell quickly into thinking of them as their assigned roles) put her finger in the chest of the other woman and got socked across the jaw for her troubles. With the choice made, the third french hen put on a red masquerade mask, complete with a set of red feathers that fanned out off the top, mimicking a hen's comb, as the deer-faced demon on top of her cage said a quick spell, allowing a door to open and the hen to exit out of the hard floor of the cube and into the dirty snow.

The french hen arrived at the stage and climbed up a set of steps to the canvas, where Nikolaos waited for her. In short order, one of the pipers arrived from the other side of the ring. Dressed in standard bagpiper's gear, the tall, muscular piper scratched at his thick, black beard with a smug smile on his face upon seeing the diminutive french hen.

"Fight!" the satyr yelled gleefully, to the unanimous approval of the assembled masses.

As Nikolaos moved to the rear of the stage, where a small ladder led up to a sitting platform from which he could watch, the crowd began placing bets with one another over the outcome of the contest. The stage itself was nearly thirty feet across in both directions and covered with a brown canvas. There were no ropes to keep the fighters in, and the crowd could press in tight to the stage, which came up to the middle of the average person's chest.

The french hen and piper circled one another. The much taller and stronger man had his fists up and out in front of him, waving them before his chest like two powerful pistons. "Come on, girlie!" he teased. "I'm gonna hate to break that pretty nose of yours, but—oof!"

While the piper was busy talking, the hen was busy looking or an opening, and when the piper got his feet slightly crossed, the hen attacked, moving in low and fast to kick him in the stomach on her way past him.

The audience erupted in delight and laughter, and the piper became visibly angry as the fickle crowd was now laughing at him instead of cheering with him. His face reddening, the piper lunged forward and the hen's strategy became evident as she easily dodged his attempt to grab her by delivering a boot to his nose, shattering it.

The event's first blood went to to the hen and the piper fell back onto his ass as his hands when to his face. Seeing her best opportunity, the hen aimed a kick at his nose. He had his hands up to block her boot, but that was exactly what she wanted, and as the foot connected with flesh, she heard bones breaking in the piper's fingers.

"Gods be damned!" he yelled, pulling his hands away from his face. The hen was on him, driving her knee into the already shattered nose, and making it bend awkwardly on his face. A second knee split the piper's lip, and the third knee broke his front teeth.

"Kill him!" someone yelled.

The hen grabbed the piper's black hair and pulled backwards, exposing his neck. Then hen reared back with her right hand and swung at the piper's neck with all of her might. She connected straight on his Adam's apple, and the piper slumped to his right, and then fell on his back.

"Unnn," he moaned.

"One!" Nikolaos roared from his seat above the mat.

The piper sat up and the hen kicked him in the face again, knocking him back to the mat.

"One!" Nikolaos yelled, restarting the count.

The piper sat up again and the hen sent another kick aiming for his face. This time, he was ready for her. The piper caught her foot near the ankle with his left hand and as he held it in place, he grabbed her knee with his right hand, and before the hen could twist out of his grasp, he pushed her kneecap forward and pulled back on her ankle, snapping the tendons in her knee and leaving her lower leg hanging.

The hen screamed in such pain that the bloodthirsty crowd went silent at the gruesomeness of the injury. The piper pushed her away from him and she fell to the canvas.

"One ... two ... eightnineten!" Nikolaos announced, motioning to someone behind the stage. As the piper rose to his feet, bloodied but victorious, the crowd bathed him in applause, barely noticing the gaggle of dwarves in ugly Christmas sweaters removing the french hen from the ring.

The satyr moved in beside the piper. "Do you wish to continue, monsieur? Or would you like to return to your holding area?"

"Bring on the next victim," he rumbled.

"Then let us see, let us see," Nikolaos smiled, "who your true love will bring to thee!"

The spotlights above all of the glass cubes were turned on, and as Nikoloas led the crowd in counting down from 5, all the lights turned off except the one above the seven swans. Dressed in a tight, all-white uniform, the petite Asian woman lasted all of five minutes, which was twenty times longer than the piper's third opponent, one of the geese, who was dressed like a ninja but fought like sleeping mouse. One of the twelve lords was next, and he lasted fifteen grueling minutes against the piper, long enough for the crowd to grow restless. When the piper finally choked out the lord, he was bruised and bloodied and breathing hard. His nose was mashed flat, his left eye was swollen shut, and his left arm was hanging.

"He should sit it out," Jill said.

"He won't," Hanna countered, and the piper didn't.

With four victories in a row and needing only one more, the piper rolled the dice that his fifth opponent would be more like the goose than the lord. The spotlights were turned on again, then shut off, revealing the drummers as the fifth opponent. Sensing a weakened piper that was ready to be defeated, there was a heavy scuffle inside the drummers' cube, and the crowd pressed in on the cube, blocking out Hanna and Jill's line of sight.

"That's one way to get the tournament to move faster," Hanna remarked.

Jill pointed to the top of the cube. "Our demon snake seems content to dig in for the long haul," she said. "What do you know about giant white and silver snakes?"

"Not a thing."

"Huh," Jill chided. "Guess it's not printed on a pamphlet."

"We need a plan," Hanna said, her eyes still on the drummers' cube.

"We should definitely try to win the tournament," Jill suggested.

"Funny," Hanna said. "Our card points out 'we shoot the weird in the face,' not 'we punch the weird in the face."

"We've got guns," Jill said, pulling an H_2O pistol off her hip.

"They don't work," Hanna said. "No bullets. No firing mechanism."

"Splitting up usually works for us," Jill said, frowning at the useless gun. "One of us needs to lose to investigate what's happening to the losers, and one of us can stay in the tournament and win it. I'll volunteer for the losing."

Hanna shot Jill a bemused look over her shoulder. "That's so generous of you," she remarked, "but I think we should try to stay in as long as possible. If we get knocked down-"

The crowd start gasping and talking in confused mutterings, bringing Hanna's attention back around to the drummers' cube. The crowd parted and out stepped a man in head-to-toe armor beneath the a dark blue coat and light blue pants of a Union soldier from the American Civil War.

"Is that ...?" Jill asked, pressing against the glass before answering her own question. "Yeah. A Nomadiri robot."

The two Americans watched the tall, metal man stroll across the stage, as confused as everyone else but for different reasons. They knew what they were seeing - a member of the Nomadiri race, a group of space-traveling aliens that had long ago been forced to place their memories and hearts into the bodies of a machine. The Nomadiri's space ship was parked in Earth orbit, as their chief scientist, Ajax Finch, tried to find a way to give them organic bodies before their big bad military leader, Darroque, tried to level the Earth. On a recent case, Hanna and Jill believed Ajax had accomplished this by siphoning off the energies of the fabled wizard, Merlin, yet here was a robot, looking very tall and ...

"Silly," Jill said. "He looks silly in that get-up."

The Nomadiri drummer moved onto the stage.

"Yes, yes, yes," Nikolaos enthused, coming down off his perch to pat the Nomadiri on the back. "Take a look, one and all, for what you see here is not a knight but an alien! Yes, a very live alien from the other side of the cosmos! And he wants to fight for the glory of your adulation! What do you say, guys and dolls, let's give this drumming drummer a big ol' 'Welcome to Earth!' huzzah!"

"Huzzah!"

The piper was less thrilled. As busted up and severely bruised as his face was, he couldn't hide the look of displeasure on his face at facing the man of metal. Whatever the Nomadiri was feeling was impossible to tell. His face was nothing but a helmet, with big, circular goggles where his eyes should have been. His mouth was a wide, but thin slot with a grate across it.

"If you give up," the Nomadiri said, "I will allow you to live. If you throw a punch, I will kill you."

"I'm dead, anyway," the piper said and stepped in to take a heavy swing at the robot's jaw. His fist connected but the only damage done was evidenced in the broken bones in his hand.

The robot reached out with his left hand, grabbed the piper's neck and repeatedly punched him in face until the piper's forehead cracked open and his brain dribbled down his face.

The Nomadiri let go and the piper fell in a lump to the canvas.

Nikolaos didn't bother with the ten count.

Two lords, another piper, and a maid were dismissed in quick order, and the Nomadiri drummer became the first combatant to claim a golden ring.

*

The War for Christmas rolled on. Hanna and Jill watched the fights, the crowd, the demons on top of the cubes, and the Steam Men behind them. After another hour, one of the lords had claimed the second golden ring, and another two hours saw one of the pipers advancing to the next round. What impressed Hanna and Jill more than anything was the way the crowd never seemed to tire. They greeted each fighter with an enthusiastic salute and each victory with explosive good cheer.

"Do you think the others know what we're fighting for?" Jill asked.

"They must have some kind of understanding," Hanna answered. "No one looks the least bit reluctant to fight, unless it's because of a particular opponent."

"There's no steam machine on any of the other cubes, either," Jill said, pointing to their unit atop the cube, "and we're the only cube that hasn't been called, yet."

"Look at you, being all detective-like," Hanna smiled.

Jill frowned and returned to her small bed.

"Hey," Hanna asked, sensing whatever Jill had been going through was bubbling to the surface again, "what's wrong?"

Jill squeezed her eyes shut, then let them slowly open, stars dancing before them. "There's something wrong with me," she said.

"You've been through a lot," Hanna said, eschewing an easy opening for a cutting remark. "Agreeing to marry a man you couldn't stand just to save your father's business, leaving home-"

"Ugh," Jill said, digging her heel into the compacted dirt floor. "Can we not do another recap? I killed my dad. I'm over it."

"Bullshit," Hanna said, moving to sit next to Jill on the bed. "I don't think one ever gets over any of that."

"Maybe," Jill said. "Maybe not. But this is something ... something else."

"That the Mistletoe Queen lady has me creeped out," Hanna admitted. "Maybe it's her?"

"She's part of it, but ... I don't know how to describe it," Jill said, rising to her feet. "It's like ... like when you're a kid and you're convinced there's a monster under the bed. It doesn't matter how many times you look and find nothing there, you can't shake the feeling. Like not seeing it is even worse than finding something creepy and crawly under there, you know? That's what I feel like's going on. That there's a monster in my head and I know he's looking at me but I can't ever see him, no matter how many times I turn around or how quickly I do it."

Hanna's own head began to thump, searching for her own monster. "Jill, you said something earlier about me helping you destroy a wardrobe."

"It was Christmas Eve," Jill nodded. "When I was 17. That was the night we ..."

"Yeah," Hanna said, her heart quickening, "I remember that, but I don't remember any wardrobe."

"Don't," Jill said, snapping around with reddened eyes. "Don't you dare play games with that."

"I'm not," Hanna said, coming off the bed to walk to her partner. "I swear to you," she said, taking Jill's arms in her hands, "I'm not playing games. I don't remember anything about a wardrobe."

"You're calling me a liar?" Jill asked, jerking away.

"No!" Hanna said, stepping back in. "I'm not calling you a liar. I'm not. I'm just saying there's something going on that we need to get to the bottom of. Why are we remembering the same event, but in different ways? That's messed up, but I'm betting that the Mistletoe Queen lady has something to do with it."

"So you believe me?" Jill asked with such a plaintive voice that Hanna half-expected to see seven-year old Jill, and not the 27-year old that had been through so much in the past few months.

Hanna put her hand behind Jill's head and pulled their foreheads together. "I believe you," she said.

The spotlight above the cube turned off, then on, and this time, for the first time, it didn't turn off, again.

"And now!" Nikolaos' voice announced to the crowd, "our first look at our sweet turtle doves! But which one will come to the stage and fight?"

Hanna and Jill pulled away from each other, but before their eyes could refocus, Hanna was already volunteering.

"No," Jill said, "I'll do it."

"You're in no condition to fight," Hanna asserted, but Jill shook her off.

"I need something to do, not time to think about things."

"It sounds to me like thinking about things is exactly what you need."

Jill fixed Hanna with an assured glare. There was still wetness in both eyes, but there was a greater confidence behind those stalled tears, and Hanna stepped back and opened her palms. If Jill wanted this fight, she would let her have it.

"But when this is over," Hanna started to say.

"Yeah, yeah," Jill said and looked up to the giant snake on top of their cube. "Let's do this, Mr. White," she said and the snake hissed out a spell to open the door. Without looking back, Jill headed for the stage.

*

Grande Veracroix was in a private cube hidden beneath a red and black tent just outside of the Candy Cane Lane carnival. Three separate machines pumped enhanced air into the tent, heightening the pleasures of all inside.

Enhanced steam was what Veracroix brought to the Progenitors, the ability to nudge and nuance a person's mind based on particles in the steam. As the Progenitors built their new society on top of the current, industrial world, they were aware that ordinary citizens and politicians would occasionally need to be pointed in the right direction and that's what this steam would allow them to do.

The Progenitors saw steam not just as a new business venture but a new way of life; it's one of the reasons Lady Jenny Carashire had invested so heavily in the Steampunk aesthetic. If they could make the fashion fashionable, as it were, they could create a desire for something the public didn't even yet know they truly wanted. There was no fashion equivalent coming from the masters of industry, and even if there were, who would want clothes and jewelry and architecture based on factories and grime?

No, the future needed to be steam.

"Lady Carashire," he mumbled. A despicable wench, he thought, but a necessary and valuable ally to have. Carashire had contacts all over Europe and money to invest. There was a downside to her involvement with the Progenitors, of course, and that was how nearly every scientist that went to live with her ended up dead. When she left England earlier in the month for parts unknown, Grande was glad to see her leave.

Grande closed his eyes and leaned back on his large bed as the fairies worked his body over. Sweat began to ooze out of his pores, creating a secondary reaction with the steam and heightening his pleasure even further. Three fairies worked over his manhood as four more flew around him, touching, kissing, and licking all parts of his exposed body. Even as he reveled in pleasure, Grande was thinking ahead. Perhaps there was something unique to these fairies that could be added to another blend of his enhanced steam ... ground up wings or diluted pheromones.

"Hello, Veracroix," a female voice said, bringing him out of his thoughts.

Grande's eyes snapped opened and the fairies buzzed up and away from his body in a sluggish surprise.

"Lady Carashire!" he yelled. "What are you doing here?"

"Tsk tsk," she teased, pulling off a white glove. The blonde woman wore a silver and gold winter's dress, done in Steampunk style of corset and cascading dress. "Is that any way to greet an ally?"

Grande frowned. He wanted to spit at the woman but he knew his fellow scientists in the Progenitors had a much higher opinion of her than he did, so he swallowed the liquid in his throat and tried his best to put on a charming smile.

"You have caught me in a compromising situation," he smiled, noting that the fairies had landed near his head. Their small bodies were overdosing on the enhanced steam.

"Oh, posh," Lady Carashire smiled. "It's not like I haven't seen it in action before." When Grande's face grew confused, she peeled off her second glove. "At the Jazz Masquerade last autumn," she reminded him. "I was in the crowd. It was hard to see you amidst all of the bodies, but I never forget a ... well, it's much smaller than I prefer, of course, but perhaps if I stay in this tent long enough and let your mechanical steam work its magic on me I wouldn't mind climbing on top of you."

"What do you want, Jenny?" Grande asked, his disdain in full sight.

"Oh, I'm just here to watch the contest," she smiled. "I do find all manner of physical acts so very entertaining to watch."

Scoffing, Grande asked, "Why are you really here?"

Lady Carashire's soft face turned hard. "I'm here for two reasons Veracroix. The first is that I want to see how you're spending my money."

"And the second?"

"Has she really been found?" Lady Carashire asked, bursting with curiosity. "The Partridge?"

Grande nodded. "She has."

"We should just take what we want from her and damn this tournament," Lady Carashire said.

"We should, but we can't," Grande said, stepping out of bed to move to a chest on the floor in the corner of the tent. The Frenchman opened the chest and pulled out a sack, which he handed to Lady Carashire.

"What's this?" she asked, accepting the bag.

"Your money," Grande said. "The man we hired to find the Partridge didn't want money. He just wanted to make sure we had a tournament to decide who gets to take the Partridge's life. That's why we've stacked this tournament with trusted allies. Whomever wins, the Progenitors will benefit."

"Not everyone," Lady Carashire said. "Hanna Pak and Jill Masters are out there."

Grande nodded. "Another condition."

"Who is this agent you hired?" the Englishwoman asked through a deepening frown.

"Didn't give a name," Grande said. "And I didn't ask. The 'man in the red coat' is what we called him."

"Where did you find him?"

"He found us."

"You're a damned fool," Lady Carashire spat.

"Rest easy," Veracroix said, climbing back into bed and picking up a fairy to put on his chest. "We have contingency plans. Now, I am tried of looking at you. Either get your clothes off or get out of my tent." He waved his hand around at the steam in the room. "You might as well stay, Lady Carashire," he grinned. "You are already bathing in my essence, after all."

Lady Carashire made an unpleasant face and did not stay. There was a third reason she was here, and it had to do with an object of power she valued far greater than what the Partridge had to offer.

*

Strange thoughts at inopportune times had been a hallmark of Jill's life and this particular moment was no different. She stood on the canvas, awaiting the arrival of her opponent, one of the two remaining swans. Her mind should have been sizing up the diminutive woman, looking for weaknesses and putting a strategy together.

Instead, what Jill was thinking about was her outfit: white boots, light-blue skirt, blue and white shirt of a design she had never seen before. Where had it come from? Was it designed solely for this occasion? As the curly redhead hit the stage with a snarl beneath her freckled face, Jill took a deep breath into her lungs and let it out slowly. On her right, the crowd. On her left, the rear of the stage. Behind her there was a tent and out in front of her and down on her left was the casualty ward. Injured fighters were led into a big, white tent by women in red winter coats.

The swan snapped her fingers as she stepped into Jill's face. "Stay on me, yeah, and I'll put you in that tent soon enough, yeah?"

Jill sniffed the air. "Did you have garlic for breakfast?"

"Huh?"

Jill pulled her non-functioning H2O pistol off her hip and cracked it across the swan's nose. As her stunned opponent's hands went to her bleeding nose, Jill short-tossed the pistol into her left hand and stepped in, delivering a heavy right hand to the swan's left kidney. Doubling over in pain, the swan made it easy for Jill to grab her hair and pull it down as she drove her knee up, connecting with the already broken nose.

The swan fell back onto the canvas and did not get up.

*

Hanna did not know how to feel except that they should not have agreed to head south when Ignatius offered them a potential client. She blamed herself — not a new thing — for pushing Jill when what her friend really needed was time off. A vacation. Instead, ever since Kraken Moor, they had kept pushing forward at an increasingly fast pace. Since arriving two weeks ago, they'd fought the Mistletoe Queen, the Krampus, Scottish vampires, Sinterklaas, and now whatever this Battle of Christmas Tournament was really about. There was no need for them to push this hard.

Except ...

Except Hanna was increasingly getting the sense that they weren't pushing, at all.

They were being herded.

"If you survive this, you may find me in Lyon."

Hanna spun around to see the Mistletoe Queen standing at the back of the glass cube. She'd pressed her emerald mask not only against the glass but through it, leaving the rest of her body outside.

"Who are you?"

"Lyon," the Mistletoe Queen said. "The day of reckoning will be at hand. We have a mutual acquaintance who lives at the End of Time."

"One of The Metronome?" Hanna asked. "What kind of Reckoning are you talking about?"

"You never should have destroyed that wardrobe, Hanna," she said before retracting her mask back through the glass.

"Wardrobe?" Hanna yelled, feeling a wave of nausea roll over her. "What wardrobe?"

By the time she'd raced to the glass, the Mistletoe Queen had faded beyond the Steam Man standing guard at the rear of Candy Cane Lane carnival.

*

A colly bird was next up for Jill. Dressed in all black, her opponent was wearing a kind of thick, but somewhat pliable vest with the letters F-B-I written in white across the front. Jill had no idea what FBI stood for and didn't really care. She kicked the colly bird in the stomach but the vest absorbed the blow, so after taking a few hard shots to her own ribs, Jill let FBI get in close. When she swung for Jill's ribs, Jill trapped colly's arm between her side and arm, slipped her leg behind FBI, and pushed her to the canvas.

Surprising herself at her own viciousness, Jill stepped on the woman's throat until she tapped out.

*

Banging on the glass cube brought the expected result of accomplishing nothing, but when Hanna turned around she saw that the one remaining french hen was standing at the rear of her cube, behind the cart selling fried bread, and looking at Hanna with a smile on her face.

"Eat me," Hanna huffed.

The hen raised an eyebrow as a smile came to her face. The hen was clearly a confident young woman just by her posture, and her brown eyes seemed to swirl with a power beyond her years. Her brown hair was tied back into a ponytail, and her left hand sat on her hip in such a manner as to suggest this was the very center of the universe.

"Eat you?" the woman mouthed back. "I'd love to," she said and then bared the fangs of a vampire.

Hanna's spotlight went out.

The vampire hen's light remained on.

*

Jill knew she was in trouble just by the way the french hen walked onto the canvas. She looked ridiculous in the white suit and red masquerade mask with it's feathers arced back over the woman's forehead, and maybe once upon a five months ago Jill might have been blinded by the silly costume and not seen the powerful woman beneath, but the stakes had been raised on her and Hanna's adventures since their time as kids. Back then, it was almost always a gas, but ever since she'd left home, this had become her life, her means of supporting herself, and she took it more seriously than she'd ever taken anything.

More or less.

When Nikolaos signaled the start of the match, the french hen got in close and took Jill to the canvas, where the women rolled around and grappled, much to the delight of the crowd.

"Stay down," the hen murmured into Jill's ear as she pressed down onto Jill's lying body.

"You stay down," Jill snapped back, not caring who heard, as she rolled to flip their positions.

The hen sighed, "Poseidon said you would be difficult," and boxed Jill's ears. Jill's hands went to her ears, and the hen double-punched Jill's kidneys, forcing Jill's hands back down. Twisting beneath the American, the french hen pushed Jill off of her and came up behind her, forcing her face into the blood-stained canvas. Slipping her lower arm beneath Jill's throat, the hen leaned her weight on the back of Jill's head as she pressed her lips to the Bostonian's ear.

"Stay down," she hissed. "Stay down and look for me when you wake up."

Jill tried to rage against the Frenchwoman above her, but she was trapped, losing oxygen, and when she looked out into the crowd, all she could see was blurred faces ...

And a man in a red British officer's Revolutionary War jacket.

She screamed until the darkness fell upon her.

*

The crowd roared their approval at Jill being choked out, and Hanna wanted to shoot all of them in that moment. When the spotlight above her cube stayed on, she was convinced it had happened through the sheer force of her own will. Stalking to the stage as Jill's unconscious body was pulled roughly off the canvas by the sweater-clad dwarves, Hanna didn't stop walking until she punched the hen in the face as hard as she could.

The hen fell back as blood spurted from her mouth. She did not get up.

One down.

*

Inside the victor's cube, a drummer, a lord, and a piper waited patiently, sitting on black sofas that had been provided for them. The piper was a young Frenchman and he said nothing to the other two as he pretended to rest his eyes in order to watch them. The drummer was a man of metal, something called a "Nomadiri robot" and the lord was a large, imposing, muscled African.

What seemed odd to the piper was that the two men clearly knew each other.

"I say," he said suddenly when the robot and lord had stopped their unspoken communicating from opposite corners of the cube, "no need we can't be civil. This is France, after all, and I am a Frenchman. My name is Remy," he said, moving to split the difference between them, "Remy Lafayette and I shall tell you a secret. That woman who was just knocked unconscious by the turtle dove? That's my sister, Julie. So what do you say you tell me you're secret, eh? How does a man of metal and an African lord know each other?"

The lord and robot exchanged a glance. The lord had a bemused look on his face.

"You are beneath me," the lord said, and turned his back on Remy. "But you may call me Darroque." He waved his hand behind him, dismissing the young Lafayette, and said, "Kill the vampire, Ilkommen."

The robot turned to the Frenchman and began his advance.

"Er, I don't think that's how the rules work," Remy said, backing up and putting the platforms with the golden rings between them.

"The only rules Darroque follows," the lord said, "are the rules Darroque makes."

*

A lord with a thunderous left hook was next.

He hit Hanna's face hard enough to spin her around, and her side hard enough to double her over, but that was his last offensive move. From her knees, Hanna delivered a hard uppercut to the lord's crotch and knocked the figurative piss out of him.

Two down.

*

The massive white and silver serpent that lay coiled above the glass cube that had contained Hanna and Jill smiled to herself as she looked past the stage to the medical tent.

The serpent was hungry and it was almost time to feed.

*

The final goose relied on speed, and was able to score hit after hit on Hanna's midsection. Every offensive move Hanna threw at the woman was easily parried and immediately followed by a kick to the stomach or thigh or forearm. What made the goose infuriating for Hanna was the woman's intelligence and patience. If Hanna laid back, the goose simply waited, unaffected by the booing, impatient crowd.

Recognizing she needed a combination move of her own, Hanna took one of her H2O pistols off her hip, took a big stride towards the goose, and threw the pistol straight at her opponent's face. The goose raised her hands to block the assault, allowing Hanna to step in and drill her with an uppercut to the jaw.

Three down.

*

"That's enough, Ilkommen," Darroque said absently as his Nomadiri ally held Remy on the ground and pounded the young man's face.

"You should let me finish him," the robot replied. "Returning to a fleshly prison has made you soft."

Sighing, Darroque reached into a pouch sewn on the interior of his vest and pulled out a triangular piece of metal. Depressing a round button at the center of the thin triangle, Darroque tossed it across the glass cube, imbedding it in Ilkommen's back. Electricity sparked from the triangle on contact and the robot's body seized up.

Darroque smiled. Neither Ilkommen nor Remy Lafayette would pose much of a challenge now.

As Lady Carashire sauntered towards his cube, a gleaming smile on her beautiful face, Darroque thought on Ilkommen's words and knew he was anything but soft in this moment.

The penultimate drummer came to the stage, already bloodied and bruised from his fight inside the cube to determine who would come and face a weakened opponent. Halfway to the stage, the mischievous water demon who controlled the drummer's cube let the final drummer out and the two men fought through the hollering, appreciative crowd.

Hanna took deep breaths of the chilled night air into her lungs, happy to watch the two men do her work for them. The shorter, black man tossed the taller, thinner Indian man into a bank of brightly-colored stuffed animals at a booth operating a game of chance. The shorter drummer jumped over the railing of the booth to press his advantage, but was met with the butt of a rifle under his chin. Staggering back against the booth's railing, the rifle's butt was driven two more times into his waist before he dropped to his knees. The Indian man stood above him, sneering in delight, and hit the black man so hard the rifle cracked in half.

"I fight!" he yelled.

"You lose," Hanna said, jumping up onto the railing and kicking him straight on with her white boots, breaking his teeth and dropping him back into a fallen pack of pink elephants and green monkeys.

"Four down," she said.

"I'd say five," Nikolaos countered with a wink, and Hanna was escorted to the cube of the golden rings.

*

Jill awoke slowly and painfully. Bringing her hands to her throat, she could feel raw bruises starting to form. Wanting nothing more than to sleep the pain away, she forced herself to sit up in the cot to which she'd been deposited and look around.

The woman who'd knocked her out said to find her, but the large tent wasn't going to make that easy. Pushing herself to her feet, Jill took stock of the triage center. There were three rows of green cots, and two wide rows between them. Nearly 100 people dressed in costumes of all the twelve gifts of christmas were in various states of hurt around the room. Arranged haphazardly, Jill was forced to walk the entire length of the row on her right, finding neither her opponent nor Hanna. At the far end of the tent, Jill made the turn to head in the other direction when a pair of hands shot out, grabbed her bloodied blue and white shirt, and pulled her outside.

"Thought I was supposed to find you," Jill said, folding her arms. Outside the tent, the thick woods were only a few feet away.

"That would take all night," the young woman smiled, pulling Jill into the forest. "Name's Julie Lafayette," she said. "We have mutual friends."

"Ignatius?" Jill asked, the words flowing too quickly and causing her to scold herself for bringing jealousy into play without any cause.

Julie looked back over her shoulder and nodded. "And his father, too."

"You're a demon hunter?"

Julie smiled as she nodded, her brown locks cascading in front of her face. "Demon hunter," she said. "Demon and hunter."

"Aren't you the go getter," Jill said, stopping as Julie pulled off her white jumpsuit to reveal a full body suit of black leather, complete with thigh-high boots and corset. "Part dominatrix, too?"

Julie laughed. "You're funny," she said. "I can see why Ignatius is into you when my guess is he hasn't been in anyone else."

"Ugh."

"Was he good?" Julie asked, stepping in close. "It's for a bet. My brother thinks he must be quite talented while I think he's likely rubbish. There's no way he can rut as hot as he looks."

"I am not having this conversation."

"Later, then," Julie said, looking around the dark woods. "We've got work to do, anyway."

"We're a team now?"

"Yes."

"What's all this even about?" Jill asked, waving her arms back towards the raucous carnival.

"You don't know?"

Jill shook her head.

"Then why are you here? I thought you knew. I thought Ignatius told you."

"We got pulled in on the road by Nikolaos," Jill explained. "No one's told us anything."

"Someone wants you here."

"Yup."

Julie crossed her arms and looked around the still forest, lost in thought.

"What is everyone fighting for?" Jill asked.

"An object of immense power," Julie said, frowning. "The winner of this tournament receives a weapon called a Universe Cutter."

Every nerve in Jill's body stood at attention.

*

Nikolaos the Wonderworker stood at the edge of the canvas and looked over the crowd, bursting with excitement. Standing on the snowy ground below him were the five claimants of a golden ring: a drummer, a piper, a lord, a turtle dove, and a maid.

"We have arrived at Round 2," the satyr explained to the giddy, but hushed, crowd. "Standing below me are the finalists, waiting to tear into one another just for your amusement! Ilkmommen the Nomadiri! Darroque the African Lord! Hanna Pak the American Gunslinger! Remy Lafayette, the Vampire Theologian! And our final winner of a golden ring, Laviolette Lazois, an actual French Maid dressed in her actual black-and-white work clothes! To be clear, they do not fight entirely for your amusement," he added, looking around to make sure the demons on top of each of the glass cubes were ready to act. Looking back down at the crowd, Nikolaos asked, "Would you like to see the object we have all come to see?"

"Yes!" the crowd erupted in unison, like conditioned members of a Catholic congregation.

"Then turn," Nikolaos ordered, "and gaze upon the Snow Globe of Nineteen Hundred and Sixty-One!"

The crowd turned to look at the globe as the demons watched the crowd and the Steam Men watched the demons.

The massive globe sat on an eight-foot high base of wood, and inside the globe, a singular tree with oval-shaped green leaves and hanging green fruit stood in the fake snow. It was, as anyone close enough to see the fruit could see, a pear tree.

"Of course," Hanna murmured. "A partridge in a pear tree."

"So very clever," Darroque smiled at her.

"I liked your old look better," Hanna snapped. "Giving up on global domination? It'd be easier to conquer the world in that body," she said, pointing at Ilkommen.

Darroque snarled. "If only Finch had awoken us decades ago. Our metal bodies have little life left."

"Ilkommen looks pretty good."

"Look closer," Darroque mumbled. "Paint covers rust and patches hide holes. He volunteered for this mission. Believe me," he confided, "once the final battle begins, he will no more be my ally than you are."

"In our snow globe," Nikolaos continued, "there rests a partridge protecting the upper branches of the tree. The goal is simple. Defeat the Partridge, climb the tree, and claim ... the Universe Cutter!"

A shimmering, golden trident rose out of the tree to float at the top of the snow globe, like the star on top of a Christmas tree.

"I don't believe it," Hanna whispered.

"How can you not believe seeing what we're all fighting for?" Remy asked. The young vampire was in rough shape after the beating at the hands of Ilkommen, but he stood bravely at Hanna's side, ready to fight with the knowledge that his healing powers would eventually put him all back together, whatever the damage inflicted.

"I didn't know," Hanna admitted. "Jill and I were shoehorned into this."

Remy nodded. "Unfortunate," he said politely, "but I am glad you are here. We have mutual friends," he said to her questioning look. "The Poseidons," he continued. "Ignatius told us we might find you here-"

"How did he know we'd be here when we didn't?"

Remy shook his head. "His father is running hard to the Gates of Hell to stop the Cutter from reaching it's destination should we fail."

"What do demons need a Cutter for?" Hanna asked.

"If only we knew," Remy admitted. Looking out through a puffed-out face, the Frenchman could not help but admire the golden trident. "It is beautiful, is it not? I never thought I would actually see one."

Hanna couldn't resist a small dig at her newfound ally. "Seen one, seen 'em all. Well, not really," she added. "They all look different."

"You've seen another one?"

"Yes," Hanna said. "We used one to bring Jill back from the dead."

Remy opened his mouth and closed it. "A story for another time," he said as the trident drifted down into the pear tree's upper leaves.

Hanna looked to Ilkommen and then back to Remy. Was it possible to have an ally in a fight such as this, with a prize as grand as the Universe Cutter, a device created by The Metronome at the end of time, and granting one person both the ability to travel through time and become immortal. Once a person was opened up by one of the Universe Cutters, their own blood was replaced by the Blood of the Universe and they could only be killed by a Universe Cutter.

If those rules seemed arbitrary, that was the way of The Metronome.

"At the base of the snow globe," Nikolaos explained, "are doors that lead inside and to the tree, and to the Partridge that guards it. Our combatants will fight one another right here, at the base of the globe, right where you are currently standing. Ah, I see your confusion, but do not worry, my friends. We have a place for you to sit! Feast your eyes on the demons that sit atop the glass cubes!"

The eleven demons rose to their feet or hind quarters and began chanting in unison. On their command, the walls of the glass cubes began expanding, connecting with one another to create a ring that encapsulated all the cubes, all the carnival booths, the stage, and the infirmary tent. Doors on the interior of the ring opened, and Nikolaos directed them to enter the new structure, which they did.

When all of the assembled humans stood inside the circular cube, leaving the central area of Candy Cane Lane empty saved for slushy snow and discarded trash, Nikolas easily scampered to stand on top of the snow globe and opened his arms wide.

"Ladies and gentleman!" he called. "I would like to thank you for attending! I hope you enjoy the show!" Nikolaos smiled maliciously. "Because, you see, you are now part of it!"

All at once, the roof of the glass circle slid aside and eleven hungry, snarling demons fell onto a confused and panicked crowd.

Hanna wet hard at Nikolaos. "Bastard!" she shouted over the sounds of people screaming in fear and pain and the act of dying.

Nikolaos shrugged and pointed behind her, and Hanna turned around just in time to take a hard left-hand shot from Darroque across her jaw. The attack signaled the start of the final round. Despite wanting to stop the demons from killing all of the people now trapped inside the glass tube with them, Hanna recognized there was nothing she could do to save them directly, and that her best hope was in getting the Universe Cutter and putting an end to this whole damn charade. Glancing in the direction of the medical tent, she could do nothing but hope that Jill was taking care of herself.

*

"Is there a plan," Jill asked as they made their way through the dark forest, "or are we just going to wander around the woods?"

"There is a plan," Julie Lafayette replied. "Remy and Hanna will do their best to win the Universe Cutter and we will concentrate on stopping the Progenitors of Steam."

"What about the demons?" Jill asked.

Julie frowned and shook her head. "I believe they are here to consume the crowd, to ensure there are no witnesses." Pausing in the dark to wipe sweat from her brow, the vampire asked Jill, "Are you Catholic?"

"I am."

"So you know of the legend of Saint Nicholas, then."

"Um ..."

"Americans," Julie said, shaking her head. "In one of his many exploits, Saint Nicholas gave bags of gold coins to the three daughters of a poor man to save them from having to turn to prostitution, as he had no money for a proper dowry."

"Yeah," Jill said, "that sounds vaguely familiar."

"That gold is a holy object of great power. It is believed that the gold is tied to another of Nicholas' exploits and has the power to bring the dead back to life, as Nicholas did in resurrecting three murdered children."

"So ... we're looking for three bags of gold?"

"Gold can be melted down."

Jill blinked and her mind had it. "The five golden rings."

Nodding, Julie said, "What the Progenitors want with the rings, we do not know, but they are not the kind of object one would want to see fall into the hands of madmen."

"Agreed," Jill said. "We should ... stop!"

Julie spun around to see Nikolaos the Satyr sprinting away from the Candy Cane Lane carnival, five golden rings hanging around his neck.

"Let's go!" Julie shouted, just before her body was hit in the stomach by an arrow.

Jill's hand reflexively went to her hip to pull out a gun, but the H2O pistol there had no life to it, and thus had no way to defend herself as a beautiful blonde woman in a French maid's outfit stepped out from behind a tree with a crossbow in her arms.

"Dois-je tuer l'Américain, trop?" Laviolette Lazois asked.

"Oh, no," Lady Jenny Carashire said, stepping into the clearing. "Jill and I are old friends and she'll certainly help us to stop that dastardly pagan satyr from running off with Christian relics. There's no reason to shoot her, too."

"I don't need any help," Laviolette said through a heavy French accent.

"If you didn't need help, my dear," Lady Carashire reminded her, "you would have been one of the first four winners of the tournament's first round and could have absconded with the rings."

"If you trusted your new lover ..."

"I trust him to win the Cutter, girl," Lady Carashire snapped.

"If I stop him," Jill said, kneeling to check on Julie, who was busy pulling the arrow free and waving Jill away, "I'm keeping the rings for myself."

Lady Carashire made a shooing motion with her hands. "Go. Run."

*

When the maid left them to chase after the satyr, the remaining four victors squared in a battle of two versus two. As Darroque reached the doorway in the base of the snow globe, Remy jumped on his back, pulling the larger man down. Hanna took advantage of the two men rolling around in the trampled snow and made it to the edge of the door, where the sight before her caused her to stop.

White and blue lights in the shape of large snowflakes swirled around each other in circuitous non-patterns, blocking out nearly everything else from sight. It was clear that she needed to enter the light storm, but between the rotating lights she caught glimpses of a large tree sitting in the cosmos, it's branches and roots extending in impossible distances to touch other worlds.

Before Hanna could wrap her thoughts around that image, Ilkommen slammed into her from behind, driving her into the light storm. The white and blue snowflakes burned her skin through her uniform as she passed through them, the pain intense but short as the robot pushed her forward into a bank of soft snow that covered their heads. Hanna began to choke on the snow and panic hit her hard as she tried desperately to find a pocket of air, but the more snow she brushed aside, the more snow fell down on top of her. Being a man of metal, Ilkommen did not need to breathe and punched Hanna from behind, drilling her right kidney with such force that she fell to her knees, the snow becoming heavier on her neck.

The robot did not relent. Grabbing her hair, he yanked backwards, drilling his knee into her other kidney and forcing her mouth to open as she screamed in pain. Snow instantly choked her mouth, and Ilkommen held her by the back of her neck with his left hand and shoved more snow into her mouth with his right hand, choking her with the frozen liquid.

"Ilkommen!" Darroque yelled. "Where are you?"

"Here!" the robot yelled, letting Hanna go. "Come through the light!"

When Darroque stepped forward, his fellow Nomadiri traveler punched him square in the nose, shattering it. Darroque was knocked backwards and would have tumbled back out of the snow, but Remy moved in at that moment, catching him and shoving him forward again.

The three men began punching and tearing at one another in the magical snow, which transparent enough for them to see each other in pixelated blurs but wet enough to be clumpy. If the pushed the snow off their mouths, the opening it created would give them a second of clean air before more snow dropped in to fill the void, like wet snow sliding down a window pane.

Of the three, Darroque was the most accomplished fighter, even in the confines of his new, flesh-and-bones body. With blood gushing down his face, the newly formed human went after Ilkommen's iron-rotted parts, tearing open the drummer's outfit and punching holes through the robot's torso. As the battle progressed, the magical energy of the snow globe began to activate, and the snow that they pushed aside was no longer filled in, and the combatants created a pocket of air in which to brawl.

Remy struggled to keep up with Darroque; though the young Frenchman had the extra strength of a vampire, he was a theologian by training, not a fighter, and after five rounds in the tournament and the beating at the metal hands of Ilkommen in the glass cube, his already bruised face continued to take a pounding from the larger human. After a handful of shots, Remy could barely see past the swelling of his cheeks, and he fell to his knees in a defensive posture, desperate for a moment's respite.

Darroque was not in a giving mood, raining blow after blow down on the vampire, only stopping when Ilkommen broke his concentration with an anguished scream.

"The girl!" he yelled, his body sparking wildly as death descended onto him. "Where did ... she ...?" The last word never exited his mouth as the Nomadiri robot gave up its ghost.

Remy pulled his swollen cheek down with one of his hands so he could look around their area and saw that Hanna had crawled through the snow away from them.

*

Jill and Laviolette tore through the woods, the satyr barely in sight up ahead of them. After the events with the Krampus, Jill had had enough of running through the French woods at night, but the stakes were higher this time around so she fought through the slush and kept moving forward.

"You really think the rings are worth more than the Cutter?" Jill asked as the two women pushed through branches.

"It does not matter," the maid replied. "This is a contract, nothing more."

"Listen," Jill said, slipping to one knee, "when we get there—"

In an act of brilliant acrobatics, Laviolette jumped forward to grab a small, but sturdy tree mostly bereft of branches. Grabbing the trunk, the Frenchwoman used her momentum to pivot around the tree, and in a flash she went from running ahead of Jill to circling back on her, kicking the American in the chest and knocking her back into another tree.

Jill's head snapped back hard against the larger tree and the world lost its focus as the maid ran on ahead without her.

*

In the snow globe, Hanna crawled through the snow, slowly rising up a hill until she burst free into a snow covered clearing. As soon as she pushed herself to her feet, the entire world started to rumble, and the snow around her began to whirl up into the sky. It seemed unnatural until Hanna remembered that she was, in fact, inside a snow globe.

The pear tree was fifty feet in front of her and she ran to the tree, determined to get there first. With each passing step, however, the snow at her feet began to disappear and and once again she saw the universe itself spread out before her, pocket images of other worlds located on different planes of reality, all connected by the tree before her. Was this caused by the tree or was it a holdover from the Exatled Waters of Sinterklaas? Looking skyward, she saw glimpses of other worlds connected through the pear tree's branches, and she realized halfway to the tree's massive trunk that the pear tree was Yggdrasil, the Norse tree of life that connected all nine realms.

"If only I could enjoy the view," Hanna mumbled.

Behind her, Darroque pushed through the snow barrier and ran hard at her, leaving the battered Ilkommen and Remy to lick their wounds. Both Hanna and Darroque knew this would be decided between them. Hanna knew she had a decision to make - she could push ahead to the tree and climb it immediately, which would put her lower legs at risk from the late-arriving Darroque. Or she could make a stand, fight him, hope to win, and then climb the tree.

Ten feet from the squat, massive trunk, Hanna saw through the swirling snow that there were knots and short branches rising up into the leaf-bearing branches that would make for an easy climb. Giving a quick glance behind her to see that Darroque had not yet reached the halfway point, Hanna decided to risk the climb. Grabbing ahold of the highest branch she could reach, Hanna pulled her body into the air, her feet slipping on several knots before finding their purchase. She could hear Darroque coming in behind her, but she pulled herself up into the canopy before he had reached the trunk.

The new human had seen how quickly Hanna ascended the tree and made to follow the same path. He grabbed the same branch and looked upward as he started to pull himself up. He had expected to see Hanna scrambling through increasingly thick branches.

What he actually saw was the bottom of the Bostonian's white boot as it slammed into his forehead. Darroque wobbled, but held tight to the tree. "I'll gut you and watch you bleed, girl!"

Hanna responded in action instead of words and stepped off her branch, dropping down onto the alien. She spread her legs to connect with both of his shoulders and as Darroque fell backwards towards the ground, Hanna fell on top of him. His back hit the snow and then her ass hit his mid-section, forcing the air from his lungs. Sitting on his chest, Hanna pulled out her H2O pistol and drilled Darroque in the temple, knocking him out.

Leaning her head back, Hanna looked up into the tree and saw what looked like miles and miles of branches just waiting to be climbed.

*

Jill pushed herself to her feet and stumbled in the direction Laviolette had gone. There was blood on the back of her head and each step made the world rumble inside of her, and within a few steps Jill couldn't even look ahead. Holding her eyes shut to dull the pain, she moved forward by feel instead of sight. This was stupid, she realized, but she kept going. Something was wrong with her, something that she thought had started when she killed her father in Kraken Moor, but the cold night air that she sucked into her lungs provided her with a larger sense of self. Each breath brought needles of pain stabbing at her from the inside and she began to think that whatever was wrong with her started earlier than the events that transpired inside that haunted castle.

Everything unsettled that had been kicked up inside of her started when Hanna brought her back to life with the Universe Cutter.

Jill had died and come back to life, her soul pulled back to this world thanks to one of the eleven blades created by The Metronome at the end of time. The Metronome - one of them, anyway, they were a collective unit of time barons that operated under the same name — had been there when she came back and though she had been brought back to life and turned immortal for only the briefest periods of time, it changed her.

She didn't remember what had happened during those hours she was dead, but she felt a loss at her temporary immortality being pulled away from her as she sacrificed that part of herself to save Hanna's life. There was some kind of ... connection with the Blood of the Universe that coursed through the Void that had taken brief residence inside of her body. She was glad to be rid of it as being an immortal had upset the balance between her and Hanna, but even though they were both back to being physical equals, Jill felt a connection with The Metronome or with the Void that unnerved her, as if ...

"Decide."

Opening her eyes, Jill saw the Mistletoe Queen standing before her, dressed in a long red jacket, trimmed with white fur and her emerald mask. In the air before her, the five golden rings floated in the air. On her right and left, Nikolaos and Laviolette were busy trying to choke the other one to death first.

"Decide," the Mistletoe Queen repeated, "who gets the Golden Rings of Saint Nicholas, and with it, the power to bring five of the dead back to life."

"Go shove a Christmas tree up your ass," Jill spat, holding her head in her left hand. "I have no interest in picking between two bad options."

"But you must."

"Go to Hell," Jill said, and turned away. "I'm tired of playing someone else's game."

Beneath her mask, the Mistletoe Queen smiled and sent the golden rings floating around Jill. The rings were positioned perpendicular to the ground and in the interior space of each of them, images began to appear.

"The rings can bring the dead back to life," the Mistletoe Queen explained. "How many have you lost that you would like to see come back to you?" As the rings orbited slowly around her, a moving image of a young boy appeared. "His name is Timmy," the Mistletoe Queen said. "He adventured with you and Hanna in your youth, until you pushed him too far and he died."

"Stop it," Jill grunted.

"You could correct that mistake," the Mistletoe Queen continued as Laviolette and the satyr died at each other's hands, their struggle for life reduced to mere shadow play. "Who else might you want to see return? Perhaps your father," she suggested, and an image of Jill's father, Branford appeared in one of the remaining four rings. "Such a good memory of him," the Mistletoe Queen said, as Branford Masters sat in a chair between a fire and a Christmas tree, handing large gift-wrapped boxes with enormous bows to his two daughters.

"Stop it," Jill repeated, her hands balling into fists.

"This is why you continue to play in Europe, is it not?" the Mistletoe Queen asked. "Instead of returning home to be with your grieving mother and sister? Oh, you sent them a letter explaining how your father killed President Johnson, and that handsome British spy, Bellingham, brought them some gold so they would not have to work, the poor things, but do you not regret killing your daddy in the bowels of Kraken Moor? Where he is now bound for eternity with all of those other demons?"

"I'm telling you to stop!"

"Is there anyone else from your past you would like to bring back?" the Mistletoe Queen asked, and as she did, the three remaining rings were filled with a rotating series of faces out of her past. "There isn't, is there?" she prodded. "That's the thing about those who think they're too good for everyone else - eventually, there is no one else who wants to be around them to be told they're inferior." Rolling her eyes, the green-masked woman said, "Well, there is the lapdog, of course," as all three unstable rings took on the appearance of Hanna.

Even though it was empty, Jill pulled the H2O pistol off her hip and pointed it at her tormentor. "I said to stop, God dammit!"

The Mistletoe Queen stopped the rotating of the rings and positioned them in a straight line in front of Jill's face. Images of Timmy, her father, and Hanna were joined by those of a handsome man in a British Revolutionary War jacket.

"Timmy, Daddy, Hanna, Hanna's love, and ... well, you know who the last man is, don't you, Jill?"

Jill studied the handsome face but did not recognize him. His light brown hair was tied back into a ponytail, though several clusters of hair fell around his face and he hadn't shaved in several days. He was screaming for help in the midst of a battle, but either no one could hear him or no one cared. Muskets were fired and smoke billowed, and the anguished man fell to his knees, where he a wounded woman in a nightgown lay unmoving in the reddened snow. The man picked up the woman to hold her in his arms, and Jill could not see the woman's face, but she could see she was bleeding heavily from three bullet holes in her chest and stomach. The soldier cursed the gods and the woman's head lolled into view.

Jill froze.

The woman in the image was herself.

"Ah," the Mistletoe Queen said, "you understand the man for what he is even if you struggle to remember his name, don't you? He is the man you have always wanted, the man you have always fantasized about in the dead of night, when your hands roamed over your own skin and between and beneath your folds. With closed eyes, your fingers became his fingers and tongue and manhood thrusting inside of you. Here he is," the Mistletoe Queen said softly, "failing to save you because there is nothing he can do. Unless ..."

The soldier placed Jill back into the snow and reached into his coat, pulling out one solitary golden ring. Placing the ring on Jill's stomach, the musket balls were pulled out of Jill's body. The wounds were healed, and Jill fluttered back to life. The soldier pulled his Jill to him and they kissed.

Jill watched some version of herself kiss this handsome soldier, and she felt her own lips grow warm. Her arms began to ache and she felt the muscles in her leg want to pull themselves apart from one another.

How was this happening? she wondered. The soldier seemed a complete stranger to her, yet complete known, as well. Was it just the power of a fantasy made real? Or a fantasy given form? Was it—?

The images disappeared.

Five empty rings hung before her in the air for a moment before dropping into the snow below them. the Mistletoe Queen was gone and Laviolette and Nikolaos were still breathing, albeit with great effort.

Without looking at either the maid nor the satyr, Jill picked up the rings and ran, leaving the maid and the satyr to die in the snow.

For the life of her, she did not know if she was running to something or away from something.

*

Hanna pulled herself higher and higher into the pear tree, long ago realizing the tree was infinitely grander on the inside than it appeared from the outside. The leaves and pears of the branches helped keep most of the snow outside, though whenever the snow had completely tapered off, the tree would rumble again, as if some giant hand was shaking the snow globe, and the snow would become heavier, even deep in the heart of the tree.

Stopping to look around and try to plan a path forward, Hanna saw a dull, green and yellow light emanating from the other side of the trunk and below her position. Realizing she'd likely climbed too high by about twenty feet, she began descending. At the same time, she heard Darroque somewhere in the branches below her, promising great harm to her body when he reached her.

When she was within ten feet, Hanna started to move towards the trunk as Darroque's voice became louder. The thick branches of the pear tree's interior granted her better footing but a more difficult time moving around them. Darroque's pace thus remained steady as hers diminished. Glancing down as she passed the trunk just above the glowing light, Hanna could see that Darroque was only fifteen to twenty feet below her.

Moving as quickly as she dared, Hanna moved away from the trunk, clinging to one branch at her waist and another at her neck as she all-but ran the length of one branch that was just above the light.

"Come here, girl!" Darroque yelled, having finally spied her.

"Just a minute!" Hanna called back, looking down into the light.

Similar to the blue and white lights at the base of the snow globe, there were green and yellow stars moving around each other up here, creating a cocoon that held the Universe Cutter, wrapped between two branches and multiple pears. Jumping down, Hanna landed on a thick branch and steadied herself by grabbing onto a branch at face level. The Cutter was just ahead of her. She reached out her hands and almost grabbed it, just as Darroque burst into the cocoon, barely ten feet behind her and on the same branch.

The Nomadiri sneered. "You'll never get it out in time, girl."

"You keep calling me 'girl,' like that's an insult," Hanna said, tugging on the trident.

With his hand firmly on a higher branch for support, Darroque began rocking up and down, causing the branch he shared with Hanna to wobble. Hanna lost her balance and had to cling tightly to the nearest branches to prevent herself from falling. Given how thick the branches were beneath her, she didn't think she'd fall all the way to the ground, but while her life would be saved, the battle would be lost.

Darroque let loose a battle cry as he stopped shaking the branch and ran straight ahead. He cared not for the fall, only the victory in claiming the Cutter first. Seeing what he was doing, Hanna heaved herself up and reached for the trident.

Together, they grabbed the staff.

The cocoon exploded, blinding them in blistering greens and scorching yellows.

"It is two that I face, then," a woman said. "So be it."

Darroque and Hanna held the Universe Cutter between them, and looked around to see they were on a platform high above a city. Skeletal framework surrounded them, and they each got the impression they were inside an unfinished structure. Over the edge of the platform and far below them, a city the likes of which Hanna, at least, had never seen spread away from her. There were brightly gleaming carriages with white lights in front and red lights at the back end. There was honking and shouting. There was-

"You would do best to pay attention to me, villainess," the woman twenty feet before them sneered defiantly.

Bruised, battered, and bloodied, the woman before them wore a costume almost exactly like Hanna and Jill's, only with a light green replacing their light blue: white boots, belt, and gloves, a light green skirt and bolo mask, and a white and green shirt with the silhouette of a partridge in the middle of her chest. When she moved her arms, Hanna could see there was a green cape on the woman's back.

"I don't know who you are," the Partridge said in a light French accent, "but I know you have my Cutter, and I will not let you use it to harm my city."

"What city is this?" Hanna asked, recognizing what had to be the future but unaware of any city with such a skeletal tower in its heart.

"Paris, of course," the Partridge spat. "Now, come, let us fight and be done with this madness, and I will send your dead bodies back to the Grenadier."

"Who's that?" Hanna asked. While this future woman's words were rough, Hanna had the distinct sense they were born out of hurt and anger, and did not speak to the true measure of her.

Darroque yanked the trident from Hanna's grasp and stepped forward. "I claim the Universe Cutter," he announced, "and if I have to kill you for it, that will be to my pleasure."

"Bigger men than you have tried," the Partridge assured him.

"By the looks of you," Darroque said, tossing the trident back and forth in his hands, "it seems the last one was particularly successful."

"Who the bloody hell is the Grenadier?" Hanna asked.

"The man who arranged this tournament for the Progenitors," Darroque explained. "He played Veracroix for the fool that he is." Halfway to the Partridge, Darroque stopped and bid her to come forward. "Come, woman, and meet your maker."

"Bloody hell," Hanna grumbled, "why does she get to be a woman and I'm a girl? She's younger than me!"

The Partridge ran hard at Darroque, who stabbed purposely with the trident. The Frenchwoman easily avoided the lunge by diving to the platform's floor and kicking Darroque's ankle with her boot. Shattering the ankle, the newly-made human jammed the trident down towards his opponent, but the Partridge was ready for him, and rolled to the side.

Fast as she was, the beating she had taken at the hands of the Grenadier had done its damage, so while her body escaped being skewered, her cape did not. Darroque pinned her to the ground, the three points of the Universe Cutter digging deep into the metal floor. Slamming the heel of his boot into her temple to knock her dizzy, he pulled the weapon free.

"I kill you," he declared, "and claim my immortality!"

"You talk too much," Hanna grumbled, jumping at him to drive her heels into his lower back and knocking him forward. The Cutter tumbled in one direction, clanging loudly, as Darroque rolled in the other direction. Though he was new to this body of flesh, he had been one of the Nomadiri's greatest soldiers and was quickly on his feet, ready for whatever Hanna had com—

"Urk!"

Hanna jammed the Universe Cutter into Darroque's throat and tore it to the side, ripping away large chunks of his neck. The black man's hands went to the injury, but they could not stop the tide of blood that gushed forth. Hanna moved over him and Darroque tried to usher a challenge or curse, but the words could not be formed in his throat. With no words of her own, Hanna pierced his heart with the trident and ended his time as a human.

"Let us finish this, then," the Partridge said, forcing herself to her feet. Wobbling on unsteady legs, she tried and failed to shake the cobwebs from Darroque's last attack.

Hanna pulled the Universe Cutter out of Darroque and dropped it to the floor, then kicked it over to the Partridge. "Not interested in being immortal," Hanna said, shaking her head. "My friend went through that for a brief time and it's not for me."

"You're just ... going to give it to me?"

"I just want to go home," she said.

"But you killed that man without a moment's hesitation."

Hanna glanced back at the still oozing body and shrugged. "He's actually an alien with plans to conquer the Earth is his big, round spaceboat," she explained, "so while I do not kill lightly, I will not lose any sleep over not having him around."

"Spaceboat?" the Partridge asked. "Are you from the future?"

"Nah," Hanna smiled. "The past. 1866. This is ...?"

"1961," The Partridge said as she sat back down, holding her still throbbing head and closing her eyes. "My life has gotten very strange since that trident crashed into my office. The last thing I remember is the Grenadier tossing me inside a small snow globe on my desk. Tell me," she started to say, but when she opened her eyes to complete the thought, the woman with the turtle dove silhouette had disappeared.

*

Grande Veracroix exited to stand outside the glass tube, filled with dead and dying bodies. The demons feasted, growing fat and satisfied at the sacrifice he had arranged for them. If the Progenitors of Steam failed to take control of the world through the power of their machines ... it would be nice to have a back-up plan.

"Has Darroque returned?" Lady Jenny Carashire asked as she moved past the Steam Men and up a small incline towards Veracroix.

"He has not."

"Darroque failed and has died at the hands of Haneul Pak," the Mistletoe Queen said from atop the glass cube. "The Grenadier found and delivered to you two powerful objects, and you failed to prove yourselves worthy of either the golden rings or the Universe Cutter. This ends our contract," she said. "If you would like to hire me, again, I shall return to Lyon. A Happy Holiday to you both."

And with that, the woman in the red jacket faded away.

Lady Carashire shook her head as the morning's first rays of sunlight washed over them. "Truly, Veracroix, I do not know if I want to hire those Gunfighter Gothic women, or burn their bodies in the ovens of Hell."

*

Hanna listened to Veracoix and Carashire, and then slid back into the woods. Searching for Jill, she quickly came upon the body of Julie Lafayette, who was being tended to by her brother, Remy.

"Did you win?" Remy asked.

"Yeah," Hanna said. "Where's Jill?"

"That way," Julie pointed.

"Will you be okay?"

Julie nodded. "When you find her, be forewarned that others will come for the golden rings. The power to bring souls back from the dead will have many suitors."

Hanna nodded, patted Remy on the shoulder, and then went in search of Jill.

It was, in multiple ways, the story of her life.

THE MAN IN THE RED COAT

ACT FOUR
THE MAN IN THE RED COAT

1866, December
Almost Christmas

A woman wandered through the streets of Lyon, her face hidden behind a painted yellow star that crossed over both eyes and mouth. Her gait was unsteady and her eyes were wild, and her green dress was dotted with round, glass baubles. Her face made a visit to every door she passed, offering a holiday salutation.

"I am the tree of Christmas past!" she yelled in English, and then repeated her words in French: "Je swiss le barbrer de Noël ... de Noël past!"

On a nearby rooftop, a man asked a woman, "How can she not speak French?"

"You really don't know Jill at all, yet, do you?"

Ignatius Poseidon shook his head and ran a hand through his thick hair. "The whole plan hinges on Jill speaking French, and she can't speak it?"

Hanna Pak shrugged and defended her partner. "She can speak it well enough."

Ignatius raised an eyebrow. "It should be pronounced, 'Je suis l'arbre de Noël passé,'" he said, "not 'The Swiss barber of Christmas past."

"Hey, we want her to catch the attention of the authorities, yeah? Well, this will do it." Hanna pulled her thick, peacoat tighter around her neck. It was cold on the flat roof of the factory, and the American born and bred Korean woman was agitated. It was Christmas Eve and she wanted nothing more than to blow their accumulated cash on a fancy hotel and spend the next week being pampered. What she did not want to do was stand on a cold roof in a terrible part of Lyon with a man that Jill had the hots for to help a woman said hot guy's father didn't want to help; it was Hanna's decision, after all, to stop having sex with Jill and it wasn't like she expected Jill to never have sex, again, but Hanna playing babysitter with some guy that wanted to get into Jill's pants was too reminiscent of their old life, when Jill was the servant and Jill was in charge.

"You care about her," Ignatius said as the wind began to pick up.

Hanna rolled her eyes and looked at the young, black man with what she hoped what professional annoyance and not outright contempt. "Listen, kid—"

"Kid?" Ignatius asked. "I'm two, maybe three years younger than you."

"Do you want to know how this is going to work?" Hanna asked, feeling the venom start to seep out of her. "Jill is infatuated with you because you're hot."

"I thought you were a lesbian."

"I am," Hanna said, "but that doesn't mean I'm blind. You're also Poseidon's kid, which means you've got the whole forbidden fruit angle working for you."

"I thought I was forbidden because I was black?"

"Please," Hanna scoffed. "Having sex with a woman is way more forbidden than having sex with a black guy. Jill's parents are progressives. Well," Hanna corrected, "her mother is. Her father murdered the president and then Jill let him die, so his opinion doesn't really count for anything. But still, he would be way more upset if he found out Jill was sleeping with me than you. He'd like you, more or less."

"Why? Because I'm strong and can take care of his daughter?"

"No, because you have a penis and I don't."

"Hrm."

"So you and Jill will do the flirting dance for a while and sleep together a few times and then she'll lose interest and be on to the next guy," Hanna said. "It's how it's always been because she loves the attention from men more than she likes the men, themselves." Hanna shrugged and jammed her hands into her pockets, her face darkening, and her voice lowering. "There was ever only one man she truly loved."

"What happened?"

Hanna said nothing, and let the seconds turn to minutes. Jill and Hanna knew each other's deepest and darkest secrets and fears and passions, and they knew damn well which of those not to give voice to, but this ... latest assertion ... Hanna didn't know where it came from. Jill had never truly loved anyone but herself, yet here Hanna was asserting Jill had had her One True Love already, even though she knew damn well she hadn't. Well, no, she realized as a buzzing in her brain gave her a headache. Without question, Hanna swore she knew why Jill treated men like she did and Jill knew why Jill treated men like she did (and why she treated Hanna like she did), yet Hanna couldn't identify the root cause.

Knowing and not knowing, all wrapped into one statement. What the hell was going on? she wondered.

"We have a problem."

"No," Hanna shook her head as much to snap out of her daydream. "You have a problem. I don't care what you two do."

"Yes, you do," Ignatius said, "but that's not what I mean."

Hanna spun in her boots and looked down at the city streets.

Jill was gone.

"Shit."

"You take the street," Ignatius ordered, "and I'll take the rooftops."

Hanna nodded and moved back to the roof's open stairwell and rapidly descended towards the street. She did not like Ignatius giving her orders, but that argument could be had later. After getting sideswiped by the Scottish vampire sailors off the coast of Brest, she thought her and Jill needed time off and not another mission to attack, but Jill was hot to impress Ignatius "on a professional level," and so here they were, tracking down the Mistletoe Queen and the Progenitors of Steam based on a shoddy lead with no one footing the bill.

Exiting the apartment building, Hanna moved quickly to her left, the cobbled streets covered in a slushy, filthy snow. Garbage stuck half out of the muck. Her mind tried to work up a metaphor about how snow could cover human garbage in a cloak of beautiful white, but then melt away to reveal an ugly interior, but it was past midnight and she was on edge and Christmas would be here in less than a week and the longer Ignatius stuck around, the more certain Hanna was she was going to spend Christmas alone.

A drunk man pissed against a bakery on her right and a fat woman pulled two sailors into an alley on her left.

"Hey, China Girl," a surprisingly handsome man said from the closed doorway of a bank, "how much for you to come back and entertain me and my friends?"

Hanna pulled a heavy H_2O pistol off her hip and shot him in the crotch with a steam bullet as she kept moving forward, not bothering to tell him she was Korean by blood and American by birth and Bostonian by upbringing, her eyes darting through the sparse crowd as her eyes sought out any signs of poorly spoken French rolling off an American tongue.

"Where are you going?"

Hanna raised her pistol at the doorway of a cheap hotel, preparing to fire.

Jill raised up her hands. "Easy, Tex," she said, wiping yellow greasepaint off her face with a towel.

"Where's your costume?" Hanna asked, seeing Jill was wearing jeans and a green t-shirt and not the Christmas tree dress.

"Ugh," Jill said, sticking out her tongue. "It was too hot and we weren't getting anywhere."

"You were out here for ten minutes!"

"Yeah, well, it was a dumb plan. Get kidnapped to find out where they're taking all these missing girls which no one but one crazy lady thinks are missing? Dumb," Jill said, tossing the towel back inside the bar. "It's probably just tied into that Krampus Society nonsense. Merci, Francois!" she called to the man who caught the discharged towel, and then joined Hanna in the street. "Come on, let's go get a real hotel and take a warm bath. Not together," she added quickly, looking around. "Where's Tall, Black, and Handsome?"

Hanna shoved her H2O pistol back in its holster and balled her hands into fists. "Are you serious?" she asked. "You're already giving up?"

"I'm not giving up," Jill said, hugging herself against the cold night. "I just don't care."

"About missing girls?"

"For ball's sake, Hanna," Jill snapped. "We're not heroes. We're businesswomen. And right now, we've got enough money to spend two weeks in a nice hotel and celebrate Christmas. Let's do that. Let's get drunk every night and buy silly gifts for one another and, you know, find a rich client to pay us to go find these missing girls."

"You're not serious, are you?" Hanna asked, shaking her head. "Of course you're serious. You're just too stupid to realize these missing girls are all homeless or headed there. There's nobody rich who cares about them. Hell, there's likely not anybody poor who cares about them."

Jill sighed, shook her head, ran her hands through her flowing black hair, and then sighed again.

"What?"

"Shouldn't we talk about what happened?" Jill asked. "We never talk about what happened." Hanna was ready to jump down her throat but she'd spent her whole life with Jill and knew when the exterior was cracking, and right now, it was cracking.

"Which 'happened' are you referring to? Your dad? Dotson? Timmy? The five magic rings you've got that can rase the dead?" she asked, and then spat in the snow. "What the hell's going on with you?" she asked.

Jill looked away, avoiding the question. "I just feel like being silly for awhile," she said, dropping her voice. "I always feel like being silly on Christmas. You know this."

"Yes, I'm familiar with that state of your being," Hanna said. "But why now?"

Jill opened her mouth to answer, but closed it, choosing to look around again for a distraction to avoid having to explain herself to her friend and partner. She found it on the roof of a nearby factory, and pointed in that direction.

"I found Ignatius," she said, reaching for guns that weren't there.

"His dick will still be there later," Hanna snapped. "Now, tell me what's going on?"

A black, metal mask, large enough to cover a person's entire face, slammed into the cobblestone street and bounced towards them, picking up slush as it skidded to a halt by their feet. Hanna spun to the roof three stories above them and one block away, where Ignatius stood next to a woman in a red robe, lined with white fur, and whose face was hidden behind a mask cut from a large emerald: the Mistletoe Queen. Ignatius stood placidly at her side, a mask cut from a large ruby sitting on his face.

"Is he betraying us, again?" Hanna asked.

"No," Jill shook her head. "I saw a man sneak up behind him and put it on his face. Then Iggy went all comatose."

"Iggy?"

"I'm trying it out," Jill said. "You like it?"

"It makes me feel nauseous," Hanna said as the Mistletoe Queen and Ignatius stood side-by-side on the rooftop, making no effort to move until Hanna pulled her electric shooter off her right hip and aimed it at the roof.

the Mistletoe Queen raised her left hand in the air and then lowered it slowly, a request for Hanna to drop her weapon. When the Bostonian refused, the Mistletoe Queen turned to Ignatius, who nodded in obedience and then placed one of his feet over the edge of the rooftop, holding it there as he awaited further instructions.

"Drop it," Jill ordered.

"Yeah, yeah," Hanna said, holstering her pistol.

The Mistletoe Queen turned to Ignatius, who backed away from the edge. She reached into her robe and extracted a small glass bottle, full of blue liquid, and handed it to Ignatius, who walked it to the corner of the rooftop and placed it there. the Mistletoe Queen pointed to the metal mask at the women's feet, then to the bottle, then backed out of sight. Ignatius followed her.

"Get the mask," Hanna said, bolting for the building with the bottle, "and watch the exits!"

Jill watched her go as she bent down to pick up the metal mask. There were four vertical panels across the front: two on the sides that fit against the side of the wearer's head, and two on the face that angled to a central line. Two small holes existed for breathing. There was an opening at the mouth cut out to look like a a menacing frown. The rest of the mask was unremarkable in its creation, but Jill felt a chill run through her that made the night feel warm.

She had a strong urge to try it on ...

"Jill! Jill!"

Blinking her eyes, Jill looked up to see Hanna standing in front of her. "How did you ... ?"

"I've been gone fifteen minutes!" Hanna snapped. "I was calling you from the roof for half that time! Jesus, what's gotten into you?"

"Ignatius ..."

"Gone!" Hanna yelled. "No obvious trace of them, but I did find a- oh, hell with it! What do you care? No one's paying us to go save him!"

Jill held the mask tightly in her hands and swallowed.

That's when the tears started.

"Jill ...?"

In a whisper, the merchant's daughter said, "What's wrong with me, Hanna? Why can't I ... why can't I love? Why can't you remember the wardrobe?"

"What goddamn wardrobe?"

The tears didn't stop until long after Hanna had wrapped her arms around her friend, and promised everything would be alright, and even though they both knew it to be a lie, they took comfort in it.

*

Jill awoke in a small bed, feeling ashamed and uneasy. Hanna wasn't there, but her presence was in the room in the form of a tray of food and drink on the nightstand: water, bread, cheese, grapes, and the bottle of blue liquid from last night. The metal mask was there, too, though Hanna had tried to hide it beneath a handwritten note.

The room itself was small and poorly lit, the bed's sheets and blankets clean but showing signs of wear. There was an effort made to decorate the room for the holidays: a wreath was on the wall opposite her, but the Christmas ornaments adorning its branches were not festive. Wanting a better look, Jill pushed back the covers and stepped out of bed, wearing a thin, purple nightgown of unknown origin. There were slippers, accessorized to look like happy reindeer, complete with fuzzy antlers. The hardwood floor was cold enough to feel through the slippers as Jill made her way to the wreath. Instead of shimmering red balls or candy canes, there were small bottles of green absinthe and vials of white, powdered cocaine spread around the branches.

"What kind of hotel is this?" she wondered aloud, her voice feeling small and coming back to her in a series of rippling, whispering echoes. Rubbing the last bit of sleep out of her eyes, she moved back to the bedside table to read the note.

Jill,
Drink the water.
Eat the bread with the cheese.
Eat the grapes.

Then drink the blue bottle (it will steady your nerves) and meet
me in the central room down the hall. I have information on Dotson.
Happy Christmas,
Hanna

Dotson? Her ex-fiancé-slash-megalomaniac that Hanna
had killed on the same night in Kraken Moor that Jill had
killed her father? What could Hanna have on Dotson? He was
dead, his soul trapped in the English estate along with every
other person that died that night.

Jill read the note again.

Jill,
Drink the water.
Eat the bread with the cheese.
Eat the grapes.
Then drink the blue bottle (it will steady your nerves) and meet
me in the central room down the hall. I have information on Ignatius.
Happy Christmas,
Hanna

Ignatius, not Dotson.

"Ugh," she groaned, rubbing her face, "where is my mind?
Stupid Christmas."

Looking around the room for clothes, she noticed a small
closet behind her that she hadn't seen in her first look around
the room. "Get it together, girl," she scolded herself, pulling
open the doors to find herself staring at a naked, gray-skinned
man with a goat's head.

"Kadul!" she gasped, recognizing the demon as she
tumbled backwards. Desperately, she looked around for
anything to use as a weapon, and found nothing. Looking

back, preparing herself for a physical attack, Jill saw no sign of Kadul or anyone else.

There was just a closet with clothes in it.

Shaking her head to clear cobwebs that she didn't even think were there, she pushed herself to her feet and then sat on the edge of the bed. Following Hanna's instructions, she drank some water, then ate a slice of baguette with a hunk of cheese on it, then popped a few of the green grapes in her mouth, and finally knocked back the bottle of blue water.

Her eyes felt as if they widened far enough to take in half the known universe, and she felt a ripple of dizziness rush from her head to her feet and back again, but then a sense of peace descended onto her. There were no more demons in the closet or bottles of absinthe and dials of cocaine on the wreath. There was only balls of green and white glass on the wreath, and an elegant crimson dress, highlighted in streaks of a dark gold in the closet; although she and Hanna had been traipsing around England and France looking like cowboys, she recognized the dress was in the emerging style called "Victoriana Nouveau" or "Steampunk." The dress had a corset on the outside, around the middle and several unnecessary straps and buckles on the cascading dress. The neck was cut low enough to reveal the top of her breasts, and the shoulders were flat, but the tops of the arms were puffy and loose, and ended no more than two inches down her arms.

There were high-cut, black boots in the closet, too, though she was disappointed to find there were no weapons strapped in amongst the numerous buckles, nor even a gun belt anywhere in the closet.

"Probably Hanna's way of making sure I go down to see her," Jill reasoned, and it made a tremendous amount of sense to her. Jill was so certain of this fact that she didn't even recall actually putting on the dress. One moment it was in the closet and the next it was on her body.

"It's the stress," she said, and that sounded more right than anything else could have sounded.

When her hand hit the doorknob, her eyes took in the metal mask on the bedside table. Wondering if she missed any instructions relating to it, she picked up Jill's note and read it for a third time. It said:

Jill,
Put on the mask.
Put on the mask.
Put on the mask.
Put on the mask and meet me in the central room down the hall. I have information on the mask.
I will carve my name on your heart with my tongue,
The Woman in the Red Coat

"Hanna," Jill chuckled, shaking her head and picking up the mask and strapping it to her face. "Always kidding around."

*

Hanna sprinted up the central staircase of the apartment building, and when she burst through to the roof, she was half-surprised to find the Mistletoe Queen and Ignatius standing at the ledge.

"I thought you would have run," Hanna said, electric shooter in hand.

"Why would I run when you were so desperate to get to me?" she asked, placing a hand on Ignatius' shoulder. "Why would I run when I have such a virile man willing to do whatever I want him to do?" the Mistletoe Queen ran a hand over Ignatius' chin. "I have already tasted of his essence," she said.

"It's the mask, right?" Hanna asked rhetorically, ignoring the sexual allusion and noting the woman's voice had an American tilt to its Britishness. "What's it do? What do you do? What are you after? Why do you always keep showing up wherever we are?"

the Mistletoe Queen stepped in closer to Ignatius, pressing her mask up against his cheek. "You should not have interfered with my performance in Bourges. You have made a habit of interfering with the Progenitors of Steam far too often for their liking, in fact, and it is time that debt is paid. Poor Olivier Farmier is dead. Poor Emil Vozhov is paralyzed."

"And what of Lady Carashire?" Hanna asked. "Is she mad at us, too?"

the Mistletoe Queen gave a small chuckle. "Lady Carashire has decided not to pursue you for murdering Darroque, and has, instead, returned to Madagascar to care for the Anthon boy. But then, you know something of the theft of children, do you not, Haneul Pak? Yes, you and Ignatius both."

Eyes narrowing, Hanna fired her electric shooter at the Mistletoe Queen in anger, but the woman in the red robe held up a hand and the blast was directed at Ignatius. The body of Poseidon's son seized up and then wobbled dangerously close to the edge of the roof.

"I trust you will not try that, again," the Mistletoe Queen said, "and we can get started with the night's festivities? We approach the day before Christmas, after all, and it is not the time of year to dilly and dally. Unless you are like me, and have all the time in the world."

Hanna gritted her teeth and holstered her shooter. "What's this about?"

the Mistletoe Queen turned to motion over the edge of the roof, and Hanna stepped forward to look down into the street, where Jill was standing completely still, the metal mask strapped to her face.

"Tsk, tsk," the Mistletoe Queen said as Hanna prepared to run back down to her friend. "Jill will be given a chance to escape that trap on her own, and I assure you," she said, motioning to riflemen on the nearby rooftops, "she will be protected."

"If you hurt her ..."

"She can only hurt herself," the Mistletoe Queen promised, snapping her fingers to get Ignatius to move away from the ledge. "I am neither villain nor saint, Miss Pak, but if you wish to discover my true purpose, you will do as I say."

"Why are you not trying to kill us?"

"Kill you?" the Mistletoe Queen laughed. "This is the bosom of civilization, my dear, not the Wild West. The Progenitors of Steam seek nothing more than to change the world for the better. I want to claim the golden rings, but I have no desire to see Jill die in the process. Killing you would bring them unnecessary attention. You have powerful friends, do you not? President Ulysses S. Grant. Queen Victoria. Bellingham. Charles Francis Poseidon. The Metronome."

"I wouldn't call the Metronome a friend. Any of them," Hanna added, letting the Mistletoe Queen know she knew the Metronome wasn't just a person but a collective of people who sat at the end of time and played god.

"No?" the Mistletoe Queen asked. "Was it not The Metronome who built the Universe Cutter who allowed you to bring a very dead Jill back to life? Was it not The Metronome who built the Universe Cutter that allowed you to kill Darroque?"

Hanna said nothing.

Beneath her emerald mask, the Mistletoe Queen smiled. "Are you familiar with Charles Dickens' A Christmas Carol? I trust you have heard of it even in the savagery of America? Below us, Jill's mind has been infiltrated by the psychotropics laced on the interior of my metal mask. It is my take on the Ghost of Christmas Past. She is facing all of her buried shame and fear and worry about her past actions. You see, Miss Pak, after three months of fighting monsters and demons, it is time for you both to face the demons inside of you." She chuckled. "I would imagine The Metronome is well acquainted with Dickens' fable of time displacement, do you not agree?"

The Mistletoe Queen reached up the sleeve of her robe and removed an Italian Medico della peste, or "Plague Doctor" mask, carved out of diamond. Handing it to Hanna, the Bostonian could see the mask was would cover the wearer's entire face, and its most striking and recognizable feature was the elongated beak that extended far away from the wearer's face. Two perfectly round eyeholes were cut into the mask, but covered by round, onyx discs.

As Hanna studied the mask, she was horrified to find a mouse crawling inside the beak.

"'Twas the night before the night before Christmas," the Mistletoe Queen said, "and all through the house, only one creature was stirring, it was that little mouse."

"You're a terrible poet," Hanna said.

"Put it on, Miss Pak," the Mistletoe Queen ordered, "and face my version of the Ghost of Christmas Present."

Hanna looked over to the unmoving Ignatius. "And that means he's face the Ghost of Christmas Yet to Come?"

"You always were the clever one."

"And if I don't the snipers turn on us instead of protecting us?"

the Mistletoe Queen nodded. "Put on the mask, Miss Pak."

Not seeing as she had any other option, Hanna put on the mask, and her world went white with snow. She looked around her, trying to get her bearings, but the snow was hitting her with the intensity of an attack. The big flakes stung her face as they whipped past, and the accumulated snow was up to her knees. All she could do was trudge forward, but Hanna was doing that instinctually. She had no idea where she was or where she was going. This was supposed to be about confronting the demons of her present?

Hanna stopped, letting the snow hit her square, and looked around at the night. The storm cut her visibility to not more than ten feet, and she had the sense of being trapped in a snow globe, where she could catch glimpses of the world but not the whole of it. What she saw through the snow were monstrous squares, rising into the sky, and then she caught a glimpse of a window.

They were houses, which meant she was on a street, and just before a woman's scream pierced the night she realized where she was.

Boston.

Standing in front of Jill's house.

Dressing in her crimson, Steampunk-styled dress, Jill opened the door to her room, expecting to see the hallway.

There wasn't one.

Instead, Jill found herself looking at a fast moving train like the Morgan steamer she and Hanna had boarded in Kansas City on the day they met Bellingham.

The train screeched to a halt, the steps at the rear of one of the passenger cars now outside her door. At the top of the stairs, a woman in a black dress and veil offered her hand. Jill took the puffy hand and rose up the steps, giving her thanks.

"Your interference cost me $85,000," the woman said, pulling back the veil to reveal herself as Mary Todd Lincoln. She was referring to the Colony List, a document containing the names of secret agents across the United States and Europe. "Dotson was going to pay me money for that list, and you interfered."

"Yes," Jill said solemnly, "I did."

"And then you died."

"I did."

"And then you came back."

"I did."

"And I still have not gotten my money."

"I am sorry about that," Jill said, and she found that she was, in fact, sorry.

The widow of President Abraham Lincoln put her index fingers against the back of her jaw and dislocated it. Her mouth sagged open and Jill saw rows and rows of sharp teeth inside Mrs. Lincoln's mouth and a snake slithering around the mouth that flicked out to lick Jill's face.

"I want to devour you," Mrs. Lincoln said, "but your father killed President Johnson, and for that, you killed your father." Mrs. Lincoln grinned, her smile seemingly wider than her face and the snake zig-zagging back and forth through her teeth. "I approve. Please, enter the car. Hanna awaits at the next stop. And Jill," she said, her grin somehow wrapping around her face, "Merry Christmas."

"Merry Christmas, Mrs. Lincoln," Jill said as she bowed slightly to the older woman, then moved inside the car. Cabins occupied both sides of the thin hallway. There were light bulbs in the ceiling by the doors of all the cars, but as the train started to chug forward, the bulbs began to flicker. Music began to play and as Jill walked forward, looking for a place to sit, she saw in the first cabin on her left a group of seven brown- and gray-furred werewolves in red coats playing string instruments: violins, violas, and a bass. On her right, a group of Sun Chasers — nearly naked men wearing yellow and black kilts, their skin scarred from their devotion to the sun's rays — played the woodwinds: clarinets, flutes, oboes, and even a bassoon.

The flickering lights cut out and a woman's voice taunted Jill from someplace beyond the car:

"Jingle Bells,

Jingle Bells,

Jingle Till You Turn Gray ..."

"That's not how that song goes," Jill said as the train rumbled forward, moving noticeably faster.

Ahead of her in the dark, a glowing green mask appeared in the darkness.

"That's the way I sing it," the Mistletoe Queen laughed. "Give me the rings!"

Jill reached for guns that weren't there, then started forward "I'm going to rip that mask off your face!" she yelled.

The lights in the train car began to flicker, but they were now blood red instead of white. When they flickered on, Jill expected to see the Mistletoe Queen standing there, waiting for her, but with the lights on, the strange woman disappeared, and when the lights went out, all Jill could see was the green mask taunting her.

"Dashing through the snow," the Mistletoe Queen taunted in a quiet, sing-song voice, as snow began to fall inside the train. Jill continued her march forward, but within three steps the snowfall was above her knees. The fashionable dress didn't help, either. She wanted to rip off the puffy shoulders and tear off the dress, replacing them with jeans and guns.

"Here's a one-horse that you did slay," she continued. The lights turned off, leaving Jill in the rumbling dark. Ahead of her, the Mistletoe Queen disappeared, to be replaced by two shimmering red eyes above steaming nostrils, and Jill knew this to be the horse she had ridden to its death at the hands and teeth of the Krampus. The horse whinnied, rising its front legs high in to the air.

"Easy, fella," Jill said. She was half a car away and covered in deep snow but the horse would have less trouble moving in it that she would.

From behind her, a make voice said, "It is not Gambader you have to worry about. It is I!" Jill turned in the snow that was now halfway to her thigh to see a half-human, half Krampus standing there with a human upper body sandwiched between a Krampus' head and its powerful, furred lower legs. The Krampus sneered at her, "You did not even know his name, did you?" he accused in a gravelly, deep voice. "To you, Gambader was nothing more than a tool to be used and discarded."

It was true, Jill knew, but she didn't think the horse would have preferred to be left behind.

The Krampus shimmered, now becoming its human host, the Icelandar Anar in face and legs, and the Krampus' torso between them. "I do not want to hurt you," he begged, "but I cannot control him ... I thank you for not killing me but I ... I ..."

Anar's handsome face distorted, cracking and bubbling as he was transformed fully into the Krampus.

He charged.

Jill took one step backwards and fell back in the snow. It was too thick for her to crab walk away but not thick enough to make it easy to rise to her feet. As she lay in the snow, the fully-realized Krampus built up steam in his approach. His snarling face drooled and snapped and howled, as his he ran forward, the train car now seeming to stretch out for hundreds of feet. Jill should have been happy with the extra opportunity to move, but she found herself stuck in the snow, almost accepting of whatever fate delivered to her, almost believing this was all some kind of dream and there was no Hanna waiting for her at the end of the hallway that was a train car that was full of past enemies.

The Krampus jumped forward, its large frame shattering the sides of the train's hallway. The heavy bulk of the beast began its descent and Jill welcomed the physical battle to come; there was something cathartic in the fight for her. Christmas made her think of her family and she found she dearly missed her mother and her sister and almost sorta kinda her half-sister, too. It was December 23rd, the night when father gave each of them a special ornament as the Masters sat around the tree, drinking warm brandy and enjoying each other's company: Father always concerned with the family's wealth and future prospects, mother chirping pleasantly about the holiday's social gossip, and Jill's younger sister, June, always smiling and singing when she was little. The image of the family Christmas now changed, and there was Branford Masters, heavier and never without a whiskey or a cigar in hand. There was Lindsey Masters, graying at the temples and now nattering on about what everyone thought of Jill's continuing status as a single woman. And then there was poor June, her love of life poisoned in her desire to not become her older sister; where Jill was carefree and individualistic, June tried desperately to be the perfect daughter, wanting to marry someone above her station and concerned with her position among the social elite of Boston.

"I want to be married by this time next year," June had announced last year. "I have found the perfect boy. His name is Dotson."

Jill gritted her teeth, the Krampus falling onto her in the slowest of motions. She looked to her left and right and saw the unique pattern of every falling snowflake as it twirled through the Morgan train.

Dotson Winters.

How much different would her life be today if Dotson had passion for June instead of Jill. Her sister would have gladly married the handsome genius and their father would have still received the infusion of capital he so desperately needed to keep his merchant and whaling businesses operating.

But Dotson was the kind of young man who wanted what he couldn't have, and so he demanded Jill, and she agreed to marry him and the Krampus' claws were reaching for her ...

They did not reach her. The horse that she had used to escape, and then watched perish at the teeth and claws of the same beast before them, dove forward, slamming his thick body into the Krampus' large frame, sending a powerful shockwave through the train car that blew out all the windows, the glass falling to the ground as snowflakes.

The car's red lights turned white. Directly on top of her, the two beasts gnashed and tore at one another. Jill lay still in the snow, and somehow the hooves and claws avoided her. What she could not avoid, however, was the falling blood that poured and dripped from each creature. The part of Jill that was too tried to move simply watched the horse and Krampus devour bits and pieces of each other, each slash or chomp taking a piece of the other one, until there was nothing left but two heads without bodies ... two heads that dropped, dead, into the red snow beside her.

The lights went out, and the Mistletoe Queen laughed low and menacing. Still on her back in the snow, Jill arched her head backwards to look at the glowing green mask taunting her from half a car away.

"O'er the fields you go ... as I laugh, laugh, laugh all the way!"

The snow melted as the car turned hot. Pushing herself to her feet, she trudged forward beneath flickering lights, each cabin revealing some other past foe or friend standing and watching, as if they were decaying zombies unsure of what to do next: the vampires of Jesus Christ, Emil Vozhov, Agent Plummer and President Grant, Ferdinand von Zeppelin, Roma, Bellingham, Poseidon, and Ajax Finch ... and on and on. With each set of cabins she passed the train grew one cabin longer until it seemed as if everyone she and Hanna had ever met made an appearance to bear witness to Jill's Christmas march.

At the end of the car, the smiling mask of the Mistletoe Queen remained, always watching and laughing until finally

Jill had passed the last set of cabins and stood face to face with the mask of the Mistletoe Queen.

Screaming at the glowing emerald gemstone, Jill lashed out, swinging her fist hard at the mask. When she made contact, a crack in the tapestry of reality emerged, and Jill watched a spiderweb of sharp angles extend away from the undamaged mask, until her entire vision of reality crashed like broken glass.

Jill covered her face as reality fell in shape shards around her, cutting her hands and dress, until the image of the train was gone, replaced by the image of a very ordinary hallway inside a very ordinary hotel.

Ahead of her stood a Christmas tree that appeared as if it had been set up five years ago and never taken down. the pine needles were black and grey, the round ornaments covered in dust or broken. The room itself was large and circular and in a similar state of decay. The wallpaper was torn and yellowed, and there were cracks in the walls. A huge bay window looking out onto a residential street was shattered. On her left, a fireplace burned a blue flame that emanated cold instead of warmth, and on the right hand of the room were four glass goblets: one appeared full of wine, two of milk, and the other of bourbon.

Hanging from the ceiling was mistletoe, and on the ground by the tree was a model of a three-masted ship, made of cast iron and laying on its side. As Jill knelt down to examine it, she remembered it as belonging to her father. Turning it over, she saw the name MASTERS etched across the hull. Her father kept it outside, near the entrance to their home in the Back Bay, to let the world know that this was the home of that same merchant whose ships left ports in Boston,

New Bedford, and Nantucket to ply his trade out in the world.

"Jill?" asked the familiar voice of Hanna, but there was no Hanna in the room. Putting the MASTERS back where she'd found it beside the tree, Jill looked at every inch of the room, as if Hanna would appear in the markings of the wallpaper if she stared hard enough, but there was no sign of her in the room.

There was only her voice, asking for her again and again, an echo that grew fainter and then louder as she circled the room. There was a door on her right and it was the door that gave her immediate pause.

She had been in this room before.

She had been in this room a hundred, a thousand, a hundred-thousand times before.

It was the sitting room in her family's house in Boston.

"Jill?" Hanna asked, and this time the voice was nearby. It was not coming from the doorway, because when Jill peered through that opening, she saw nothing but the cold emptiness of the Void staring back at her.

Turning away from damnation, Jill's eyes took in the bay window, where Hanna was standing, her body appearing not in color but in sepia tones of cold browns and pixelated whites.

"Hanna?" Jill said, moving past the blackened Christmas tree on her left to stand at the window. Hanna was just on the other side, looking at Jill with squinted eyes.

"Jill? Is that you?"

"It's me, idiot," Jill said, trying to inject humor into the moment, but failing. Her words came out choked and ... muted, it seemed to her. Almost as if she could watch them form in the cold air being let in by the broken window and then slip away into the storm that was raging outside.

"Jill!" Hanna yelled, growing taller. "What's happened to you?"

Looking up, it took Jill a moment to see that it wasn't Hanna that had grown taller, at all. She'd shrunk, down to the size of a child. No, she realized after looking at her hands, not the size of a child ... she'd become a child. Her Steampunk dress was gone, replaced by a dirty pair of blue overalls she liked to go adventuring in because she didn't care if they got dirty. Hanna's parents had given her those overalls, which meant Jill's mother didn't mind if they got dirty, either.

"What's happening?" she asked, looking up at Hanna, who had to strain to hear them against the whipping wind and the vagaries of displaced time.

A voice from out of the past said in a low, seductive voice, "Hello, little girl."

Terror gripped Jill, and she spun around, looking back to the doorway that revealed the Void to this world. Hanna began screaming above her to "Run!" and "Get out!" and "Goddamn it!" but the person who stepped out of the Void and into the Masters' sitting room had eyes only for Jill.

"Do you remember me, my sweet girl?" he asked with a grin. The man was a tall and ruggedly handsome British officer, dressed in the black boots, white pants, and red coat of a Revolutionary War soldier. His hair was dirty blonde and pulled back into a ponytail, yet loose strands of wild hair hung down the side of his face. His stubble was several days old, but his smile was fresh, intoxicating, and dangerous, like when the warmth of a fire turns to burning when one has been drawn too close to the heart of the flame.

Jill pressed her back against the wall beneath the window, crying and sputtering and screaming, but no sounds escaped her lips. Paralyzed by fear, Jill could do nothing as the man she knew only by his title, The Grenadier, fully entered the Masters' sitting room.

"Of course you remember me," he smiled wickedly. "How could you forget someone who has always been near you?"

The Grenadier placed his hands together in front of his body and then opened them wide. A band of light bridged the expanding hands, and then escaped into the air when the Grenadier let it loose by dropping his left hand, moving through the air like a ribbon caught in the wind, weaving in and out as it advanced across the room.

The white light began to change, then, and Jill saw moving images of her own past slide out of the Grenadier's right hand ... when she was a baby, left alone in her crib for the first time and a man in a British military uniform stepped out of her wardrobe to stand over her ... when she was almost two and learning how to talk and told her mother about "the red man" and her mother didn't believe that Indians would dare enter the house ... when she was four and moved into a new room with new furniture and she began to hear a voice in the dark, and then footsteps in the hallway, and then the silhouette of feet by her closed bedroom door ... when she was five and awoke in the basement without understanding how she arrived there ... the next night when she did the same ... the next night when she did the same and finally saw the old wardrobe that she was sure had been in her room at some point ... the next night when she invited Hanna in to watch over her and nothing happened, save for the smiling presence of the Grenadier always standing two feet behind Hanna, never letting the Asian girl see him ... when Jill was seven and a boy down the street gave her a black eye, and three days later when his body was found on his doorstep, hung to death by a noose made out of intestines from his father's butcher shop, and the red coat of a British soldier vanishing into the darkness as the boy's parents screamed in anguish.

Aging in tune with the moving memories, Jill tried to close her eyes but the images kept coming, one after another, moments she remembered and those she didn't, wondering how she'd ever forgotten them except they seemed somehow both new and old all at once.

When she was eight and his inviting voice called her to an abandoned house down the street, and he made images appear out of thin air, and she watched the Revolution play past in glorious color.

When she was ten and almost died for the first time as her and Hanna were chased around one of her father's whaling ships by an Egyptian mummy, and she returned home, relieved and thankful, only to have the Grenadier pull her into the back of her wardrobe, slamming her body against the wall as he choked her, threatening her to never do that to him again, or he would finish the job she so recklessly started.

When she was eleven and had the wardrobe removed, and when she was twelve and it came back.

When she was thirteen and in the company of two older boys who lured her away from a Christmas party and meant her harm, and the Grenadier was suddenly there, in the library of the strange house, and peeled off each of the boy's skins while they screamed. And the next day when each of them arrived separately and apparently unharmed at the Masters' house to offer their sincerest apologies. And three months later when one of them was committed to an asylum, and two months after that when the other boy was found at the breakfast table one morning eating his own intestines and masturbating.

When she was fourteen and began spending nights in Hanna's bed, for fear of the man in the red coast watching over her.

When she was fifteen and brought a boy back to her bedroom for the first time to play a kissing game, and how the bright, charming boy never smiled again.

When she was seventeen and a new boy moved to Boston, and how she fell deeply and truly and madly in love for the first time, for the only time, in her life. He was handsome and charming and wealthy, and everything he did made her cheeks turn red. Jill forgot about adventuring and refused to let Hanna meet him and forgot about being independent and wanted only to marry him and be whisked away and make babies and travel the world and look down on everyone else because she felt like the center of the universe when he held her in his strong arms and passionately kissed her lips and squeezed her breasts, first over her shirt and then beneath it, his hands somehow soft and powerful at the same time, and how he reddened more than just her cheeks, and how her hands explored his body ... the tightness of his neck, the solidity of his chest, the muscles of his arms, and then on to other places, lower places, forbidden places, throbbing places that beckoned her, pleaded for her, needed her and only her hands and mouth ...

And the Christmas Eve of 1855 in her bedroom, when her parents were gone to a party at Mayor Smith's and her sister was asleep in her bed down the hall and all of the servants had been given the night off to have their own Christmas dinner, when Jill and her heart's only love were at last completely alone in the world and she pulled off his black pants and blue shirt and winter boots and they pressed against one another, her hands running endlessly through his short hair and building a rhythm into an orchestra of grunts and groans and sobs and sweat and exaltations.

When she told him he loved her and he told her he would love her forever and always had and always will and now they laid together in the darkness, falling asleep, awoken only when Hanna's voice could be heard on the stairs, calling to her, and how Jill hated her in that moment because her lover - her lover - rolled out of bed and put on his clothes.

Only they weren't the clothes she had pulled off him.

The clothes he pulled on were black boots, white pants, and a red coat, and his face was no longer his face except that it was his face, only now it was a decade older and his hair was longer and pulled into a ponytail save for the few strands that hung by the side of his face. His clean-shaven visage now had a few days of stubble and somehow she knew the boy with no name was the man in the red coat all along.

And how he came back to her in that moment, with Hanna's footsteps getting ever closer, and she opened herself to him and moved on top of her to place his thumbs at the bottom of her rib cage and then they were inside of her, penetrating her skin and then so were his fingers, enclosing over her ribs so that he held them in his strong hands. And she knew what was coming and she wanted it even more than she'd wanted him inside of her during their lovemaking. He pulled open her rib cage, snapping her sternum and tearing her skin as if it were nothing but poorly made cloth until her heart was laid bare before him and she loved him and feared him and loved him even more because of it as he told her words she would never forget and never remember:

I will carve my name on your heart with my tongue.

And how he did, and then rose to his feet and walked across her room, opening her wardrobe and climbing inside just as Hanna opened the door to find her friend crying inconsolable tears and joined her in bed.

And how Jill realized in that moment, pressing against Hanna, that love was not so easily defined.

And how Jill never slept again without one eye being on the wardrobe door and how she feared it opening and how she longed for it opening and how she once opened it herself and stepped inside and the man in the red coat was waiting for her back there in the deep darkness.

And how once became more than once.

And how he never came out but always made her come in, and how the man in the red coat was now something more than a hazy recollection and temporary guest into her life but the reason for it, and how she hated herself for doing it but couldn't stop, not understanding what he was but craving it, and long after she realized everything he made her feel had nothing to do with love but everything to do with the primal part of her soul that craved danger and excitement she still went to him.

And how, after the twentieth time or the thirtieth time or the hundredth time, when she had turned 19 and her parents' fears about her never marrying reached a crescendo, when she went into the wardrobe one night, a Christmas Eve she seemed to recall, and gave of herself one last time and then climbed off the Grenadier and started taking back her independence, and as the midnight bells chimed back out in the real world and she left him her clothes, and turned herself into a memory, telling him he would never see her again.

And how she stepped out of the wardrobe that night to find Hanna standing there with an axe in each hand. Hanna, who somehow knew without ever being told what was happening, and the two young women took apart that wardrobe with those axes until there was nothing left but slivers and shards.

And how they carried those slivers and shards to the fire and let it rage.

And how the man in the red coat could be heard screaming all the way back down the hole to Hell.

Or was it all the way up to the End of Time?

And how they never talked about it again.

And now an image of a woman in an emerald mask stepping through the curtains of the Jazz Masquerade, seeking the man in the red coat and finding him, tied to a tree in a New England forest as the Revolution raged around him.

And now an image of her cutting him down and giving herself to him in the midst of battle, the world ignoring them because they ignored the world. He is behind her and she is facing through time and space at Jill Masters sitting alone in a haunted room in a haunted house, now all grown up but still stupid and forgetting and remembering all and nothing, and wondering through her fear how memories could never have happened and always have happened.

And now she has been shot by three musket balls and she is dying and he has the golden rings and he saves her and she kisses him.

And now the grown woman in the Steampunk dress is not looking at what was, but is looking at what is. She is back in the present, inside the image of her parent's house, watching a man wearing only a red coat thrusting behind a woman wearing only an emerald mask and she knows and doesn't know and has always known exactly what it is she is seeing, and knows above and behind her outside this damned house is Hanna, who also knows and doesn't know, and knew even before Jill did that there are more sides to love than there are Christmas wishes.

And now the whisper of the Mistletoe Queen floating to her as the Grenadier finishes his thrusting that it's all been an orchestral lie, that she is not some petty trickster dependent on silly boys with silly dreams giving themselves silly names, but that she is in the control, she is the one pulling all the strings, and the Progenitors dance her tune unaware because that's how she wants it, because they were never her Purpose.

And how Bellingham is a fool for ever bringing Jill back to life with the Universe Cutter because the blade that gives eternal life to the dead was built by The Metronome, and once the beings at the end of time give you a gift, it is always for what they get back and what they get back is your soul and your body and they get it all, not just from the moment that blade cuts you open and fills you with matter from the Void, but for always and ever and forwards and backwards through time and space and that is how a memory can be both new and old, both the truth and a lie.

And now a cast iron, three-masted merchant ship with MASTERS inscribed on its side is tossed through the front window of Jill's family home, skidding to a stop exactly where the model Jill found lays on the floor, and the past and the present are pulled back together in between moments and Hanna is jumping into the room and the forest fades away and the four of them look at one another.

And now the Grenadier and the Mistletoe Queen are standing with their clothes on, the man in the red coat and the woman in the red coat are holding hands, and the woman in the green mask tells Hanna that Hanna was right and Hanna was wrong, and that Jill did face the Ghost of

Christmas Past and Hanna she did face the Ghost of Christmas Present, but it is not Ignatius fighting the Ghost of Christmas Yet to Come because he is inconsequential, because the Mistletoe Queen is the Ghost of Christmas Yet to Come and she is here to show Hanna and Jill what awaits them if they continue on this path.

And now the Mistletoe Queen' hands are unzipping her red coat, the zipper invisible beneath the trim of white fur, and she is opening the coat wide, revealing herself to the world, but it is not a shirt the world sees or a naked torso but a rib cage cracked and opened, revealing a beating heart with the name "Grenadier" carved into it by the tongue of a man who reached the end of time.

And now the Mistletoe Queen is pulling off her emerald mask.

And now the mask is dropped to the floor.

And now Jill Masters stands looking at herself from both sides of the room, her past and future selves beside her two great loves, neither of them enough and both of them too much.

And now Jill is screaming and Hanna is screaming and a man who became one of The Metronome is smiling in his red coat and the latest woman to become Metronome is running a hand through her graying hair as she turns to kiss him beneath the hanging mistletoe.

And now a bell rings.

And now it is Christmas.

END

NEXT IN GUNFIGHTER GOTHIC

<u>AMERICAN VALKYRIE</u>

It's the summer of 1867, and after almost a year overseas, Hanna Pak and Jill Masters have returned to the United States. The women of Gunfighter Gothic are ready for some rest and relaxation, but they enter the city of San Francisco during a time of turmoil: the United States Army is in charge, prisoners are vanishing from the city's jails, and even though it's the middle of August, a supernatural chill has enveloped the city.

Hanna and Jill quickly become entangled with the glory-seeking Colonel Washburn, the widowed hotelier, Kerstin Demoff, and the operator of a local den of vice, Madam Lhong. As the two Bostonians investigate the mystery of the vanishing prisoners, a new player takes the field: Andi, a strange Indian woman in Viking armor, who appears out of thin air to kill the city's men and shepherd them to Niflheim, where they will serve her mother, Helreginn.

The Nordic priestess has more in mind than the conquest of San Francisco, however. She has built an army of zombies, ghosts, and giant white worms for a more personal purpose: the murder of Hanna Pak. But why does a witch they've never met want Hanna dead? And what secret does Helreginn keep from her daughter about Andi's true origin?

Caught between the machinations of the Nordic priestess and her warrior daughter on one side, and Washburn, Demoff, and Lhong on the other, Hanna and Jill fight to save both the city and the soul of the American Valkyrie!

The Works of Mark Bousquet
Ordering details at themarkbousquet.com

Spooky Lemon
The Masks of Saturday Morning
Haunt It or Flaunt It
Hootdunnit?
Parachutes & Ladders
Old Man's Treasure

Gunfighter Gothic
The Train Where Jill Died
Western Demons
Absinthe & Steam
The Man in the Red Coat
American Valkyrie
The Bandolier

Other Novels and Collections
The Haunting of Kraken Moor
Used to Be: The Kid Rapscallion Story
American Hercules: The Hunt for Zeus
Harpsichord & the Wormhole Witches
Dreamer's Syndrome: Into the New World
Face Your Yesterdays

For Kids
Adventures of the Five: The Coming of Frost
Adventures of the Five: The Christmas Engine
The Bear at the Top of the Stairs

CPSIA information can be obtained
at www.ICGtesting.com
Printed in the USA
LVHW031848071220
673554LV00016B/2322

9 798669 779047